DISCARD

I RISE

J. G. JAKES

ARCHWAY
PUBLISHING

Archway Publishing books may be ordered through booksellers or by contacting:

Archway Publishing
1663 Liberty Drive
Bloomington, IN 47403
www.archwaypublishing.com
1 (888) 242-5904

ISBN: 978-1-4808-6312-5 (sc)
ISBN: 978-1-4808-6311-8 (e)

Library of Congress Control Number: 2018905792

Print information available on the last page.

Archway Publishing rev. date: 05/25/2018

Contents

Prologue

An unexpected raid. A strong left foot kicks open the door of the small house. Arms raised, pistols and AR-15s held eye-level and steady, selected members from the Sheriff's office and Wesleyville, Georgia P.D., bursts in and storms the property.

"Hands up!" orders the task force sergeant. "Down on the floor!"

The man under arrest slowly lowers his hands, cocking an eye towards the back door. Anticipating he may be looking for an escape route, the officer yells, motioning with his pistol. "I said, 'Hands up!'" He motions to the floor. "Down on the floor! Face down! Hands behind your back. Now!"

The man quickly drops to the floor. Another officer quickly cuffs the man's hands behind his back as a wave of tension fills the air. The downed man's response sounds like he's been there, done that. "You have no right to burst into my house like this! I demand to see your search warrant. I have my rights!"

"Yeah, your rights—ain't lawyers great?" says one of the team, rolling his eyes.

As the law officers strategically infiltrate the smoke-filled house, the commanding officer scans the room. On the table nearby, various drug paraphernalia, including a smoking bong, along with methamphetamines, fentanyl, and bags of marijuana are out in plain sight.

The commanding officer points to the evidence. "Search

warrant?" The officer's jaw tightens as he motions his assistant. "Show the man the search warrant."

Suddenly, another officer, searching through the house, opens the bedroom door. His voice quickly escalates. "Sergeant! Get in here quick!"

"Hold him," the commander orders an officer. On the floor, a woman has collapsed and appears not to be breathing. A toddler, approximately three years of age, is lying lifeless on the bed.

"Oh, good God. I think we've got a victim of marijuana smoke here." The other officers nod. They've seen it before: dosed by an intentional puff of marijuana smoke blown into the child's nostrils, the toddler is probably the victim of a method commonly used by partying drug users—they blow marijuana smoke up the child's nose in order to induce sleep.

Solemnly, the sergeant backs out of the room and instructs one of his comrades to call an ambulance. He strolls over to the prisoner. Snatching him up, he glares into his eyes. He instructs, "Get him out of my sight."

1

A Push Instead of a Nudge

"Mom! Why are we stopping here?" asks Gracie, daughter of Sarah Cole, "the most audacious and gritty mother in the world," as Gracie calls her. "Mom! You don't have to start work for another two days! Have you forgotten we are meeting the movers this afternoon?"

Gracie asks, "Why did they choose you, Mom, to pull this agency out of the mud?"

Sarah laughs. "Maybe because they recognize my invincibility and insidious prowess. Or maybe, they feel I enthusiastically reject the central premise of laziness and don't mind inundating those who avoid responsibility." She casts a whimsical glance towards her daughter. "Who knows? Maybe I'm the only one they think is stupid enough to come here."

Sarah smiles a beautiful smile that makes her bright bluish-green eyes glow against her long, pin-straight dark brown hair that lies gently across her shoulders. "Besides, we have the rest of our lives to settle in to our new house."

Gracie, who is as beautiful as her mother, only with eyes dark as coal instead of blue and wavy and black hair parted in the center, contends, "You may have the rest of your life here, but just as soon as I begin college this fall, I'm out of this dump!"

"Now, Gracie, you know that you have stay close to me. You

are my baby girl." She grins. "In fact, you are my only child." She laughs as she checks her lipstick in the mirror. "Besides, who would have my back if you are not around? You are the one who always shows up when I need a push instead of a nudge."

"In all seriousness, I suppose someone has to keep you grounded since you love to go after bad guys. However, I guess that is your expertise."

Sarah retaliates with a hint of jest. "Okay, so I am pragmatic and sometimes lethal. However, in my defense, I am learning to be gracious in my victories. Although I do enjoy taking down the bad guys who mistreat and abuse their children. There are a lot of things in this world I can tolerate, but child abuse and neglect are not in that category. There are too many children that need taken out of their homes before the worst can happen."

"Mom, tell me, can you save every child? You know you can't save the world."

"I know that, sweetheart. But those I do save will be better off for it."

Gracie laughs. "Yeah, you are right on that account. And, that's another reason you want me to hang around. I know that you are a tough cookie, but I also know that you are still vulnerable. You have a heart bigger than the third rock from the sun, and because of that, your heart gets broken when others hurt. You need me to help you pick up the pieces and heal again. And I'm not just talking about how sad you get over children who have been the products of broken homes."

Sarah turns to her daughter. "You are wise beyond your years, my Gracie. I have the feeling you are referencing mine and your Dad's relationship. Honey, you need to stop hammering me about divorcing your dad." She takes Gracie's hand into hers and looks deeply into her eyes. "Your dad is what I refer to as a really bad life choice. He was a disastrous mistake." She smiles. "However, that disastrous mistake gave me the most beautiful, wonderful daughter I could ever ask for. That is, you, pumpkin. Besides, you shouldn't define me by the worst thing I ever did in my life—marrying him. If you give me a definition, do it based on my merits."

She motions to the building that houses the Office of Safe Families. "In the same manner, the true reason this state hired me to clean up this office is because of my merits, not giving me any favors. The problems in this county concerning the abuse and neglect of children have escalated. They need answers and they need solutions. So they gushed over my portfolio and decided that if anyone can turn this institution around it would be me. By the same token, I want you to define our relationship based on merits, not mistakes."

She pulls Gracie close and they embrace. "I love you, Gracie Cole. Always, remember that you are first in my life. And if you are having any misgivings about us moving here and you want to go back home, then we'll back out of the parking lot and cruise on down the road and never look back. Your happiness is that important to me. Compromising my work which I am passionate about is not near as important as my dedication to you."

Gracie lays her head on her mother's shoulder. "That's okay, Mom. I'm here for you." She jokes, "Of course, it's going to take some indulgence, but I guess I can take Yoga and deep breathing lessons to help reduce the stress. And if that doesn't work, I'll do acupuncture."

Sarah laughs at her daughter's frivolity. What would I do without this teenage epitome of warmth, delightfulness, and mischievous energy, she thinks. "Acupuncture?"

Gracie continues. "Yes. Desperate times call for desperate measures. I will willingly become a human pincushion to relieve my despair and release some mind control." She casts a glance at Sarah, who is about to explode with laugher.

"Just kidding, Mom. I can chill out and tolerate this for a while. Stay here for as long as needed. I'll just tough it out, even though I don't like this place. I don't like our neighborhood and I'm not too fond of this hick town. So, I'm hoping it won't take you long to turn things around here." Gracie frowns.

Sarah grins. "You are just a chip off the ol' block. I know this is hard. But it's what we do. I guess we are both tough cookies." She pauses. "I need you to stick around, Gracie, at least for a while simply because I do need you. You are always my constant, my go-to, my rock, but more than that, you are my very best friend. When you do leave for college, I will miss you terribly for the rest of my life."

"Okay, don't over sell it. Enough said. I guess I can tolerate this place for a while." She grins. "Besides, we both appreciate a gentle nudge and not a hard push. Right?"

"Right. So, are you ready to give me a push out of this car and let's begin this epic journey?"

"Might as well. Let's go."

Sarah and Gracie walk up to the front door of the red brick building that houses the Office of Safe Families, a facility whose responsibilities, says their mission statement, "help promote child well-being by preventing child abuse and neglect," as its mission statement says.

They stop at the door, take a deep breath, and enter into the lobby and receptionist's office. Quietly, they walk around, whispering. Gracie asks, "Cars are in the parking lot, but where are the people?"

"I don't know. It's as quiet as a mouse in here."

Suddenly, the sound of breaking glass could be heard. Sarah

blurts, "I'm going down the hall to see from where that noise is coming."

Gracie grabs her mother's arm, pulling her back. "Maybe you shouldn't walk down that corridor."

Sarah pulls back. "Why? Because when I open those doors, all the answers will come tumbling out?" She smirks. "I have to start somewhere." She casts a discerning eye towards her daughter, demanding, "Stay here, Gracie."

Gracie's eyes dart from one side of the room to the other. Eyes wide, she says, "Not by a long shot! I'm going with you!"

The commotion gets louder. Sarah skirts down the hall, with Gracie close behind, stopping short of the door of the room from which all the turmoil came. Sarah snatches the door open and quickly jumps back, narrowly having her face obliterated by a whirling vase. As the vase crashes against the wall, Sarah yells, "Stop! Stop this right now!" She glances around the room littered with broken glass, files, and paper clips. Hands on hips, she demands, "What is going on here?"

Grinning, Gracie's eyes beam as she snickers, "Hot dog! A fight! I love a good fight. A good fight is a thing of beauty. Don't you think, Mom?"

"Shhh! Gracie!"

The two apparently responsible for the mess remain frozen. Both women, standing with mouths open, stare at the woman who inserts herself into the middle of their fight. Finally, both point a finger at each other, trying to inject the blame on the other.

Sarah continues to rant as Gracie peers over her shoulder. "This"—she motions around the room—"is completely unethical! This is hugely inappropriate. The two of you have totally obliterated this room. Look at this office. You have completely destroyed it."

One speaks up—the taller and perhaps older of the two. "It's not that big of a mess."

"Seriously? This is not a mess? Oh, let me guess. You can't see? You've lost your contact lenses during the fight? What about all this stuff on the floor?" She glances at a picture hanging on the wall, tilting to on side. She points. "And that?"

The older woman answers rather coyly, "Our equilibrium is a little out of whack?"

Sarah dismisses the remark, glaring at the two women. "Let me make myself clear. This *is* a mess! And, you *will* clean it up! Then, come to my office and we will discuss this, whatever this is, that happened here today."

"Your office?"

"Yes, I am your new supervisor."

Wide-eyed, both women look at each other and gulp as if completely aware of the kind of problems their altercation has caused.

Sarah turns to leave the muddle, but notices oozing blood from the younger woman's arm. "Except for you. You may have glass in that gash. You get to the ER and get some stitches. I'll see you later."

Looking over her shoulder, she bumps into Gracie. She whispers, "I thought I told you to stay in the lobby."

Having a hard time hiding the excitement on her face, Gracie grins. "And miss this? No way!"

Suddenly, a frown etches its way across Sarah's face. Looking almost embarrassed, she turns back to the women. "By the way, where is my office?"

The older of the two motions down the hall in the direction of Sarah's new office.

Sarah nods. "Thank you," she grumbles, slamming the door

behind her. The next door on the right has a name plate on the door: Ethan Ericson, Supervisor.

Sarah looks at Gracie. "I guess we can take this sign down. Mr. Ericson is a supervisor of the past."

"Mom, do you think—" Suddenly, Gracie's words seem to stick in her throat. Sarah opens the door to her new office, looking over her shoulder and talking to Gracie, unaware of the scene before her.

"What's wrong, Gracie? You look pale, like you have seen a—"

"Oh, nothing. It's just that your timing is impeccable!"

In an instant, Sarah turns around and notices the sight upon which Gracie's eyes remained fixed: another room, another mess, another evidence of disorderly conduct. This time, it's a young couple making a crude attempt to frolic on top of the desk— Sarah's desk.

Sarah yells, "Oh, my gosh! What the heck did I just walk in on? What are you doing? And on my desk!" Stuttering, she chokes, "Get . . . get off my desk!" As she tries to block Gracie's eager eyes trying to peer over her mother's shoulder, she yells, "Gracie, get to the car. Right now!"

"Mom, do you have any idea how unfair this is? You are always wanting to have the 'talk,' and now I get to see what happens firsthand. Heck, Mom, this is better than sex-ed."

"Gracie!" Sarah shouts.

"Okay! Okay! Knock it down a few decibels. I'm going!" Taking one last peep at the embarrassed couple, she slips away with her hand cuffing her mouth, stifling giggles. "Boy, this is totally mind blowing! This day couldn't get any better!"

Sarah turns to the young lovers. The volume in her voice intensifies. "What have I just walked in on?"

No answer from the startled couple, whose wide eyes look like those of two goats caught in a headlight.

Sarah's outrage continues. "As for two of you, right now, I'm taking my daughter home. I will be back in this office in the morning, and I expect both of you here if you want my response to this incident. As for me, I want closure to the hub-bub I've seen. As soon as I find out what is going on in this office, we *will* move forward. For now, my best advice is *not* being late. If you are one minute late, I will hunt you down. I will hunt you down and pull you back here by your ears! Understand?" Suddenly, she stops in her tracks. "By the way, spray my desk down—with Clorox!"

"Yes, ma'am."

She slams the door and walks down the hall, bumping into one of the women she had caught in the fight a few minutes earlier. Sarah pushes by the humiliated woman and snarls, "Get out of my way!"

The older of the two women says, "Ma'am, I realize that this is a shock, but if we stand back and regroup, we can make the most of this, and perhaps forget it?"

Sarah chuckles. "That's your best defense? Total denial? Forget it? I don't think so! See you in the morning!" Slamming the door behind her, with heavy steps, she trots to the car. Flopping down in the front seat next to Gracie, she exhales an exasperated "Whew!"

Gracie, hesitant to speak, manages to say, "Well, so much for catching your employees with their pants down!"

"Gracie!"

"Yes, Mother. Forget what my all-knowing eyes have seen, what my delicate ears have heard, and erase from my mind all manifestations of evil bestowed upon me today. Anyway, back to your staff. I guess this will be one of those situations when you need to keep you friends close and your enemy closer?"

Sarah leans her head back against the head rest. She takes a deep breath. "You've got that right. In all my years, I never thought that stranger things could happen." She sighs. "Coming here seemed like the right thing to do. Now I'm not sure. I'm thinking this is going to be a colossal waste of time. This rabbit hole runs down much deeper than what I thought."

She reaches for her daughter's hand. "For now, I'm getting you out of here. I'm putting you on the first bus, plane, boat, or whatever that will take you back home."

Gracie smiles. "Are you trying to get rid of me? Forget it, Mom, I'm not going anywhere. And, you aren't either. You signed up to do this job and you are going to see it through. Since when are you a quitter? Sarah Cole does not quit, and neither do I. I'm like you in so many ways. She sees things through. She perseveres. I am not going to allow you to tuck your tail and go crawling back to that fabulous, wonderful job in Florida and our beautiful, upscale townhouse. Where is your sense of pride? Are you just going to sit back and allow this place to continuously beat you and you not even tried to make a comeback?" She giggles. "Besides, there is always acupuncture! They say needles are great to help one fix their out-of-whack thermostat." She sits back and folds her arms behind her head. "I think I am going to like it here."

"What happened to the girl who said she couldn't wait to get out of this hick town?"

"Maybe I've changed my mind. At least for a while. After all, this place is pretty exciting. I mean with all the cat fights and the—"

"Gracie!"

"Oh, Mom! Can't I poke a little fun without you getting all out of whack? Besides, not every dream is meant to come true. Yep, I'm thinking this will be quite an interesting little town."

Sarah smiles as her daughter offers humor as a brief respite. "I'm glad you have decided to stay for whatever the reason. I need you to stick around because I do need you. Remember? To keep me grounded."

Sparkling with enthusiasm, Gracie concurs, grabbing her mother's hand. "Do you really think I could ever leave you? Of course, you need me. I'm your greatest support system. I'm the one who gives you a push instead of a nudge!"

2

No Excuses

Sarah, stone-faced, looks over the rim of her reading glasses at the man and woman who have just walked in the door of her office. As she tries to keep an emotional distance between herself and the day's previous events, she says, "You are a little bit late, aren't you? Come in and sit down. For all concerned, let's make this as quick and painless as possible. Let's get down to business and start talking. We'll start with you, Mr. Hardy. You look like you have something profound to say. Just spit it out."

Jim Hardy asks, "There is no point in speculating, is there? I mean, do you think there is a possibility you did not see what you think you saw?"

"Do you see this smile on my face, Mr. Hardy?" Sarah asks, smiling, pointing to her face.

"Yes."

"It's fake! I don't make speculations, Mr. Hardy. Speculations are a waste of time and are nothing to smile about. Without a doubt, I saw what I think I saw." Fumbling through the man's files, Sarah adds, "However, the fact remains, sir, you did get caught with your pants down!" She lays the files down on her desk. "I've been looking over your personal files. Lucky that neither of you are married. I would hate to fire you if there were families involved."

Hardy comes right to the point, as he remarks, "With all due respect, ma'am, aren't you going a little overboard with this? You don't have to be so melodramatic. Do we really have a problem here? Exactly how far do you plan to take this? After all, we were two consenting adults." He chuckles. "At least your daughter got a kick out of it!"

Sarah adjusts her glasses. *He's sorta nice looking, but this man is too cocky for his own good. What a despicable man!* Her fiery eyes look as if they could throw darts at the man. "You think that's funny? Not only are you shallow, but you are thoughtless and irresponsible. With all due respect, sir, you are beginning to irritate the heck out of me. First of all, in what universe do you think we don't have a problem here, unless you want to get bogged down in trivia? You may not have a problem strutting around this office as if you are the barnyard rooster, but I'm not wired that way. I won't stand and watch you run this place deeper into the ground. And as for being two consenting adults, Mr. Hardy, what you do on your time and at your place *is* your own business. However, when you bring it to this office and you are doing it on the State's time, then it becomes *my* business. For that reason, Sir, I don't need or want your kind working under my supervision."

Hardy steps up his defense. "Are you calling my bluff because you can't use this against me? If you fire me, I can get a lawyer and take you to court. I will be exonerated because this little issue will be thrown out. After all, it is your word against mine and you have no witnesses. That's my recollection of events and I am sticking to them."

Sarah leans back in her chair, crossing her arms. "Are you making threats, Mr. Hardy?"

"Maybe. If you want to call them that. I'm just saying I'm not going down with a fight."

Sarah rubs her forehead. "Hm. So, I have no witnesses? I

suppose you have forgotten about my daughter? You know, the one who you say 'got a kick out of it'?" Sarah reaches into her purse and extracts her cell phone. Saying I have no witnesses is archaic, Mr. Hardy. Don't you realize that we live in a digital age?" She taps in a photo, holds it up briefly, then makes a swift right swish—all the time praying her bluff will work.

"My daughter has this quirky habit of taking quick pics. You know, for memory's sake. The way I see it, you'd better end this before it starts. I have admissible visual evidence against you—some that won't get thrown out in any court of law. I understand you are grasping at straws, but you need to listen to my voice of reason. I am getting rather tired of your righteous indignations, so turn in your resignation and do it now. Just walk out of here and this whole thing will be over."

Jim Hardy slumps down in his seat across from Sarah. "I guess being sorry is out of the question? Would there be a chance that you would kindly accept my apology for my rudeness today and let's act like this never happened?"

Sarah, shuffling through Hardy's file, continues, "There is no need to get all warm and fuzzy with me, Mr. Hardy. Apology accepted. I've been challenged and tested many times. I've been forged in more fires that I can count. You are definitely not the first. However, forgetting this little incident never happened is definitely out of the question. Not in this universe, anyway."

"Then do you mind if I say something in my defense, ma'am?"

Sarah looks up from Jim's files and nods. "Go for it. Why don't you try to vindicate yourself so you can get on with your life?"

He points to his partner, Kathy Harmon, who had been caught on the desktop with him. "My relationship with her is a sham. She tricked me into a fraudulent relationship. Not only is she despicable and toxic, but she is a lowlife."

His partner in the previous day's events, sitting quietly, speaks up. "No, Jim. Our relationship is difficult." She glares at Hardy. "You're a cold-hearted jerk. And I wouldn't offer you a cookie if it was the last thing you ever had to eat."

Jim ignores her and continues, "I'm not trying to boast, Mrs. Cole, but I am a rather handsome man and she just can't keep her hands off me."

"You're not trying to boast? Doesn't sound that way to me."

"I know I'm not exactly destined for sainthood, but neither am I responsible for everything that has happened here. I was coerced. The woman is nothing but a femme fatale, master of the art of feminine manipulation who made a power play for me." He motions towards his partner-in-crime sitting next to him. "In fact, she is nothing but a slutty train wreck. She's the one who is always flirting with me and trying to seduce me. Besides, she has a personal vendetta against me. Everyone in this office thinks I am the monster, but she is far more sinister than I am. If any lose their job here today, it needs to be her and not me."

Tears trickle down Kathy's face. "How can you say those things about me, Jim? How can you do this to me? What about your general, pathetic record? All the rotten things you have done to me in the past are just erased from your memory?"

Sarah intervenes, saving Kathy from further humiliation. "Sounds like you are the one with the personal vendetta, Mr. Hardy. Explain yourself. I'd like to hear where you are going with this."

"First of all, those files you are holding in your hands have not been updated in years. I am married and she is mad at me because I chose my wife over her. She won't give it up and she is always tempting me, making it hard for me not to give in." Another hard glare with a condescending eye makes its way towards the woman sitting next to him. "You know how some women are, Mrs. Cole."

"No, I don't know how some women are, Mr. Hardy. Enlighten me."

"They prance around in front of you with short skirts and low-cut blouses and . . . and make it hard for a man to concentrate. She is toxic. She ruins everything she touches. She employs her stuff and takes advantage because of my vulnerability."

"Poor Mr. Macho Man. Woe is me!" Sarah exclaims. "Mr. Hardy, you just informed me that not only do you have a hard time staying focused, but you lack in strength of character and you are also deficient in the morals department. You are not the man you think you are. You can't spend the rest of your life focusing on yourself and making excuses for your actions. You took an action and because of the consequences, there is going to be a lot of pain to live with."

Mr. Hardy, looking the part of a broken man, concedes, slouching in his seat in a way that telegraphs, "My mouth has overruled my brain this time."

"Are you a churchgoer, Mr. Hardy?" Sarah asks.

"When I can. I don't go as much as my momma wants me to."

"That's a shame. Especially for your wife, who probably sits at home every day, preparing your dinner, mending your socks, and waiting on her husband to come home—the husband whom she trusts and believes in his fidelity with her whole heart." She folds the weepy man's personal file. "Thanks for stopping by, Mr. Hardy. If you'll excuse me, I have another discourse to conduct."

He stutters, "What—what do I do now?"

"I sincerely wish you the best. I hope you find another job where you can make lots of money—so you can indulge in your passion of seducing beautiful women!" She shakes her head. "I'm sorry, Mr. Hardy. I don't mean to be so sarcastic. May I give you my best advice?"

"Please do."

"How much is it worth to unburden your conscience, sir?"

"I don't understand what you mean, Mrs. Cole. Do you want me to clear my conscience?"

"Yes. For your sake, not mine. Sometimes a clear conscience helps the person who is keeping the secret. I'd like to suggest you go home and tell your wife what a louse she has married before she finds it out on the street—after you go by the unemployment office."

He nods and slowly meanders his way towards the door, beaten.

Sarah advises, "Mr. Hardy, take the last option and think really hard about doing what you momma wants you do. Go to church! By the way, Mr. Hardy."

"Yes, Mrs. Cole?"

"Not all men are created equal."

Waiting their turn, sitting nervously in the lobby, were the two glass breakers. The blonde-haired woman, the older of the two, asks Hardy, "How did it go?"

Subdued and quite downcast, the man answered, "Jackie, I'm writing this meeting off as a loss."

"Are you going to schedule another one?"

"No. It will just run off the rails like this one. Besides, she is radically opposed by self-centered glory-grabbing people."

"Hmm, I don't like the sound of that. Tell me about it."

"Well, we had a rocky start and an even harder ending. She came down on me like the wrath of God. I am the one who usually takes control, but, believe me, that woman is a force of nature." Remembering the supposable cell phone photo, Jim adds, "Besides, she has enough proof to send me to the unemployment line." He chuckles, waving his arms. "And, she will write it in the sky! So, don't make the mistake I made—not being agreeable. It makes her uncomfortable. Definitely, don't miscalculate about her. She is determined and persistent. She has strength and courage to stand up for what she believes is right. I told myself that I wouldn't break, but I did. I broke like a ton of rocks." He sighed. "Other than her insulting my manhood in the end, we cleared some ground."

What do you mean?"

"The Lord certainly does work in mysterious ways."

"Meaning?"

"She cut me down to size after telling me to resign. She took me to school, so to speak, and made me admit that maybe I am not the macho man I thought I was. I am just a man. And, come Sunday, ladies, I am going to church!"

The taller woman gulps as a collective gasp fills the air.

Sitting across the desk from Sarah, Kathy Harmon, biting her nails, mutters, "I am so nervous."

Sarah asks, "We have a lot to talk about." She motions toward the brewing coffee. "Would you like to take a coffee break? I'd like to tap your brain."

Kathy shrugs. "No, ma'am. Let's begin and get this over."

"Okay, then let's begin by you telling me exactly what is your relationship with Mr. Hardy and please don't try to pad your resume the way he did."

Kathy begins to explain. "No ma'am, my life is boring and uncomplicated."

"Sometimes, boring and uncomplicated is a good thing." She

sighs. "However, let me share this—passion always fogs good judgement."

Kathy chuckles nervously. "We are just friends. That's all, Mrs. Cole."

"Huh. Looks like you are more than just friends to me."

"I guess I deserved that. I can't imagine what went through your mind yesterday when you walked down that corridor and opened that door."

"No, you can't, but thank you for validating my outrage."

"I'm sorry. I made a really bad choice."

"You bet you did!" Sarah thumbs through Kathy Harmon's files. Without looking up, she asks, "Is being impulsive part of your personality?"

Kathy answers, "By that, do you mean do I always leap before I look?" She contemplates how to answer. "Yes, ma'am. I guess I do. At least, to some extent." She seems to be choosing her words carefully. "Mrs. Cole, I admit responsibility for my part in this little incident. I admit that I am deeply flawed, but you have to understand, it's just the kind of relationship Mr. Hardy and I have."

Sarah's brow crinkles. "The only thing I understand, Miss Harmon, is that kind of a relationship is not permissible in any office, much less this one. I hold this office to a standard—a benchmark to measure up to on how we are to conduct ourselves." She bites her bottom lip. "Here's the rundown. I was sent here to clean this office up. I won't lower my expectations or nor make a string of broken promises. I *will* fulfill my duties. If I have to remove some ruffled feathers, then so be it. It is nothing I haven't done before."

Sarah's mouth tightens. Kathy hears Sarah's attempt to soften her voice and remain poised and professional. "Mr. Hardy is a hypocrite and you are irresponsible."

Kathy doesn't expect Sarah's next question. "What price do you put on your dignity, Miss Harmon?"

The petite woman sitting across from Sarah holds her head up and says, "I'm not a bad person and I'm not a coward, either. Neither am I a hypocrite. It's just that things between Jim and me have never been simple. He is wild, irreverent, feeling the flush of manhood, and on the prowl. I am youthful, maybe naïve, and was thrilled to meet someone I thought truly cared for me."

"If he really cared for you, Miss Harmon, he would not have thrown you under the bus. He is not what you would refer to as a real winner. Mr. Hardy is the kind of man you cannot count on. He will always break your heart. He is committed totally to himself, not to you. Besides, you don't need a man like him to validate your existence."

The heartbroken woman wipes a trickling tear. "What is sitting here before you is a woman who made a bad choice. And, now I realize my choices have consequences. If given the opportunity, I can turn my life around." She points to the files Sarah is holding in her hands. "I need this job, Mrs. Cole. I hope you give me a chance to prove my worth. I will work really hard to put my life back on track."

"I hope you do have worth. But, Miss Harmon, you have to be stronger than the darkness inside. It is going to take a lot of resolve, but I honestly believe if you try hard enough, you can put your life back on track." Sarah leans back in her chair. "Do you think I was unfair to Mr. Hardy?"

Without hesitation, she answers, "Maybe. He is not perfect, but he tries to be a good person. He hears me and understands me. At times, I can trust him."

"Don't oversell it, Miss Harmon. He is wasted space and you know it. He put you in a precarious situation. To me, that means he is far from perfect. Besides, he is a grown man. He makes his own choices. You don't have to bail him out every time he gets in trouble. Every time he screws up, I'm betting you are the first to forgive him because he always makes you believe that he will do better." She frowns. "What he said about you was cold. It was arctic. For me, it would take that a long time for those comments to thaw. However, you still defend him."

"Yes, ma'am. I know."

"It takes grace to stand by someone especially when they run you down. I am not going to look at you through rose-colored glasses, Miss Harmon. I know who and what the two of you have done, but right now, I want to know who you are at this moment. So, point-blank, tell me why you need this job. Tell me why this job is your calling and why you were meant to do this kind of work?"

Without hesitation, pushing her dark hair away from her mahogany-colored eyes, Kathy slowly begins to unfold the story of her life. "I have not had an easy path in my life. Maybe that is what has caused me not to have a real and trusting relationship." Sniffing back falling tears, she slowly continues, "What you are made of is what you need to do. I put my life and my heart into being a social worker because I, too, was an abandoned and abused child." She clears her throat, wiping a fallen tear. Quickly, she fumbles for a tissue. "My mother would stay drunk more than she would stay sober. You can imagine what kind of life I had growing up."

"It's interesting the links an abused child, now an adult, will make to help other abused children."

"Yes, it is. It's almost like having a driven purpose in life. However, I have made peace with my childhood and have put it behind me."

Careful, Sarah thinks. Don't allow your emotions to cause

a distraction from your job at hand. She asks, "Where was your father?"

"I don't know. I never knew my father. Anyway, when I graduated, I left home, got a student loan, and worked my way through college. I wanted to make a difference in this world. I wanted to help children who were hurting just like me." She dabs her eyes. "I got a job here, met Jim, and thought I fell in love. I thought he was in love with me." She sniffed. "I thought we were in love with each other."

"My condolences!"

"Okay, I deserved that. But, he told me we would get married one day. However, his other girlfriend, his wife, came up pregnant. So, he married her." She turns to Sarah with pleading eyes. "I know what I have done is wrong and I regret the choices I have made in my life. I wish I could just select the "alt delete" button on this entire period of my life. I know now, after listening to him talk to you, that the narcissist never loved me. My voice of reason is just now beginning to tell me that Jim is only a footnote in the bottom of my life. All I can do at this point is try to work on my faults and make myself a better person. I realize that many times I try to do the right thing, but it turns out to be the wrong thing." She pauses. "So, I would appreciate it, ma'am, before you get too hard and cynical, will you look beyond my faults and give me a chance to prove myself. Give me a chance to be a better person."

For a moment, Sarah sits, absorbing the heart-wrenching story she just heard. "Huh. That's exactly the resounding pledge of confidence I am looking for. However, I can't be responsible for your insecurities, Miss Harmon. I am not inclined to sympathize, but I am paid for my discretion. I'm going to sleep on it tonight and I will make my decision in the morning." She motions to the door. "Come by the office then and I will let you know what I have decided."

Kathy stands, nods, and walks out into the lobby where Natasha Woods, one of the coworkers caught in the office fight, is waiting. She asks, "What's the verdict?"

"I don't know. She will let me know in the morning. Whatever she decides will be for the best. She's a good woman, steady as a rock, solid through and through, and very conscientious about her position. Take some advice and don't play her. She polished, intelligent, and has a lot going on." She points to her head. "Don't throw her any curve balls. She can handle anything that you throw at her." She chuckles slightly. "She is definitely not the journalist type. She doesn't write anything down. Anyway, everything comes straight out of her mouth. It's about time this office hired a supervisor with more sense than God promised a goose."

Jacqueline Karr—"Jackie"—standing nearby, crinkles her forehead and asks, "So, you are saying it is better to keep her close as a friend than an enemy? Is she a manipulator?"

"No. I don't think she is capable of deception or manipulation. She shoots straight. Definitely, don't try to manipulate her. She'll quickly figure out your game plan."

"Do you see if there is a chance to normalize things?"

"If 'normalizing things' means having you kicked out of this office, then yes, she will normalize things."

At that moment, Sarah, standing in the doorway, calls out for Jacqueline. "Mrs. Karr, I'm ready for you. You can come back now."

Jacqueline answers, "You don't want both of us to come back so you can talk to us together?"

Sarah answers, "No. One at a time."

Jacqueline looks at her counterpart, Natasha, and shrugs her shoulder. "This is not good. Not good at all! I think we've gotten ourselves into a mess."

Sarah patiently waits for Jacqueline to saunter down the hall. Once inside the office, Jacqueline begins an assault against Natasha. "Mrs. Cole, before you start asking questions, I have a plausible excuse. Furthermore, I'd like to say that nutcase sitting out there in the lobby has a vendetta against me and any allegation she makes against me is baseless. She is a pompous idiot and a horrible person. Don't let her gut-suck you and take you in with all of her lies."

Sarah interrupts, sighing. "This is beginning to sound like the same Hail Mary pass that the previous employee was trying to do on his counterpart. So, let's hold on and wait a minute. No one here is going to gut-suck me—especially you. I don't live under a rock. So, why are you taking all of your rage out on her, undoubtedly spawned by some cruel hatred against someone who is not even in here to defend herself?"

With fiery indignation, Jacqueline continues, insisting that her coworker is the one at fault. "At the risk of repeating myself, this wreckage is all on her. I just wanted you to know that I didn't start that fight, but neither was I going to walk away from one, and I'm not taking the blame for it. Understand?"

Sarah stands and walks to the door. As she opens it, she motions outside. "I understand more than you think, Mrs. Karr. Your attitude smells like a three-day old, dead fish. It just won't bite with me. You see, Mrs. Karr, there are certain standards by which a person's behavior is measured. Honesty is one of those standards. The thing I condemn most is hypocrisy. I have a tendency to lose respect for those who maintain a façade of purity but who at the same time are telling lies. You can try to deceive me, but no matter how successful the self-deception may seem to be, you cannot escape the fact that you are being dishonest. Perhaps I am subtle in my psychological rationalization, but what it amounts to, Mrs. Karr, is that I detest a liar." She motions towards the door. "Have a good day."

Jacqueline stands, muscles tensed, and slowly walks past Sarah. She stops and turns. "I guess I blew it, didn't I?"

Sarah says, "You've got that right. You blew it right out of the water! I'm sorry to inform you, Mrs. Karr, that your services are no longer required. Tell your associate to come on back, please."

Jacqueline wavers. "Yes, ma'am."

As Jacqueline walks past the lobby, Natasha asks, "Is everything okay?"

"No! I just got fired! That'll be the title of my new memoir. The stars are definitely not aligned in my favor today. Nope, I wouldn't call it a win. I would call it a travesty!"

"Wow! You actually said a three-syllable word!"

"Whatever! Anyway, everything is definitely not all right. That did not go well, at all. In fact, it was nothing but a huge failure. I guess I was too strong-armed."

"Whatever do you mean?"

"It is called 'inconceivable and indefensible behavior.' I went in with the goal to save my job no matter what. Sorry, Natasha, if that might have meant throwing you under the bus, but I need the job. At the time, I didn't realize that she is not the type of person to bend the rules, not even for her own gain. Therefore, my plan backfired. I played right into her hands and now she's sending me packing." She smacks her lips. "Hardy tried to warn me." She sneers, "By the way, be careful that your stitches don't get infected and your arm rots off."

"Thanks. I love you, too."

Jacqueline snarls, "I would tell you that you are a nice person and I have enjoyed working with you, but that would put me one step further from honesty."

Natasha responds, "Why, thank you, Jacqueline, but I am not going overboard with a sense of gratitude."

Jacqueline glances over her shoulder as she storms away. She yells out, "What do you want me to do? Smack a smile on my face and pretend that I like you?"

Natasha sighs. *I'll never have to endure this type of verbal abuse again.* She looks down the hall at Sarah, who is impatiently waiting on her. "Well, here goes nothing." She walks in and sits down in the same chair where Jacqueline had bombarded the new supervisor only a few minutes earlier.

Sarah looks directly at her bandaged arm. "How's your arm, Natasha?"

The young woman smiles. "It only took a few stitches. Thanks for asking." The soft skin around her dark eyes crinkles.

"That's good. Now, let's talk. And, please do me a favor—no lying. It's been a long day and I am tired of being annoyed. Where do you want to begin?"

Natasha shrugs. "From the beginning?'

"That's always a good place to start. Tell me, what's your story?" she asks Natasha.

"I don't have a story, Mrs. Cole. I admit that I was part of the fight that started yesterday in Jacqueline's and my office. I admit that I was selfish and shallow and a little bit out of control. I'm sorry. I will replace the things that were broken."

"I admit, I am surprised by your humility. First, I want to make my position perfectly clear before you start hurling accusations. I respect honesty and I expect you to be completely honest with me. I guess I am a stickler for that. However, once you lose trust in another person, it's hard to gain it back."

"What do you need from me?"

"I need answers. That is what I need." She glares directly into Natasha's eyes. "I need the truth. Did you start the fight?"

"No, ma'am. I did not. I am not proud of my altercations with Jacqueline, but I did not start that fight."

"What if I told you Jacqueline says the opposite and places all the blame on you?"

"That sounds like something she would do. Nevertheless, I am being completely honest with you. I didn't start it. I am guilty of throwing a few things. I had to defend myself. Still, I understand that is no excuse."

"It's a relief how truthful you're appearing to be with me." She seems to weigh Natasha's answers, then adds, "I am sorry if I have been sounding coarse. I want you to know that I am not naïve. My head is not in the sand. However, I have a job to do, and at the moment, I am desperate for honesty."

Natasha's tense muscles relax. "Whew. It's good to know you are human."

Sarah bites her lip, refraining from laughter. "Oh, I see that I am being perceived as being insensitive."

Natasha giggles. "No, ma'am. I wouldn't call you insensitive." She bows her head, almost shamefully. "I have a little boy at home and I am a single parent. I really need this job. It might not sound like much to you—I mean coming from me—but I would walk a mile to save a child's life."

"Tell you what, Natasha. I'm not supposed to start my job until tomorrow. That will give me time to sort out things and make my decision about keeping you on. In the meantime, I'm going home to help my daughter unpack. Until tomorrow, I'll focus on taking care of my life. You focus on taking care of yours. However, that being said, I'll see you back here in the morning. I'll let you know your fate at that time."

Just as Natasha reaches for the door, she hesitates and turns back to Sarah. "Even if you decide to fire me, I will know you are making the decision you feel is best. I'm glad you are here. You mentioned 'focus.' Safe Families in Wesleyville seems to have lost its focus. Maybe, you are just the person to turn things around." She smiles and then she is gone, closing the door behind her.

Sarah whispers, "Hm, she probably just saved her skin—simply because she offered no excuses."

3

New Beginnings

Sarah's tires softly connect with the pea gravel driveway as she pulls in to the little house she now rents on the edge of town. The quaint, well-crafted, earthy style house has a country vibe—freshly painted white siding and a deep front porch, its front side enhanced with shuttered windows and graced with simple columns that sit on brick piers. There is a chicken coop in the backyard. Far from any delusions of grandeur, the abode is everything Sarah has longed for all of her life—a refreshing open-door invitation to the natural world, with big, oak trees dripping with Spanish moss and its quiet historic charm that eludes noisy neighbors. To her delight, it is the perfect home, feeling friendly, approachable, and seamlessly connected to the surroundings.

Gracie meets her at the door. "Welcome to our unwelcoming home, Mom. Good timing. I can use someone on my side right now. The electricity has not been cut on yet. Boxes are still stacked head high everywhere, and it is too darn hot in this house to do any work." On this hot, steamy summer day, she wipes the perspiration from her forehead. "Mom, I'm here to tell you—I'm not going to spend another night sleeping on the porch with those mosquitoes. We're packing up and going to a hotel."

As the temperature begins to spike, Sarah looks over her sunglasses slipping down the bridge of her nose, tosses her hair to one side, and then decides to pin it up off her neck as her face begins to flush in reaction to the heat. Cringing at the conglomeration of clutter, misplaced furniture, and unopened boxes set before her, she attempts to make light of the situation, cackling at Gracie's frivolousness.

"Hey! There's a thing as a little too much enthusiasm. You pay too much incomprehensible time to minute details. Besides, I'm glad to see you, too, my dear. Where are those words I couldn't wait to get home to hear? Like 'I missed you, Mom, glad you are home,' or how about my favorite, 'I love you, Mom. Sit down and take a load off while I bring you a glass of tea'?"

"Had a rough morning, huh?"

"The worst of the worst. It's always a downer when you have to fire someone from a job they depend on for their livelihood."

"Yea, I would think it would be a downer—much like a lousy train wreck."

Sarah, remembering Jim Hardy's accusation slung at Kathy Harmon that insinuated she *was* a train wreck, cringes. "Please don't mention 'lousy train wreck.' It makes me want to throw up!"

Gracie places a consoling hand on her mother's shoulder. "You seem rather distraught over the morning's events. Hey, let's sit down on the porch and you can tell me all about it. I am prepared to listen for hours to your tales of woe."

"Thanks for your concern, my dear, but it's a long story and I'm not sure you want to hear the whole story."

As usual, Gracie opens the way for Sarah to vent. "Skip the long story and get to the bullet points. I know the mounting stress your new job is imposing upon you. I know you—at times it'll be challenging and at other times depressing, but in the end, making a difference in a child's life is the reward that always makes it worth the trouble for you."

Sarah kicks off her shoes as Gracie adds, "And, Mom, I know

your disposition—sensible and sometimes a little callous on the outside, yet warm and compassionate on the inside. You're perfect for this new position of supervisor over Safe Families in Wesleyville.

Sarah perches cross-legged on a rocking chair and begins to relax. Lilly, the family dog, part schnauzer and part dachshund, jumps in her lap. As she begins to rub Lilly's long, shaggy black hair, the dog affectionately licks her hand and the tension begins to recede. Her heart opens to Gracie, whose warm, delightful, and mischievous energy always changes the outlook on her life dramatically. "The first person I had to let go this morning was Jim Hardy. He was the man—"

Interrupting, Gracie sings out, "The man who was scrambling around trying to find his pants and clambering around to look for Clorox?"

Sarah chuckles. "Yes. He's the one." Then her tone becomes more serious. "He has a wife."

"You mean the pig is married?"

Sarah sits up straight. "Yeah, that's the word I'm looking for—pig! Anyway, I figured all four employees knew I couldn't fire everyone. That would leave me empty handed and there could be no way I could accomplish the job I was hired to do. I had to leave a couple of social workers to fill me in on all the information I need. So, I narrowed it down to two." She throws a leg over the arm on the rocking chair and leans her head back, basking in the messy tranquility of their new home. "Anyway, Mr. Hardy, pig, whatever, comes into my office and immediately starts ranting about why he is all innocent and his partner is the one to blame."

"What nerve! Doesn't he know it takes two to tango?"

"Undoubtedly not. Anyway, right off the get-go, I realized he is not a keeper. He acted so high and mighty and ethical, but all the while, his true colors kept him rolling around in the gutter.

I think I knew immediately what kind of man he is. He is a real lowlife with an IQ just above room temperature. If he were a decent guy, he would have done the right thing and left Kathy alone. Not only is he a womanizer, but he manipulates her feelings and tries to destroy her character. I want someone on my staff that I can trust, not someone who is so self-absorbed."

"So, his tango partner stays?"

"I didn't give her a definite answer, but I think so, Gracie. Sometimes, the complexity of a situation should be viewed in its simplicity. Anyway, I am trying to see things from her point of view. She has the heart for trying to help others and all that our job encompasses. She not only understands what we are up against, but she has lived it. She carries grief because of her own mother, at best neglectful, and at worst, abusive. Because she can relate, I truly feel that she will be an asset. I honestly believe that some people can make a change for the better." She smiles. "That's probably why I am so naïve. Anyway, I told her I'd sleep on it tonight."

Gracie whispers, "Yeah, I hope it's in a hotel."

"What did you say?"

Gracie swats a mosquito, sweating copiously. "I said, 'it's nice out here.' What about the two women who were propelling rocket grenades at each other? Did they go down without a fight?"

"Not hardly. At least, the older woman didn't."

"What do you mean?"

"Well, almost immediately, I picked up that the older woman is an intelligent, perceptive person. However, she rambled too much and spoke in metaphors. Rather than telling the truth, she is the kind of person who assumes the worst about everyone and takes joy in other people's misery. Immediately, she began a coldly manipulative and pragmatic setup. In a vain attempt, she tried to extricate herself by downgrading the other woman, placing all the blame on the girl I instructed to go to the ER. I have no tolerance for backstabbers. If they stoop as low as to sabotage another human being, they'll do anything to protect themselves, especially by lying. Lying about something had her name written all over it. I need people whom I can depend on and trust. You trust that the other person will have your back. You trust that you can depend upon each other. Trust that no matter what happens, you will always be there for each other. That's true because *trust* always wins out. For that reason, I'll always choose truth over diversity."

"So she is out? Sounds like she is a real nut. You know, the kind of woman who uses too much hair spray. All that aerosol eventually kills the brain cells!" Gracie giggles as she continues to question her mother. "So, the other one is in, even if she was a little bit out of control the day before? What's going to happen now? They won't consider it departmental bias. Do you think that since everything is out in the open, you'll be able to work together?" Before Sarah can answer, another question follows quickly. "You going to have to sleep on that one, too?"

Suddenly, the lights blink, flicker, and blink again. Gracie and Sarah look up at the ceiling fan above their heads. It stops, then starts.

"Oh, Lord, please," begs Gracie. "Let there be light!"

Then, with full velocity, the ceiling fan begins to suck out the humidity on this hot summer day, blowing cool air to on their uplifted, welcoming faces.

"Thank you, thank you," Sarah and Gracie say in unison.

Elated, Gracie jumps up and says, "I think we deserve a celebratory drink. However, if you choose to abstain, all the more for me!"

Sarah laughs a little. "We all know that alcohol lowers your inhibition."

Within a few minutes, Gracie trots back with a cool rag she places on her mother's forehead and a couple of bottles of water, preserved in an ice cooler in the kitchen. She opens the cap for her mother and offers a toast. "Here's to new beginnings."

Sarah smiles at her daughter. "That's your strong suit, isn't it?"

Gracie chugs down a walloping swallow of the cold, refreshing liquid. "What is my strong suit, Mom?"

"Taking care of yourself. Taking care of me. That's just what you do." She reciprocates the toast. "Here's to new beginnings."

4

That's just how Life Works

On a sweltering midsummer morning, Sarah walks into the Safe Families building. Kathy and Natasha are standing inside, waiting. Sarah directs, "I want everyone in my office in five minutes."

Kathy looks at her coworker and says, "Does this sound like we are going to be interrogated? Do you think we are going to need a lawyer? Because I have the feeling this is not going to be an easy conversation. Things are fixin' to spark." She casts a discerning glance towards Natasha. Muttering glumly, she asks, "Do you think we should call 911?"

Natasha answers, "Don't be so melodramatic. This is what it is."

Quietly, Kathy and Natasha enter and sit across the desk from their new boss and supervisor, Sarah Cole. Nerves are frayed as they listen intently.

"Let's get down to business. We have a lot to talk over. First of all, I want to make sure that the ground underneath us is solid. It's time for us to be realistic. Can you understand that?"

With a slight nod of the head, both women whisper, "Yes."

Sarah continues, "Both of you put your careers at risk. Your careers could be horribly over. However, because I am the type of person to assume nothing, I believe in everything. There has been a lot of blame going around here for some reason. However, I don't feel as if you are the ones to blame. Therefore, I have chosen to keep the two of you on board, simply because I can't go into this new position alone. I need staff on hand, at least, until I can hire new employees. Till then, it's up to you. I generally don't believe in second chances, but both of you have been given a second chance."

Both women exhale a silent breath of relief.

"With that said, let me remind you—three strikes and you are out. By my playbook, you have two. So, don't let me down. More important, don't let yourselves or your family down."

"Yes, ma'am."

"Here's the rundown. I have rules. If you work for me, you have to abide by those rules. If you are going to break the rules, you have to face the consequences. I demand respect in this office and I demand the truth. You have to have trust to build any kind of relationship. If you can't abide, then maybe you'd better hit the door." Sternly, she glares. "However, as I see it, this is the perfect opportunity to reinvent yourself and get rid of all that old baggage. If you need time to think things over, then do it. Your choice may be a life-altering decision. What do you say?"

Kathy was the first to speak. "I'm staying!"

Natasha rings in with the same response, "Me, too!"

At this point, Sarah chooses to test their genuineness. She asks, "Do I strike you as the kind of boss whose vanity can be exploited?"

"Yes." They answer together.

She chuckles as she continues to probe. "Normally, I would punch anyone for saying that. You don't have to like me, but you have to respect me."

No comment, just nods from both.

Sarah smiles, "Okay. Then let's move forward. At some point,

you need to know why I was sent here, and it is best you hear it
from me. I was sent here to clean up this office. In other words,
to pull it out of the mud. This institution has suffered nearly
irreparable damage. That's not going to happen on my watch. As
we speak, this family service is rated the lowest in the state for
preventing child abuse. In fact, this county has the highest rating
for child abuse and misplaced children in the entire state. For sure,
we are not as populated as most cities and towns, but the ratio
of percentages of the number of cases per population is soaring
right here around us. I want to know why." Her glare sends chills
through her co-workers.

She continues. "Every day, over five children die because
of child abuse in this country. Every day, over three-and-a-half
million cases of child abuse and neglect are reported in this
country—most with serious injuries, some even resulting in
death. The sad part is those statistics are only generated from the
reported cases. How many out there go unreported?"

Sarah stands and paces the room with hands on hips. "Here's
the deal. I need you, but it is not beneath me to fire you if I have
any more trouble from either of you. I've always been the type that
likes to rip the Band-Aid off really quick. You know, to get it over
as rapidly as possible. Therefore, if you can't come to work every
day and give our mission 110 percent, then you have to go. If you
can give that, we can forget everything that happened yesterday.
We will put it in the past. However, if you do not dedicate yourself
completely to the cause of cleaning up this county and making
it safe for our families, then out you go. Do you agree to these
terms?"

Both reply, "Yes."

"I feel like this office has a good chance to make a difference
in this community—a good chance, but it's going to take having
you do your job the way it needs to be done."

Natasha interrupts. "I don't understand. I thought we were doing our part. We do our visitations and follow-ups. We provide continuous assistance, counseling, and support when our clients are confronted with unemployment, financial stress, or an unhealthy psychological state of mind. We help single parents and those who are victims of domestic violence. We even provide services for those who are victims of substance abuse. What more can we do?"

"I don't know yet, Natasha. All I know is that the State of Georgia sent me here to try to solve the problems and figure out the reason why the office is so unsuccessful. This agency is so far down a rabbit hole it is going to be hard to pull it up and out. But, that's exactly what I was sent here to do. My main priority is keeping this office on top. I will do whatever I have to do to keep it there. I get rid of trouble. That's my expertise."

She looks at both women. "I am asking you to look at this objectively. Every day, you are going to have to prove yourself to me. Like I said, if you want to stay on board, then you are welcomed. But, I need dedicated, hard-working social workers who are more than willing to put everything into this project. As long as you stick to the routine and stay diligent, then you can keep your job. However, I will not, nor will I allow you to, stand by and allow another child in this county suffer another day. They are out there, hurting and waiting for someone to save them. We are the only hope they have. I don't want lowered expectations or a string of broken promises from either of you. Understand?"

"Yes, ma'am."

"I am glad you understand that. Undoubtedly, we are up against a few law enforcement officers who are turning a blind eye to this outrageous societal problem. May I say these men are a waste of time and a waste of taxpayers' money?"

She continues, "It will not be easy when you have mountains

to climb and fires to fight. We all face decisions and great spiritual crises at times that test the limits of our faith. But we will be strong. Like Job in the Scriptures said, 'Yeah, though you slay me, I will rise again.' So will we. You've heard this before but you will hear it again. The choice is yours, ladies. You are on board with me or you are not. If you are not," she motions, "then there's the door."

The women are silent. Sarah notices that no one attempts to move towards the door. "Well, I guess this means that both of you are on board?"

Kathy says, "I will speak for both of us. I know we are just dipping our toes back into the pool of being the best social workers we can be, but we respect your decisions and will support your choices. Whatever you tell us to do, we will do it."

"Yes, ma'am. We are with you all the way," says Natasha. "I believe in my work here with this agency. I have seen so many hurting families." She begins to tear up a little. "I would walk a mile to do everything in my power to help them. Thank you for allowing me to continue with the work I feel called to do. I am really thankful to be a part of your team. I am honored to stand by you. Thank you for believing in me and giving me a second chance. I will be eternally grateful for that."

Sarah replies, "I have no doubt that your concern is genuine. However, I must add, regardless if you are doing a great job, there will be no monetary gain in return. Your only reward is knowing that you have saved a child from a horrible fate."

Kathy looks at Natasha and nods. "That's all the reward we need." She lowers her head. "I know I will always feel guilty about what happened here, but I will learn from it and do something useful with my life."

"There's one more thing," Sarah adds. "My name is Sarah.

Only people under the age of twenty-one refer to me as 'Mrs. Cole'."

Kathy and Natasha nod and they each smile. Natasha is the first to ask, "Sarah, Kathy and I have something for you in our office. Do you mind if I go get it?"

"Is it anything lethal?" Sarah smiles.

Both young women chuckle. "No."

Sarah nods her permission. She turns to Kathy as soon as Natasha leaves the room. "There will never be a good time to have this conversation, but I might as well get this over with."

Kathy cringes, unsure of where this conversation might lead, thinking it may be a prelude to a serious breach of trust which Sarah has only recently bestowed upon her.

Sarah begins. "Here comes some reality for you, and for the sake of expediency, I will be blunt. When life seems overwhelming, you need to stop and think about consequences. Listen to that 'still small voice' and rectify the wrongs in your life. Following a useless man around is not the way to deal with the emptiness you feel inside of you. The love you might think you feel is not necessarily real. However, I am not here to be your conscience or your guide and I am not here to judge you. Besides, who am I to throw stones? However, I am here as your boss. With that said, this whole routine of yours—using this office for anything but business—is not going to fly here. Decisions have consequences. Therefore, the next time you get involved with a man, keep it at home and out of this building."

Embarrassed, Kathy drops her eyes, avoiding Sarah's piercing ones. "Do you believe it is possible for hearts to change, Mrs. Cole . . . Sarah?"

"When you make up your mind to become resilient and make the effort. It takes a hard mindset and determination to move forward with your life, but I am a firm believer that all things are possible when you are determined to do so."

"How do you know if someone's heart has changed?"

"An outward sign is always a reminder of an inward change. That's just how life works."

"Last night, I did a lot of thinking about what Jim said about me. My opinion of him has drastically changed. Other than loathing him on a visual level, I have no feelings for him anymore. I'm really just hoping he will self-destruct."

At that moment, Natasha bursts in the door, carrying a present in her arms. Beaming, she said, "Kathy and I bought you a housewarming gift."

"What an unexpected surprise." Sarah accepts the wrapped gift bound with a blue ribbon. Slowly, she opens the box. "Wow. How nice. A toaster!" She smiles and her voice softens. "I love it. I promise whenever I make toast, I will think kindly of you."

Natasha giggles. "Even if the toast burns?"

Sarah glances at Kathy, still reeling from the previous conversation. She winks. "Of course, that's just how life works."

"I think she's a good human being inside," Natasha says with a smile as she and Kathy walk together to their desks. They talk quietly about Sarah and how her courageousness, humility, and self-deprecating manner echo in their ears and pound in their hearts, driving them to follow willingly and not falter.

"She's our leader," says Natasha.

Kathy agrees. "I think she'll be our mentor and I'm glad she's reiterated the common denominator of this force that makes up this agency.

They begin their day's caseloads with it a sense of communal responsibility and desire to help the weak and give hope for their tomorrows—hope to rise again. They tell each other that Sarah Cole's entrance into the supervisor's position at this office marks a resurgence of influence and respect. "We will stand beside her, and we'll make it our mission to go to places needed. It's time for each of us to be a savior to children who are hurting," they promise each other.

5

No Turning Back

Sarah turns into the parking space in front of a row of city housing. Quickly checking the name on the files with the address on the building, she confirms that she is at the right client's house. Just as she opens the car door, she catches a glimpse of some all-too-familiar activity occurring at the end of the street. A young man, standing on the street corner, nervously paces back and forth. In an instant, a black Ford F250 truck with jacked-upped chrome wheels skids to the curb and stops. After an extremely brief conversation, the truck speeds away but not before a suspicious exchange takes place. Sarah cannot see what was passed from the person in the truck to the person on the street corner, but she can see a wad of bills shoved into the driver's hand.

She shrugs and thinks, "No matter where you move to, you can't move away from some things—looks like this is a hotbed for drug activity." She meanders her way to the apartment door. Softly, she knocks. A young woman, with wide brown eyes opens the door. "Hello. My name is Sarah Cole. I'm from Safe Families. May I come in?"

The young woman—the file lists her name as "Tabitha Renew"—nervously glances around. "Where is Jacqueline?"

"Jacqueline?" Immediately, Sarah, uncomfortable with

Tabitha referencing Jacqueline by her first name, frowns and says, "Do you mean Mrs. Karr?"

"Yes. Jacqueline Karr, the Safe Families social worker. Why didn't she come?"

"Mrs. Karr is no longer with the agency."

"Do what? She is only person from Safe Families who is supposed to visit me. What happened to her?"

The astonished look on Tabitha's face, along with the intense nervousness which adds suspicion, causes concern for Sarah. She proceeds with care, all the time being extremely observant. "I am sorry. She no longer works with our agency. For now, you'll have to settle for me." She motions to the chairs. "Do you mind if we sit down?"

"Oh, yeah. Sure. Sure. Where are my manners?"

Sarah sits down and pulls out her file on Tabitha Renew. "The file Mrs. Karr has on you states that you and your baby are doing absolutely wonderful." She fumbles through the papers. "She noted that you have been clean from any drug use for almost a year."

Nervously, the young mother comments, "That's right. Yep. All that information in my folder is correct. I'm clean. Definitely clean."

"I see that you are scheduled for a follow-up court hearing in a couple of weeks."

Twirling her fingers around a strand of hair, Tabitha continuously nods. "Yep. That's right. Will Mrs. Karr be coming back to work? She and I get along so well together. I would really like to work with her."

Sarah frowns, wondering why the insistent curiosity about Jacqueline Karr. "No. Mrs. Karr will not be coming back. She has been terminated and is no longer associated with Safe Families."

The woman asks, "So you are going to be my new social worker?"

Sarah looks up from the files she is holding. *She seems very nervous.* Taking off her reading glasses, she explains, "For a while. At least until I can find a replacement." Almost within the same breath, she asks, "Is your baby asleep? I'd like to meet her."

Tabitha answers, a bit too quickly in Sarah's judgment. "Yes, ma'am. She's asleep. I mean, no, ma'am. My . . . my neighbor took her to the store with her. You know, to give me a break."

"It's good to have neighbors that are always willing to help out. Sometimes, those little breaks can be a good thing."

Before Tabitha can answer, the sound of a crying baby can be heard. Tabitha jumps, looking as if she realizes she is caught in a lie. Eyes wide, she fumbles for words. None come. Only a look that says, "I've been caught!"

Sarah remains composed, although she can barely hide a quivering upper lip. "Do you mind if I get her? I am not only to meet with you but I am supposed to see the baby, as well."

No answer from the distraught young mother. Sarah ignores her and takes the initiative. Ambling her way towards the bedroom, she is aghast at the abhorrent sight before her eyes. A quick glance in the kitchen, bathroom, and bedroom, gives evidence that the grubby house has not been cleaned in quite a while. Following the sounds of the crying infant makes her feel faint, knowing that this child is being raised in such a detestable environment. Finally, she finds the crib. The baby's cries are weak and feeble. As easily as she can, she lifts the infant and cradles her in her arms. "Sssh. Hush, little baby. Everything will be okay. I promise." She whispers, "Please, Lord, don't let this little one become a casualty of hopelessness in this home."

The smell from the infant's room is atrocious. Soiled Pampers left in wads around the room are coupled by the odor emitting from the child. Sarah bites her bottom lip, attempting to control her anger.

Anxious, Tabitha walks in and begins picking up strewn clothes, trash, and wet Pampers. "Excuse the mess. I just haven't had time lately to clean." She holds out her arms for her baby. "Do you want me to take her? She needs a diaper change."

Sarah snaps, "You think?"

Tabitha lays the baby on the bed and removes the dirty Pamper. It's quite obvious to Sarah that the baby has not had a clean diaper in quite a while. "Don't you think you need to clean her skin before—" Her eyes holding back tears, Sarah exclaims, "Tabitha, this baby has the worst case of diaper rash I've ever seen. She has welts on her bottom and they look to be infected!"

"Yes, ma'am. I ran out of wipes and couldn't clean her properly."

Glancing around the room, Sarah spies a container of baby wipes. "Then why don't you use a warm bath cloth?"

A noise from the living room makes her cringe. *Footsteps? Someone else is in here.* "I'm leaving now, Tabitha. I will be back tomorrow. In the meantime, I think it would be a good idea if you cleaned this place up—after you've given that baby a bath!"

Tabitha only nods, nervously adjusting the Pamper. Almost within the same moment, her eyes widen. Quickly, she rolls down her sleeves, attempting to cover track marks and scars that pepper her arms from years of what Sarah recognizes as heroin use. However, it's too late. Sarah notices that Tabitha must surely be in the throes of addiction.

Sarah anxiously paces. "Tabitha, I'm going to have to call Child Protective Services. This baby not only has a serious infection, but she also appears to be malnourished. I'm sorry, but I have no other choice. She needs to be removed from these premises, taken to a

hospital for immediate care, and I am going to recommend Child
Protective Services begins to look into family placement."

Tabitha cries out. "I can't let you do it, Mrs. Cole. I can't let
you do it! She is my baby."

"All I can say, Tabitha, is that you should have thought about
this before you allowed this child to get in this situation." She
bites her bottom lip. "I have no other choice." She glances down
at Tabitha's scarred arms. "Secrets rarely stay kept. It is how they
come out that can destroy you. It is obvious that you still have a
serious addiction, Tabitha, and this baby is suffering because of it.
Don't wait until you hit rock bottom. Rock bottom is death. The
only way you are going to survive this is to move from misery to
wellness. You need rehab and you need it now!"

"Please, Mrs. Cole. I've been *clean* for several years."

"Really? Could have fooled me!"

Tabitha wails. "I am handling my problem."

Sarah cocks an eye at the blubbering woman.

Choking back tears, Tabitha murmurs, "Well, occasionally I
do go there." She continues to plead. "Despite everything I have
done in the past, I know I can change."

"Are you listening to yourself right now? Do you hear what
you are saying? No, you are *not* handling your problem! You
are *not* handling your problem at all." Sarah pulls her arm from
Tabitha's grasp. "Do you want me to believe that you have this
under control? Do you want me to believe that you will be better
in a month? A week? No, Tabitha. You have to go into rehab. You
can't get yourself clean on your own."

Tabitha begs, "Please, Mrs. Cole. I promise I'm going to get
help."

"When were you going to get help? When you get stopped
for a DUI, get caught for possession, or maybe accidently kill

someone? Of worse than that, if this baby was to die while in your care?"

"I promise I am going to quit."

"That is what all addicts say. You *will* quit and you *will* quit immediately because if you don't your life is going to be a living hell."

"I am going to kick my dependence. Please, I don't want to lose my baby."

"Whether or not you lose your baby is going to be up to you. As for right now, that baby needs to be out of here."

"What are you going to do, Mrs. Cole?"

"Like I said, I'm going to call Child Protective Services and then I'm going to see the judge."

Tabitha collapses on the floor and begins to cry, heaving heavy sobs.

Sarah focuses on her responsibilities and braces for the inevitable. As she walks back into the living room, a young man is standing there—the same one who she had spied earlier making the exchange with the man driving the black truck with the jacked-upped chrome wheels. Without saying a word, Sarah scoots past. Stopping shortly on the porch, her gaze lifts upwards. "Dear Lord. What is going on in this house? Please guide me to do the right thing—especially for that baby."

She hurries back to the office in her gray Mitsubishi, grabbing Tabitha's files and slamming the car door behind her as she nearly runs to the front door. As she opens it, Natasha is standing at the receptionist's desk. Sarah barks, "In my office. Now!"

Natasha, on Sarah's heels, anxiously follows. Sarah slams the door behind them. Natasha asks, "What's wrong, Sarah? You look like something or someone has upset you."

"I am so glad you asked. I want to know all *you* know

about Jacqueline Karr. Put all the cards on the table and start talking. Now!"

"I don't understand. What do you mean?"

"I mean 'spill the beans.' Give me an update and tell me the truth. I want to know everything about Jacqueline Karr's work here with this agency. I was trying to stay out of your business, but I think you'd better start explaining the reason for the fight. You know, the one I walked in on the other day. Remember? The one with the flying vases?" She motions to the bandages on Natasha's arm. "Does the word 'stitches' ring a bell?"

Natasha begins to wring her hands and paces nervously back and forth. Sarah takes the incentive. She slaps Tabitha Renew's files down on her desk. "These files are terribly misreported. In other words, these files are a pack of lies. I was in this girl's home about an hour ago. According to Jacqueline's notes, she visited Tabitha five days ago and reported that the house was immaculate and the baby was properly cared for, clean, and nourished. 'A complete positive, encouraging visit,' she states. Bull crap! That house has not been cleaned in weeks, probably months. And, the baby! She is left unattended and lies in crusty poop because she hasn't been changed in days. The rash on her skin is so severe, she needs immediate medical care."

Eyes narrow with anger as Sarah moves in close to Natasha and glares. "Tabitha has fresh needle punctures all over her arms. I had to contact Child Protective Services to get that baby out of there immediately and put in placement. Fast! My question is why hasn't this problem been addressed before now? Like I said, Natasha. Start talking!"

The visibly frightened social worker stutters, "You don't understand, Sarah. If I tell you what I know, it could cost me my little boy's life. I may be a lot of things, but I love my little boy with all of my heart and I can't risk putting his life in jeopardy."

"And, I, like a total moron, believed in you. I didn't fire you the other day because of that sad soap opera story about your conviction. I believed that when you saw a child in trouble, you would walk a mile to save it. No! I thought you would run! I guess I was totally wrong when I believed that if I kept you on here, you would be an asset to this department. Am I wrong?"

Natasha beats the desktop, choking back tears. "What right do you have to judge me? I kept quiet because I need this job. I—I just happened to be in the wrong place at the wrong time. Telling you is just not worth it."

"That's crap! Tabitha's baby desperately needs our help, Natasha. Jacqueline Karr closed a blind eye and now that baby may die from malnutrition, complications from infected sores, or worse because of a drugged-up mother who is incapable to taking care of her. That baby's condition is beyond horrific. In fact, whatever is going on in that house is wrong on so many levels. And as soon as this conversation is over, you and I are going to start preparing enough documentation and evidence against Tabitha Renew to legally put that baby in foster care."

"There must be another way, Sarah. I would sacrifice myself to save her baby, but I can't sacrifice my job. Don't you understand?"

Sarah sits at her desk and places her head in her hands. Soberly, she says, "I understand. Really, I do. I can't chastise your behavior when I would react the same way. I could sacrifice myself, but never the daughter I love. I would lay down my life for her."

"Are you going to fire me?"

Sarah lifts her head and looks at Natasha. "That's a little cheesy, don't you think? I mean, asking a question like that. Talk is cheap. You are a coward and you do not have the character to qualify you as a member of this team. I don't recognize you anymore. I don't feel like you have a real purpose here anymore. The person I thought I knew is resourceful, and you definitely are not. I demand a staff that is always forthcoming with me. How can I believe anything you say to me ever again? Does that answer your question?"

Natasha swallows hard. "I see you as strict yet fair, predictable but unconventional. I understand well that I'll have to reap the consequences of deliberate disobedience. I realize that I deserve all of your anger."

Sarah cocks an eye and sarcastically comments, "Thank you for validating my rage." Sarah looks up into the distraught woman's eyes. "Is that supposed to make me think better about you?"

"Maybe if you don't, that's a good thing."

"Maybe it is," Sarah says, as she gathers Tabitha's files.

"What are you going to do?" Natasha asks.

Sarah places the files in her briefcase. "I'm not going to sit around and do nothing. I am going to make sure that baby has been taken out of that home, and then I'm going to see the judge about an emergency shelter hearing."

"I've lost your respect, haven't I?"

"Respect is all about trust and it takes a lot to win my trust. I thought I stressed to you and Kathy that trust builds a good working relationship. If you can't be real with me, Natasha, and let me in to what is going on with you, I can't respect you."

Looking rejected and downtrodden, Natasha sniffs back a tear.

Sarah is quick to notice her genuineness. Despite her feelings of distress, she says more calmly, "Here's the thing: truth is objective. It has been proven through the ages that being truthful does not always win out but it's the only alternative that helps a person sleep at night." She shrugs, moving steadily away from the woman who betrayed her.

Sarah slips out the door and to her car, leaving Natasha with her thoughts. Just as Sarah starts to turn the key, the passenger's door opens and Natasha scoots in.

Although not surprised, Sarah chuckles. "You sure have been an element of surprise today!"

Natasha replies. "The first day I met you, Sarah, I recognized your inner strength. I knew immediately that you were the best person for this job. I am not as strong and centered as you, but maybe if I hang around, I will learn to be brave and not be a coward. Maybe I will learn how to make my life better because what I do with my life will be the person I become."

Sarah smiles. Her wrath subsides and tender mercy prevails. "You have tested my limits, but I am going to take a substantial risk on you. I'm on my way to Child Protective Services. Do you think you are ready to jump on board? From this point on, no more secrets and all things are legit and above board. You have to agree to my terms and there is no turning back." Sarah grins as if she already knows Natasha's answer. "This is your mission. Do you choose to accept it?"

The door closes. Natasha salutes. "Yes, ma'am. I accept the mission. I'm on board."

"Are you sure about this? No second thoughts?"

"No. None whatsoever. I'm in this for the long haul. Let's go."

6

A Trying Day

A couple of days later, Gracie drives her red Taurus to the local grocery located in the center of Wesleyville. As she parks in front of the store, she notices a young woman about her age exiting the building carrying a couple of grocery bags filled to the brim. Suddenly, Gracie notices another car wheeling directly towards the young woman. Two boys jump out, surround her, and knock her groceries out of her arms onto the pavement. Cans roll under the cars—eggs in a carton crack, and to add insult, one of the boys smashes a loaf of bread with his foot. The thugs jump back in their car, tires squeal, rubber burns, and laughter and hoots are louder than the rumble of the engine.

Gracie approaches the distraught young woman, noticing her wavy brown hair and sad, teary blue eyes. She stoops and begins to pick up the salvageable grocery items. "Hey, what's going on? Are you okay?" Gracie asks the woman, who is wiping tears on her cheeks. *She looks both destitute and broken. Those malicious thugs . . .*

She glumly mutters, "Don't worry about it. It doesn't matter. I'm used to this."

Gracie shakes her head. "No! I hear what you are saying. It sounds as if you have been down this road before. However, it does matter. What those idiots just did to you is wrong and no human being deserves to be treated this way. It's incomprehensible." She hands a bag to the girl and looks around at her surroundings. "Where are the police when you need them?" She smirks. "This is a bummer. A real bummer!"

The wretched young woman shrugs her shoulders. "Who knows?"

"You say that you are used to this? Has this happened before?"

"Something always happens. It just depends on where they see me. It used to happen at school. Finally, I was at a low point in my life, had enough of the bullying and I officially became a sixteen-year-old dropout. Now, it happens wherever they see me, walking down the street, whatever—they treat me as if I was raised by wolves."

"This cannot be easy."

"No, it's not."

"It is cruel. It is mean. I'm so sorry that this is happening to you, but those boys are bullies and they need to be stopped." She wipes the egg whites from her hand and holds it out to the flustered young woman. "My name is Gracie. What's yours?"

"Nice to meet you, Gracie. My name is Angela." Gracie thinks, Angela appears to be a simple girl, but despite her shyness, her eyes are sparkling and yet wary at the same time, as if she is unaccustomed to being friendly to strangers.

A smile dimples Angela's cheek. "Thanks for helping me. I really do appreciate you stepping in, but I guess I'd better start for home."

"Where is your car?" Gracie asks.

"I don't have one. My boy—my brother tells me I have to walk wherever I go. He says the exercise is good for me and it will keep me from getting fat."

Gracie takes a bag out of Angela's hands and places it in the back seat of her car. "Excuse me for saying so, but it sounds like your brother is an insensitive jerk. In other words, he is shallow, thoughtless, and cruel."

"Don't let him hear you say that!"

"Believe me—I'm not scared. I've never met the guy, but I really don't care about what he thinks. Pathetic, right? That's just me. Anyway, you are in no frame of mind to walk. Get in. I'll take you home."

"You don't have to do that. Honestly, I am okay."

"You don't have a problem with what just happened to you? Really? I don't believe it. So, hop in. I am not going to let you walk home. Not after what I just saw you go through. Besides, I want to do this for you. That's what friends do."

"You are my friend? Since when?"

"Since just now. That is, if you want me to be."

"I've never had a friend. I never went to summer camps and made friendship bracelets."

"Well, you have a friend now." Gracie opens the car door. "Come on. I. can listen if you want to talk on the drive to your house. They say I'm a brilliant conversationalist.

The drive to Angela's house is short. Traveling at a country pace down a two-lane road, past an old rundown motel, Gracie notes a BBQ restaurant marked by a small crowd of people waiting out front, blocking the sidewalk, eager to go inside. On the next corner are ramshackle gas stations and a few dilapidated buildings.

Slowly Gracie drives. A series of turns brings her onto a dingy back road, which gives way to farmland. Gracie rolls into the driveway of a small home with cedar shingles on its front side and a metal roof topping it. The house has been thoughtfully restored, discreetly updated, and yet it is a gentle example of a torn down mentality. Gracie notices a large steel building in the back of the lot near a tree line. Next to the building is a group of emaciated cats playing among heaps of trash.

Sitting in the shade of a nearby tree, she spies an old man rummaging around in the pockets of his frayed, faded overalls. He pulls out a bone-handled pocketknife and opens a blade that appears sharp enough to shave a cat. Holding the knife in front of him, he stares at Gracie with cold, challenging eyes. As he rubs his thumb along the knife edge, he smirks. Finally, he snaps it closed. The sharp click makes her jump.

Gracie walks away from the man and suddenly notices a black Ford F250 truck with jacked-upped tires and chrome wheels parked in the back yard. She exclaims, "Wow! Love the truck! Talk about a conversation starter! To whom does that belong?"

"It belongs to my brother." Angela is talking in a near whisper.

"What's his name?"

"Bobby. Bobby Wright."

"All I can say is that Bobby Wright must make a pile of money. I'd like to have a job working where he works. By the way, where does he work?"

"He doesn't work anywhere. In fact, like me, he didn't even graduate from high school."

"Really? Then where does he get the money to burn like that?"

Angela explains, "I don't exactly know. He stays in that shop just about all night and sleeps most of the day. He won't allow anybody in that building except for Uncle Ham." She motions to the man sitting under the shade tree holding the pocketknife. "Gracie, if you want to remain my friend, please don't get fired up on curiosity. There are too many secrets around here. Believe me, it's not a good idea if you start asking questions."

Stunned, Gracie replies, "Sure thing. No problem. Just remember something, Angela. No secret ever stays buried. It always comes out and it generally hurts the people involved."

Quickly she scribbles on a piece of paper in her console and hands it to Angela. "This is my cell phone number. Any time you can't get a ride to the grocery store or anywhere, just give me a call." Once again, she fumbles around in the console. "Here's some pepper spray and a whistle. Take it with you on your next trip to the grocery store. Use it if those boys come after you again."

"You are sticking your neck out. I think it was pretty cool of you to step up for me like that. Even though I appreciate what you are trying to do, you can't possibly know how dangerous being my friend can be."

Gracie grins. "It's my neck."

Angela reciprocates. "Thanks, Gracie. This means a lot. And, thank you for rescuing me today."

"You're welcome. My mom says I've always been a sucker for . . ." She stops, catching herself just shy of being totally embarrassed.

Angela intervenes. "A sucker for losers?"

Gracie smiles—though she doesn't feel at all like smiling. "Something like that. I'm going to take off, but just remember I am a phone call away if you ever need me."

Angela turns to walk away, then turns back to face Gracie. She smiles. "Thank you."

As Gracie backs out of the drive, her eyes lock with those of Angela's brother, who is exiting out of the steel building that Gracie figures is probably used as a shop. Wearing fatigues and boots, he locks the door behind him—odd for someone with supposedly nothing to hide, Carrie guesses. His keen blue eyes find those of Gracie's. For some unknown reason, she shivers. Cautiously, she drives away.

Gracie begins to walk down the hall to her mother's office. Suddenly, the phone on the receptionist's desk rings—only there is no one to answer. Without hesitation, she scoots behind the desk. "Hello. Yes. This is Safe Families Services. May I help you?" She takes a notebook out of the top drawer and begins to write. "Of course, I will make sure she gets the message. Thank you and have a nice day." She hangs up.

Standing in the hallway and eavesdropping on Gracie, who sounds more proficient than any receptionist they've known, are Natasha, Kathy, and of course, Sarah. Kathy whispers, "Hire her, Sarah. We are in dire need of a good receptionist and she is so darn professional sounding. She is the best!"

Natasha adds, "Yeah, I picked up on that right away. Gracie is a very intelligent and perceptive person. She would be an asset. So, give her the challenge. If she succeeds, I have to tell you, it would be a beautiful thing for a mother to see."

Her heart bursting with pride, Sarah replies, "I'm not allowed to hire relatives, but if I could, she would be in."

"Then don't officially hire her. Just keep her around to answer the phone until someone else applies for the job. You can pay her by adding to her allowance. We'll help you." Natasha pleads. "At least, let her work until she starts to college this fall. Just think, Sarah, what an added benefit she would be."

Ears perking up, Gracie smiles from the desk as she looks at the paper in front of her. "I hear you talking about me. I'm right here. I can hear everything." She continues teasing them. "I'll take the job and you don't even have to increase my allowance."

Grinning, Sarah asks, "What's the catch?"

Continuously glaring at the paper before her, Grace adds, "I don't wash the dirty dishes for one month."

"That's too easy. Is there something else?"

Acting aloof and unconcerned as she scribbles on the paper, Gracie answers, "Let me think a minute. Oh, I know. I would like two tickets to the next Justin Bieber Concert in Jacksonville. Front row seats."

Sarah grins at her outspoken daughter. "How can you say '*no*' to a girl like that?"

Within that same moment, the receptionist's phone rings again. "Safe Families. This is Gracie. May I help you?" Quickly, she takes notes. "Yes, sir. Immediately. I understand. I'll make sure she gets the message. Thank you, sir, and have a nice day."

The group in the hall anxiously waits for a response. Gracie turns to the women and explains, "Mom, that was the DA. He said he is sorry he keeps missing you. He says he is out of court for the rest of the day and he'll be waiting on you at the courthouse. The two of you can go in to see Judge Sloan in his chambers. He wants you to bring all of your documents and evidence against Tabitha Renew to move forward on the emergency shelter hearing. He says to come immediately."

Sarah turns to Kathy and Natasha. "Kathy, please do a follow-up with your client that lives in the same projects with Tabitha. Natasha, you come with me. I want you to have the chance to shed some light on Jacqueline Karr's illicit behavior. Let's ride."

Natasha grins, gratefulness and respect for her new supervisor lighting up her face. "Okay, boss."

7

An "A-Ha" Moment

Sarah and Natasha shoot up the steps to the courthouse. Frantically, Sarah glances around. "Let's find the DA's office and get a quick briefing." Once inside, she asks the DA's secretary, "We are here to see Mr. Hines. Is he in his office?"

"No. He had to leave unexpectedly. He said to tell you that it was a matter of strict importance and could ultimately lead to solving a case."

"I see."

The secretary continues, "However, he wants you to go upstairs to Judge Sloan's office and present him with the evidence necessary to move forward with an official hearing on the Renew case."

Sarah looks at Natasha, standing nervously by her side. "We have no other choice. Can you handle your part?"

Natasha nods, affirming. "Yes, ma'am." She cast a discerning eye towards Sarah. "Do you think our case is weak?"

"No. Definitely not weak. It's a slam dunk!"

After asking for brief information, they are directed to Judge Sloan's office on the second floor of this historic building, its style dating back to the turn of the century. The steps leading to the upstairs office begin to creak. The smell of the cedar paneling on the walls tickles their noses. Shortly, Sarah knocks on the door.

"Come in," says the voice from the other side. A large, pompous-looking figure sits in a chair behind a large oak desk. He motions for the two to sit. "Please be seated. Let me clear up something before we begin. I have decided to keep this meeting informal, but the custody of the Renew baby will be solved today." He clears his throat. "I understand that you have some evidence on the Renew case you'd like for me to review, Mrs. Cole."

"Yes, I do, Your Honor. She reaches across the desk, placing Tabitha Renew's files in front of Judge Sloan. "I would like to present these files and affidavits to prove that Tabitha Renew is unfit to be a mother and prove that this warrants her baby should be removed from her custody as soon as possible. Could you expedite this and get the ball moving, Judge? That baby's life depends on it."

"And why is that?"

"I have reason to believe that Tabitha Renew, one of our clients from Safe Families, is using drugs again and using them in her home where she cares for her six-month-old baby girl. On a home visit with Miss Renew the other day, I noticed that the baby is not getting the proper care she needs. I was afraid if she didn't get medical attention, and soon, there will be some dire consequences. Therefore, I called in Child Protective Services to remove the baby from her home. The statements you have before are from that agency attesting to the fact that the Renew baby definitely was in need of medical care when they arrived at the home. Furthermore," she pointed towards the other file, "these are the medical records that state the baby was in need of medical treatment when she arrived at the hospital. These affidavits are signed and attest to the fact that Tabitha Renew should not be around her baby."

"Where is the baby now?"

"She is still in the hospital, seriously ill. I am here today, Judge, to present evidence to have an official hearing to look for family placement. If none, then I'd like for her to get into the foster care system."

He slides his glasses back from the tip of his nose, and scans through Jacqueline Karr's files on Tabitha Renew. After a short review, a frown contorts his face as he begins his assessment. "After reviewing this document, it seems to me that Miss Renew is not showing any signs of drug abuse or that she is neglecting her child. In fact, it reads extremely complimentary of her character, the condition of her home, and the excellent care she is giving her child."

"May I intercede, Your Honor?"

He pulls off his glasses and glares into Sarah's eyes. "You appear to be confident, prepared, and intelligent, Mrs. Cole. I will do what I can as long as it's in my range of authority."

"Those files of Jacqueline Karr's you have just completed reading are unreliable."

"What do you mean, Mrs. Cole? They look legitimate to me."

Sarah moves closer. "The social worker, Jacqueline Karr, who monitored Miss Renew for over a year, falsified those reports." She turns to Natasha. "Miss Woods shared an office with Jacqueline Karr. Not so long ago, Miss Woods found out that Mrs. Karr was on the payroll of one of the drug dealers in this community. She was paid to look the other way and to falsify records that might cast suspicious lights on the sale of drugs. She did this in more cases than one."

The judge says, "At this juncture, I need to speak to Miss Woods."

Sarah looks at Natasha. "Tell him everything you know."

At first, Natasha hesitates as if afraid to come forth with incriminating evidence that could put Jacqueline Karr away for a long time. She took a deep breath, remembering her promise to be more proactive, which could spur Judge Sloan to write a court order for an emergency shelter hearing to keep baby Renew away from her mother. Her dedication and trust in her new supervisor, Sarah, inspires her to move forward. "Judge Sloan, what Mrs. Cole is telling you is the truth. Furthermore, Mrs. Karr threatened to have bodily harm done to my son if I went to the authorities with this information."

"So, you restrained? Putting your job at risk?"

"Yes, Your Honor. I was desperate, I panicked, and I was afraid of what might happen to my family." She pauses as she motions to Sarah. "However, I have learned to respect my new boss, Mrs. Cole, in more ways than you will ever know. She has encouraged me to take a good look at myself and to do the right thing. There is a baby's life at stake and I want to do everything I can to save her."

Judge Sloan scratches his chin. "Do you have any proof other than your conversations with Mrs. Karr to authenticate these accusations? Did you ever record any of your conversations with this woman? Is there someone else that heard your conversations and can verify the validity?"

Natasha stutters. "No—no, sir. I only have my word and the fact that Mrs. Cole walked in on one of our fights over the matter."

He turns to Sarah and inquires, "When you walked in on this fight, did you overhear any of the conversation between the two? Did you ever hear Mrs. Karr admit and then record that she was acting illegally?"

Sarah, quite aware where this questioning is headed, lowers her head. "No, sir. I didn't actually overhear or record their conversation."

"Miss Woods, did you ever consult with any of our law enforcement on this matter?"

"No, sir. I did not. I don't have too much faith in the authorities."

"And, why is that, Miss Woods?"

"I didn't know which ones I could trust. I am also aware that a couple of officers of the law here in town are crooked. On the take, sort of speak. That is, they were also on the payoff roll from the man bringing drugs into our county."

"Do you have any proof of those suspicions? Do you have any evidence of these accusations that could hold up in a court of law?"

Looking weary, Natasha squirms. "No. I do not. Moreover, I strenuously object to this line of questioning against me. This is beginning to sound like an interrogation. I'm not the culprit here."

Judge Sloan crinkles his brow and leans forward across his desk. "Miss Woods, do you know how many cases without sufficient evidence and sad washed-up stories come across my desk every day? Do you think I commit them to memory? No! I discard them with the rest of the trash." He turns back to Sarah. "Do you have anything other than questionable proof you'd like to share, Mrs. Cole? All I have heard so far is completely circumstantial in proving that the mother is on drugs. Tabitha Renew has the right to hire a legal attorney and if you have no legal evidence that she is using drugs and putting her baby in harm's way, what you have given me today will not stand up in court. Her parental rights are still protected under Georgia law and the child will go back to her."

Sarah stands her ground. "Yes, I do, Your Honor. I have other evidence. After Mrs. Karr was fired, I followed up on a visitation with Tabitha Renew, the client in question. As I drove up to her apartment, I noticed a drug exchange taking place. It took place on the corner only a few apartments down from Miss Renew's apartment. The drug dealer was driving a black 250 Ford truck with jacked-upped chrome wheels. He was handing a Ziploc bag to a man filled with items which I could not see—the same man I saw in Miss Renew's home a few minutes later."

"Did you take pictures? Did you alert the police to the scene?" Sarah stands. "No. I didn't!" She bursts out, "Like Miss Woods, I didn't know which cops I could trust." Never taking her eyes off those of the judge's, she directs Natasha, "Let's get out of here. I know where this is going."

The judge contends, "I realize that tempers flare in cases like this. Protecting a child brings out all kinds of emotions. However, this court is tasked with acting in the best interest of the child. While serious allegations have been made against Tabitha Renew, there is not enough collaborating evidence that will warrant arresting Miss Renew or taking her baby out of her custody."

Judge Sloan holds up the file of Tabitha Renew. "I was just wondering, Mrs. Cole. Why didn't you change or add to Mrs. Karr's files on Miss Renew before you came to see me?"

On edge with this relentless conflict, bluntly, she answers, "I live by a code, Judge Sloan. I do not fabricate records or lie under oath."

"I respect that. I also have a code of my own," he comments.

Natasha whispers to Sarah, "Could have fooled me!"

"What did you say, Miss Woods?"

"Nothing, Your Honor."

Judge Sloan stands. He extends his hand. "I'm sorry, Mrs. Cole. I can't grant a court order for an emergency shelter hearing. There is not enough evidence to back it up. All you have given me is speculation. Nothing proves innocence, and unfortunately, nothing proves guilt. There is no reason to deny Miss Renew custody of her child. Therefore, I will be awarding full and legal custody to Tabitha Renew and your request for an emergency family shelter has been denied."

Once again, Sarah blurts out, "Your Honor, you can't give that baby back to her mother! She is dangerous. That home is not fit for that baby. She will surely die!"

"I'm sorry, Mrs. Cole. I would like to begin by stating a very simple truth. Tabitha Renew is the mother of that baby. My decision is final. It is based on the fact that you have no real evidence to show me that she is a danger to her baby."

Sarah's nostrils flare. "I disagree vehemently with you, Judge Sloan. However, thank you for your diligence." She speaks with fiery indignation, her eyes narrowed, her forehead furrowed. I am beginning to harbor complete and undeniable desire for retaliation towards Judge Sloan, she thinks.

"Mrs. Cole, you are a smart, meticulous woman. This case is getting too personal to you. Because you are so emotional about this, are you sure you are going to be able to follow this all the way through regardless of the outcome?"

"Maybe, but I can handle it. Let me make myself clear about something, Your Honor. I don't know what the solution will be to getting that baby away from that house, but I will figure it out. And you can bet, it will be legal and on the up and up, so as you can't come back and say it was all circumstantial."

"Watch yourself, Mrs. Cole. You are missing the point here."

"Then please get to the point, Your Honor. Or is this an order or a threat, sir? Either way, I haven't even started. As for right now, I am done talking about this. Good day." As Sarah storms out the door, she remarks over her shoulder; her voice, clear and composed, "Tell that to baby girl Renew. Tell her that you don't have enough evidence."

As the two women storm down the stairs, Natasha asks Sarah, "Don't be so hard on yourself, Sarah. You tried your best to talk him down." She stares at Sarah, noticing the tense muscles and narrowed eyes. "Are you okay?"

"No! I am so mad at that sanctimonious idiot, Judge Sloan. I am mad with the sheriff's office and the inept police department that overlooks justice. I am angry because that baby doesn't seem to have a chance—all based on supposed lack of evidence. All I know right now, is I've got to get out of here before they come after me with torches and pitchforks."

"You can blame me for what happened. You've got to put your anger somewhere. As far as getting anywhere with the judge, that ship has sailed."

"No! That ship caught fire and is burning up in some Viking sea." She casts a discerning glance towards Natasha. "I'm sorry. I don't mean to seem as if I'm overreacting. Give me some time. Although right now it seems like a defeat, I'll get over it. Besides, throwing down on the mighty judge would only compound the problem." She pointed to her head. "Talking with the judge gave me a migraine."

Natasha reaches inside her purse for an aspirin. She makes a bold statement. "I have some serious speculations that Judge Sloan might also be on the take."

"Said the spider to the fly." Sarah chuckles. "I was being facetious. Actually, I was thinking the same thing."

"Sit here for a while and nurse your headache, Sarah. Try to stay calm and quiet. The judge may have thrown a wrench in the works, but I have something up my sleeve."

Sarah frowns. She asks, "Whatever do you mean? Where are you going? I know you have an agenda but I don't know what your agenda is."

"I'll explain when I get back. Right now, someone has to stay here and look all innocent. I nominate you. I have a suspicion. Tell you in a minute." Quickly, she scurries away.

Patiently, Sarah waits in the car, wondering about the sudden urge of Natasha's to slip away. Soon, Natasha is back in the car beside Sarah. "Well?" Sarah asks. "What's the big secret?"

"Just a suspicion. I thought I heard a click on the phone system while we were in Judge Sloan's office. And I was right. Judge Sloan's secretary was listening in to the conversation we were having with the judge. I walked in her office and pretended as if I was looking for something. She was standing at the filing cabinet with another secretary, spilling all that she overheard."

"Hm," says Sarah as she backs out of the parking space. "Seems like there is no one in this whole legal system in this county we can trust." She turns to Natasha. "By the way, I admire your resilience. I am really glad you are moving forward with your life."

"Thank you, Sarah. I am doing my best." She sighs. "What do we do now?"

"Nothing at the moment. We will find another way. Not all is lost. Right now, I'm going home to take an 'a-ha' moment."

Sarah wheels into her drive, slams the car door, and heads for the shower. Gracie follows close on her heels. "What's the rush, Mom? Where are you going?"

"Straight to the shower. I need my therapy."

"Back to the shower? Tell me, how does that work for you?"

"I don't know. I guess when I'm in the shower and the water is rushing around me, it takes me to a different place, where everything becomes serene, a little ruminative, and a whole less anxious. The water turns off that switch in my brain which allows me to go into a drift mode, sorta speak. I have one of those 'a-ha' moments." She closes the bathroom door behind her. "Now, if you don't mind, my dear, give me some desperately needed space so I can reduce some of these stress hormones that are eating away at my insides." She flips on the shower knobs.

Gracie presses against the door, talking from the other side.

"Is it anything I have done? Have I made you mad or something? You are wound up tighter than a snapping turtle, ready to snap."

Suddenly, the swish of the shower goes silent. The bathroom door slowly opens. Peering out is Sarah, wrapped in a towel. She speaks softly to Gracie. "There is nothing in this world you could ever do to make me mad with you, Gracie Cole. We might have our disagreements at times, but nothing, absolutely nothing, can ever make me mad or disappointed with you." She reaches for Gracie's hand through the opening in the door. "You are my strength. My reason for doing the things I do. You empower me and give me the drive to be the best I can be."

Gracie quickly wipes a fallen tear before her mother notices. "Thank you, Mom. I love you."

"I love you, too." She smiles. "Now, if it's okay with you, I need to focus on my bath."

Sarah stays in the shower for almost thirty minutes until the water heater's heating element is sent into overdrive. She moseys out on the porch with a towel wrapped around her head and a robe covering her body. Sitting in the swing is Gracie, leisurely wrapped in her own robe as she waits for the shower, with Lilly in her lap. Sarah sits down, looks up, and begins to swat at the insects swarming overhead. "There is one thing I definitely miss about living in the city—the trucks that make the rounds spraying for mosquitoes."

Gracie agrees, "Me, too. By the way, did the shower take you to the O-zones and make you feel better?"

Sarah deeply exhales. "Yes, I feel so much better." She props her leg up in the chair. "A good, hot shower always comes through for me." She smiles, totally relaxed. "Sometimes, Gracie, the stress of my job really gets to me. When a child's life is on the line, it wears on my heart and mind." She leans back and listens to the whippoorwills strumming their melodious nightly tunes. "When you lose a helpless young soul, all the hope for that child's life is squashed. Whatever future they had is cruelly snatched away. I am that baby's only hope. This is my job and I am failing the Renew baby, Gracie. It's not an easy thing to deal with."

"Mom, don't dwell on the ones you have lost or might lose. Dwell on the ones you have helped. The ones you were responsible for. You gave them hope for a promising life."

"I try. I really try, but sometimes . . ." Her voice trails off.

Gracie stands and gives Lilly to Sarah, whose wagging tail shows she is happy being shared between the two. Sarah asks, "Where are you going?"

She answers, "Since we don't have an in-house masseuse, I am going to the shower to have my 'a-ha' moment."

8

Point of No Return

Stopping at the door of Kathy's and Natasha's office, Sarah enthusiastically commands, "Come into my office. Quick!"

The two women pour into their supervisor's office as requested. "What's up, Sarah? You didn't get enough sleep last night?" Natasha asks.

"No! And, I'm on fire to take down those hoodlums and that ungracious mother who parades behind a string of falsified documents. Are the two of you game?

"You bet!" Kathy shouts. "And have I got some news for you!"

"If it's good news, then spill it. If not, keep it to yourself. I don't need anything else on my plate that will cause me to regurgitate."

"I promise, you'll appreciate this. It's the icing on the cake. I followed up with a couple of my clients that live down from Tabitha. I asked a lot of questions and got some pretty interesting answers. It seems that Jacqueline had another client or two who was paying her to, let's say, look the other way and even falsify records so that the drug transactions could continue."

"Then, we need to give each one of Jacqueline's clients a little visit. And soon."

"What can we do or say without making them suspicious?" asks Natasha.

"Tell them the truth. We are stepping in for Jacqueline and doing her visitations until we can hire more social workers. We just need to introduce ourselves and let them know we will be following up with her cases. That will give us a chance to scope things out and see what is going on in their homes, if you know what I mean."

Kathy inquires, "Do we take a chance and get law enforcement involved? You know, in case we get in over our heads and need backup?"

"No. Not until we figure out which ones we can trust. Until then, we are going to have to rely on each other. Our best option right now is to be careful and not do anything stupid. We have to be cautious and not go out there like a barrel on fire seeking justice, forgetting who we are up against and letting our guard down."

She turns to her two employees, whose attitudes toward each other suggest a newly formed bond. "You both need to understand something. Things might get a little dangerous from here on out. I want you to make sure you are ready for this. We are at a point of no return."

Kathy and Natasha look at one another and say in unison, "We are ready!"

Kathy s voice shows her determination. "We'll follow you to Hades and back if we have to."

Natasha concurs. "We would fight giants and follow you through any storm. You are loyal, courageous, and will never back down from anything you judge as a right thing to do."

Both then repeat, "We are ready."

"Thanks. I'm beginning to believe I can count on you. It is nice to have both of you supporting me, having my back, and being protective." She bites her bottom lip. "I am so proud of the character you two are demonstrating. While I am gone, dig through Jacqueline's files and divide up the questionable one."

"Where are you going, Sarah?"

"First of all, I am going to find that black F250 Ford truck and follow it around for a while. The next time the owner makes an illegal drug exchange, I will take a picture and have the proof in the pudding. That man is a thorn in my side and I am not going to rest until I find out the truth about what this person is up to. I am not going to stop until I have enough evidence on him so that Judge Sloan can't find some little technicality, blow the case, and release him." She pauses, then adds, "By the way, Gracie will be here in a minute. Don't discuss any of this with her."

Unknown to the threesome in Sarah's office, planning their mission, Gracie has already arrived and is standing in the hall within earshot. She whispers to herself so they won't know she is there. "Mom, I hate to tell you, but your cell phone camera won't zoom in and get close-ups. You are going to need help getting a good photo." Before she is noticed, Gracie eases back to her desk. *Mom, you have always come through for me. Now, it's my turn. You are right about one thing. This is the point of no return.*

Lunch break does not come soon enough for Gracie. As the digital clock clicks over to twelve noon, she scurries out the office to the only pharmacy in town, which also operates as a gift shop and coffee shop. As she strolls up to the counter of the gift department, she catches the eye of a familiar face—the old man sitting under the tree at Angela's house. As he with other older men drinking coffee, she notices that he pulls out of his pocket the same bone-handled pocketknife. She shivers as he runs his thumb down the sharp edge of the blade, all the time taunting her as he looks at her with evil, unyielding eyes. She swallows hard, determined not show uneasiness.

The woman behind the counter asks, "May I help you?"

"Yes, ma'am," Gracie replies. "I'm looking for a digital camera—one with a zoom lens."

"Sure. I have one you might be interested in." She pulls a camera out from the behind the counter. "How do you like this one? Do you think it will do?"

Gracie examines it carefully. "This will work. This is exactly what I am looking for."

"Would you like for me to wrap it up or just drop it in a bag?"

"It's not a gift, so a bag will be fine."

The clerk asks politely, "And how would you like to pay?"

Gracie realizes, well, here goes my Justin Bieber concert tickets. "My mother opened a charge account here the other day. She has me listed on the account. So, if you don't mind, I'd like to charge this camera, please."

The clerk inquires, "Okay, no problem. What are the names on the charge account?"

Gracie whispers so the old man with the pocketknife will not hear. "Sarah Cole and Gracie Cole."

As the clerk searches the computer for that information, Gracie glances at the old man drinking his coffee and watching her every move. She shivers.

"Sure, here it is," says the clerk. She places the camera in the bag with the receipt. "Have a nice day and come back to see us."

Gracie nods and scoots out the door. As she turns to catch a glance at the old man, she bumps into a stranger—though something about him seems familiar. "Excuse me," she says apologetically. "I'm so sorry." She freezes. She is face to face with none other than the young man she plans to capture on camera, the owner of the black Ford 250. His face sports an incredulous grin.

Quickly she gathers herself. Taking in a deep breath, she regains her composure. "Hello. You are Angela's brother, aren't you?"

"Yeah, and you are the one who was admiring my truck the other day, right?'

"Of course, I was admiring your truck. Who could blame me for coveting? It's a beautiful, flashy vehicle. Anyone who appreciates the finer things in life would dream of having a ride like that. Yep, it's definitely a conversation starter. However, there's no way I could afford anything that nice—at least, not on my measly salary."

The man asks, "Where do you work? Anywhere around here?"

Gracie lies, "Down at the convenience store on the three-way."

"The three-way, huh? I bet you don't even make minimum wage working there."

"You've got that right." She proceeds, reminding herself that this man could be dangerous. "You don't know where I can make a little extra money on the side to stay afloat?" She winks. "Like I said, anyone would love to have a ride like the one you own."

The man's lips curl as a smirk crosses his face. "Are you looking for real work, or perhaps, just an easy payday?"

"An easy payday? Sure. A little extra money will always come in handy—especially when you are drowning in bills." She looks up into his eyes, flirting with him. She purrs, "I guess you don't have to worry about paying bills, do you?"

"Let's just say I just came into a lot of money. I get to indulge my passion."

"Which is—shiny trucks?"

"And beautiful women." He reaches for her hand, smiling seductively. "Everybody needs a little help sometimes. I could use you to run errands and other things."

"Then I'm your girl."

"Listen, I've got to go inside and get my uncle. Why don't you come in with me and I'll buy you a cup of coffee? We'll get a table, talk so I can tap your brain, and discuss your *easy pay-day*." Suddenly, he remembers, "Oh, I'm sorry. Where are my manners? My name is Bobby Wright." He extends his hand. "What's your name?"

Gracie's throat muscles tighten. She cringes as she remembers the man with the pocketknife, who undoubtedly has as issue with her. "My name is Gracie and I can't go inside with you, Bobby. I'm sorry but I really need to be going."

Bobby asks, "Is something wrong? You look a little pale. I'm confused."

Gracie is quick to answer as she touches her abdomen. "I'm just feeling a little off. You know, it's a girl thing."

Bobby scratches his chin. "Huh, that's an old excuse used many times over. There are two schools of thought here, Gracie. One is saying you could be faking, the other is that you are sincere." He glares into her eyes. "I hope you are being sincere because I don't like girls who play games with my emotions."

Gracie holds her ground, never blinking, yet returning the stare. "Of course I am being sincere. Why would I lie about something like that? I just don't want to unburden all my pain and misery on you."

"Okay. Go ahead and leave. Maybe another time? Is that okay with you?"

Her eyes drop to his hands. She notices dirt underneath the nails. Bobby notices her interest. He makes a weak effort to explain, holding up his hands. "What can I say? I am a dirty-thumbed gardener. You know, the kind that loves to plant vegetables and chrysanthemums. I think I'll plant some daisies. Daisies remind me of you."

Gracie balks, not remembering a garden on the premises. She tries for a quick response. "A daisy has no scent, no great beauty. It's just a glorified weed. Like I said, I'm not feeling well. We'll talk about this another time."

"And here I am I thinking I was being so clever. Would you forgive my ignorance and maybe go out on a date with me? Just because I really don't know anything about flowers and I'm not a nine-to-five guy, shouldn't give you any reason not to go out with me." He seems to rethink his position. "Don't get me wrong. I really like routine. It keeps me focused." He grins again—seductively. "Don't tell anybody I said that. So, I guess I'll be seeing you soon?"

She purses her lips—a time-buying maneuver. "You better believe I will be seeing you soon." With that thought etched in Bobby's mind, Gracie excuses herself and walks quickly to her car. She thinks, that Boy Scout veneer that Bobby Wright is hiding under does not fool me.

For a minute, she considers the conversation with him. *What kind of a precarious situation have I gotten myself into? All my deceptions are about to be exposed. I accidently gave him some ammunition to use against me. I think I have really gotten myself in a mess. Like you said, Mom, 'we are at a point of no return.'*

9

When Looks Deceive

"Hello. Safe Families. May I help you?" Gracie asks. "Yes, sir. She is in. Hold on and I'll switch you to her extension. May I ask who is calling? Thank you, sir. Hold on for just a minute."

Gracie rings Sarah's extension. "Mrs. Cole, Paul Hines from the District Attorney's office would like to speak to you."

Sarah blurts, "Well, it's about time! I've been trying to meet this man for days."

After a brief minute of conversing with the DA, Sarah walks out of her office. Gracie asks, "What does Mr. Hines want with you, Mother?" She jokes, "You are not in any kind of trouble, are you?"

"No, I'm not in any trouble, but you are," Sarah says, returning the banter.

Gracie muscles tighten. She thinks, oh, gosh, she's found out about the camera!

However, to her surprise, Sarah sheds light on the reason for the phone call, and, thankfully, the purchase of the camera is not the topic of the conversation. "I've been invited out for dinner and you've got to close up the office and wash your dinner dishes tonight. I'll just add an extra free night to our agreement."

"Whew! Thank goodness!"

"Thank goodness? What do you ever mean by that? I thought you would be upset."

Gracie sighs with relief. "Not me. I don't mind washing dishes." A quick pause. "So, I assume it's a business meeting? You haven't been around long enough to meet any hunks." She sighs. "Not that there are any around here. Tell me about Mr. Hines. Is he married, engaged, or single and loving it?"

Sarah laughs. "He's single and you are definitely right on the other two accounts. It is a business meeting—a long overdue one—and there are no hunks around here." She bends over and kisses Gracie on the cheek. "You only have about ten minutes until time to close the office. Since this is a business meeting, I'm going straight to the restaurant. I told Mr. Hines I'd be there shortly."

"Will do. Try to enjoy yourself, Mom, and try not get caught up with business, even though just relaxing is not your forte."

Sarah walks out, waving behind her, and thinking, that's my daughter! Within a few minutes, she parks in front of the local barbecue establishment. When she enters, she notices a man motioning for her. She walks over to his table. "Mr. Hines, I presume."

Paul Hines holds his breath as his eyes devour the beautiful woman standing before him. He mutters, "Scrumptious!"

Sarah hears his remark. Paul attempts to stand and pull out her chair, but Sarah waves him off. "No, please. I'm an independent woman and I don't need your assistance."

"If you don't allow me to pull out your chair, won't you think I have atrocious manners?"

"Mr. Hines."

"Call me 'Paul.'"

"Okay, Paul. After that smart remark I heard you mumble—you

know the one—I already know you have atrocious manners. And I don't find you charming at all."

"I apologize, Mrs. Cole. It slipped out of my mouth before I had time to think. I am always opening my mouth and inserting my foot. I hope you excuse my rudeness and let's have a nice dinner. Besides, I would really like to have the opportunity to get to know you better."

"Cut the nonsense! When you called me, I was thinking you were up to something. Just tell me what you want, why you are buttering me up, and what is it going to cost me. Furthermore, Mr. Hines, I am not here to create a Hallmark moment with you. Understand?"

Paul, who Sarah reluctantly acknowledges is a rather good-looking man with a hint of gray in his hair, scrambles to make amends. "Okay, I can see you are strictly business, so we'll get down to business. I happen to know all the details about your visit to Judge Sloan." At that moment, the waitress interrupts but Paul motions her off. "Come back later to get our order. But you can bring us something to drink." He looks at Sarah. "What would you like?"

"Unsweet tea, please."

Paul chimes in, "Same here."

"Don't leave me flapping in the wind, Mr. Hines. Give me the bullet points on what you do know about my meeting with Judge Sloan, and please, don't bother to tell me how you know. I'm sure it will disgust me and kill my appetite," Sarah adds, remembering the meeting with Judge Sloan and the secretary that had eavesdropped on their conversation.

Paul Hines begins. "First of all, your agency is under scrutiny along with my firm. Both have received critical evaluations recently. Safe Families had a social worker on the take and more and more children in this county are being abused and neglected because of it. The Wesleyville law enforcement agency has a couple on the police force with a tendency to drive the opposite way when they see a certain black truck. The way I see it, we need to work together to solve our problems. I know for a fact that this once-peaceful place has been interrupted by an illegal drug trade—one generating thousands of dollars or maybe more. I, for one, will not be tolerating illegal drugs in this town, and I am not going to sit around and do nothing. I have spent the better half of my life trying to uphold the law and bring criminals to justice. Now, it just seems to fail because the problem continues to fester."

"What are you suspecting?"

"I am saying this drug trafficking is an endless cycle. Drug use leads to an increase in violence, crime, and abuse. I would even venture to say that around ninety percent or more of all prison detainees are there for some drug-related cause. The way I see it, Sarah, you and I have to work together to get to the bottom of this. Unfortunately, I can't depend on working with the local law enforcement."

"You mentioned cops looking the other way. Cops on the take. Like I told the judge, Paul, a couple, maybe more, of Wesleyville's fine law enforcement officers are receiving a payoff to avoid areas where the drug traffic is going down. Why would you want to pull any one of them into the loop until we know who is not in the loop?"

"There are only two on my radar. The rest are okay, I think. Besides, I mainly work with the sheriff's department. The sheriff and his officers are highly professional. I trust them explicitly."

"Who else is in the loop of the good guys?"

"The Regional Drug Enforcement office, which is a staffed by the Georgia Bureau of Investigation drug task force, along with our task force officers, selected from members of the county sheriff's office and the Wesleyville PD. These agencies are on the cutting edge of immobilizing traffickers and dismantling their operation. It's their vital mission to dismantle drug trafficking."

"Aren't we slowly beginning to win this war on drugs? Especially the opioids? I mean, just recently, one of the big pharmaceuticals announced it would no longer market Oxycontin to doctors. Besides, I don't understand why you need my help. Seems to me as if you have an army standing behind you."

"It takes an army. And to answer your question, we may have won a battle but we still have a war to fight. As for us, our battle front is right here in this community. That's why I need your help. Because some of your clients are known addicts, you have accessibility to help us nail the little guy who can lead us to the big guy."

Paul leans forward on his elbows and whispers. "The reason why I couldn't meet with you the other day was because I had an important secret meeting with an undercover officer from the drug task force agent who works with the GBI. He is keeping me abreast of all the information he has accumulated. He's working hard to get to the bottom of this. I have a good feeling that we are very near closing in on the whole operation."

"What's the holdup?"

"You met him the other day. Judge Sloan. He's a stickler when it comes to having only circumstantial evidence. He's thrown out more cases and exonerated more criminals than I can count. He's the main reason we can't botch this operation. I have a feeling he is a poisoned judge."

"Yes, I got the same impression. Paul, you mentioned a black truck. Do you think there is a connection?"

"I sure do. I am almost positive. But I can't seem to catch him."

"Do you have anyone following him?"

"My undercover officer is handling that part of the investigation." He scratches his chin. "Right now, the owner is not my major concern. He's not the one pulling the strings on this operation. Still, I'm going to make sure he spends the rest of his miserable years in jail."

For a moment, Sarah remains quiet, realizing that the DA's request for her to work with him warrants consideration. Still, she decides to continue to weigh Paul's request for the two of them to join forces.

Paul sips his tea that the waitress has placed on the table. "I like you, Sarah. I like the way you think. You give a good first impression. You seem very sincere and that's difficult to fake." Once again, he leans forward on his elbows. "I would like for you to come in on this case with me—before anyone else has to suffer. What do you say? You are no sucker, Sarah, and I'm no fool. You and I want the same thing. We want to clean up this mess that Safe Families and the DA's office is being blamed for in this town. And we both want to get the sole source of the mess off the street—drugs. Do you know how many sad, washed-up people come through that courtroom every day? So many I can't even commit them to memory. I am hungry for bringing down the drug people in this town. Let's begin with the law enforcement. Let me help you restore your faith in them."

"Paul, I'm a long way from having my faith restored in Wesleyville's law enforcement. So, let me put it to you in a way you might understand. What you are asking will require you and me to work closely together. I'm not completely sure I will be able to handle that."

"How can you dismiss me? We are on the same side, remember?"

"It's easy to dismiss you. You opened up our initial conversation by making an uncouth comment, which I perceived as being a come-on. Then, you let me know that no one in that courthouse knows how to keep confidential information confidential. If other people are aware of the information I shared with Judge Sloan, how long do you think it'll take the crooks, who need taken down, to keep from finding out that I am onto them?"

She drinks a swallow of her tea and dabs her mouth with a napkin. "Suddenly, I have lost my appetite, Mr. Hines. I am going home. This conversation is over, I am done talking about this, and I am out of here." She stands. "Find someone else to annoy. I will do my part from my side of the street and you stay on yours. This situation is just too contentious."

Paul mumbles, "You are not exaggerating when you say things are contentious." Paul stands and looks directly into her eyes. "Sarah, I realize we got off on the wrong foot and my behavior is keeping you at arm's length. I was just so taken with you that I wasn't thinking straight. Besides, I never have been very good at using my manners when it comes to good-looking women." Paul glances around the smoky room that reeks of smell of fresh-cooked pork and a hint of beer.

Paul chuckles as he winks. "This is not exactly what I call a couple-centered establishment. How about us going somewhere cozier? Like my place? We can surrender ourselves to the circumstances and enjoy ourselves."

"I don't think this is funny, Mr. Hines!"

"I'm joking!"

"I'm certainly not!"

"I did it again, didn't I? I overstepped my boundaries."

"Did what?"

"I crossed that line, didn't I?"

"You've got that right!"

"Please, Sarah. I admit that I thought I was being romantically clever, but now I realize my invitation to take you to my place is audacious, unexpected, inconceivable, indefensible, and yes, contentious. And not funny. I put you in an extremely awkward position."

"You think?" Sarah looks deep into his eyes. Her message is clear. "As I told you earlier, you are not charming, Mr. Hines. In fact, I find you to be quite despicable. I hate to say it, but you set yourself up to be the bad guy. You have made me feel that I have to be really cautious with you."

"Boy, you sure do get your buttons pushed easily, don't you?" He sits back down and to his surprise, so does Sarah. He continues, "My mother always told me if I was going to be stupid, I needed to learn to be tough. I'll probably never learn to be tough because I'm probably going to continue saying inappropriate things and doing stupid things, but I promise, I'll never deliberately hurt you."

"Maybe not, but when you show me disrespect, you put the possibility of our working together at risk."

His eyes plead. "You are right. I am always saying something I can't take back without thinking about the consequences. Will you reconsider and take your blinders off and see this situation for what it is? And, please, I want you to know this about me—I am an optimist at heart. If I have disappointed you, it won't be because I lied and have been dishonest with you. To add to that, I put two things above everything else—truth and trust. I believe relationships, work or whatever, win out when it is based on those two things. You trust that the other person will have your back and will always be there for you. You trust that you can depend upon each other always to be truthful, regardless of the consequences. No matter what happens, as long as you have those, a relationship has a chance."

He searches her eyes for a sign of agreement. "How's that for restoring your faith in me? Do you feel like you can trust me and believe what I say is the truth?"

Sarah remains silent.

Paul continues to press. "What happens next is not up to me. It is up to you. Stop dismissing me and acting out in anger because my mouth overshot its boundaries. Please don't let that interfere with doing what is right by making assumptions that I am a pervert. You and I have a job to do to bring this case to a close." He pauses. "The Renew baby was dismissed from the hospital this afternoon, Sarah. She was placed back into the care of her mother. You know what that means. Time is of the essence. Please, don't throw a wrench in the works."

Sarah responds. "You are right. This situation between us is awkward, so let's just agree not to agree. It is important that we work together to solve these problems, so let's agree that even though we can never be friendly, we still can disagree." She smiles. "Or agree. As for me and you working *closely* together, I reserve the right to take my time and think about this arrangement. Does that work for you?" She looks questionably at Paul. "I've had an emotional day. At the moment, I am not thinking clearly and to prevent our relationship from becoming more pretentious and difficult, I'd like to have a few days before I give you an answer."

"Okay. I'm willing to follow those rules. Take your time. I am fully aware you have the discernment and intelligence to make up your own mind."

She says, "I'll be in touch."

He mumbles under his breath, "I'm already counting the minutes."

Sarah whirls around. "What did you say? Tell me! Don't make me speculate."

Once again, Paul mumbles the words.

Sarah demands, "Man up, Mr. Hines, and own this. At least, you owe me some manner of respect. However, it seems that every time you open your mouth, and I think you can't get any lower, you dig!"

Paul slaps his own face. "Dang it! Here I go again! When I start thinking something complimentary about you, instead of keeping it inside, it comes out of my big mouth. You just have that effect on me. You are one of the most provocative and beautiful women I have ever met."

"Don't you think you are setting the bar too high?"

"No. I think you can handle it." Realizing another he's made another blunder, he beseeches, "Can we get past this? I am so, so sorry."

"Somehow, 'sorry' is not the vibe I am getting from you right now."

Paul adds, "I would like to extend an olive branch."

Sarah chuckles. "I think you know what to do with that olive branch."

"You don't pull any punches, do you, Sarah Cole? You come straight to the point."

Sarah stands and picks up her purse. "Your mother told you if you are going to be stupid, you need to learn to be tough. My mother told me to be tough, don't assume anything."

At that moment, the waitress walks up. "Are you ready to order now?"

Sarah answers. "I'm not going to order, ma'am." She motions to Paul. "However, he is ready. Order him the works—for two. The man has an ego to feed." A cynical smile crosses her pursed lips. "Enjoy your night. Alone."

Paul cannot keep his eyes off Sarah as she walks out the door but not his life, he hopes. His heartstrings tug. Is she strictly unconventional and hardcore, or is she warm and permissible on the inside and all that cynicism is pretense, he wonders. He scratches his chin. *Huh! Sometimes looks deceive.*

10

Nothing Else Matters

The warm summer air fuels a storm with a strong, sudden electrical discharge. Lightening pops as Sarah rolls into the gravel drive of her country home. Their small dog, Lilly, sitting at the window and watching the storm, scampers to meet her at the door. Suddenly, a thunderclap, louder than the others, shakes the house as lightening rips across the sky. Lilly buries her head in Sarah's chest.

Gracie stands up to greet her mother, and Sarah sees she is trembling. "Gracie, honey, are you okay? I've never known of you being frightened by a storm."

"Me? Oh, no! Not me!" Grace is eager to hide her fear, not only of the storm but of the possibility a certain man is probably watching her from his black Ford F250. She quickly changes the subject. "All dishes are washed and I have lots of time to sit and listen about the night's events." She blurts, "Is Mr. Hines crushing on you, Mom? Did you get kissed tonight?"

Sarah laughs at her daughter. "The subject of my love life is off the table, my dear." She punches Gracie on her arm. "No one got kissed. No one was wooed or charmed, especially me. I will have to admit that after an initial frisson, our relationship might have settled into a genuine understanding—a working relationship, and that's the limit."

"Wow! He must have been a real bore."

Sarah cackles. "No. He wasn't a bore. Just a little too outspoken for me."

"Then what did the two of you talk about?"

"Business. Strictly business."

"Well, tell me. I'd like to know. Give me an update. I haven't heard anything exciting all day."

Again, Sarah laughs. "I am going to word this as carefully as I can. Remember, nothing personal. Remember, I love you. However, the business I discussed with Mr. Hines tonight is office related, and for now, I need to keep it quiet. Now, let's change the subject. I need someone to talk to about other things. More important things. Do you have any smart, daughterly advice you can give me?"

Gracie plops down in a chair. "Sure, I do. Why don't I go fix us some coffee? We can indulge until we get sober."

Sarah laughs a belly laugh. Humor always does offer a brief respite from the pressure of her daily life. "Yes. Coffee would be wonderful." Suddenly, she yells out to Gracie who is walking to the kitchen. "Oh, by the way, bring us something to snack on. You know, something that is loaded with sugar. Since I don't drink, I might as well get high on carbs."

Gracie sticks her head around the corner. "What? After that *scrumptious* dinner, you just ate?"

Remembering the word muttered by Paul Hines when they first met earlier, Sarah whispers, "Yuck! She could have used a better choice of words!" She leans her head back, cradling her head, feeling the onset of a major headache.

Soon, Gracie is handing her a cup of hot, steamy coffee, heightening her senses, along with a handful of cookies. "Now, don't overindulge, Mother. Remember, too many sweets give you a splitting headache."

"Thanks, my dear. Sit down with me, okay? I want to tell you something while it is on my mind." She smiles at her daughter. "You are the best thing that has happened to me in my entire life. Do you realize what a special person you are?"

"Oh, Mom, I'm not special. However, if you want to believe that I am, then please be my guest."

"So, you don't think you are special? Tell that to someone who has known you since diapers!"

"Okay. I'm special. All that I am and all that I hope to be is because of you, Sarah Cole. You made me and you have molded me." She smiles at her mother. "I have to confess. You are a strong presence in my life."

Sarah beams. "While we are having this deep, psychological, uplifting conversation, allow me to share something else with you."

Gracie sits back and awaits the new upsurge of winsome advice from her omniscient mother. "I am proud of you because you define yourself. You don't let others define you. You live, love, and speak boldly. You harness your will and hold nothing back. Most importantly, you always do the right thing and you never let others influence you to act wrongly."

Gracie holds her breath. *I have to tell Mom the truth about purchasing the camera and the black Ford F250 I'm intending to spy on.* The unintended sins of "thou shalt not lie" and "children honor your parents" are hitting her heart strings hard. Therefore, she decides to be honest. Slowly, she starts. "Mom, I have something I need to tell you. I—"

Suddenly, Sarah's cell phone rings. As Sarah sees the name of the caller, she exhales with exasperation. "What the heck is this? Me. Living my life. I am fixing to tell Paul Hines to stay out of my business and to quit bothering me." She frames the answer button, "Hello, Paul!" Within a second or two, her voice changes—panic ensues. "I'll be right there."

"What's wrong, Mother?"

"The worst-case scenario. There has been a 911 call issued from Tabitha Renew's home." She trembles; her voice strained. "Paul says the Renew baby has died."

As Sarah jumps up and dashes to her car, Gracie looks out into the darkness, eyes searching for a black Ford F250.

Sarah drives hard and fast to Tabitha's apartment, where she meets the ambulance, sirens blaring, speeding to the small community hospital. Whirling onto the street leading to Tabitha's, she notices police are on the scene and cop cars' siren lights are flashing. Joining them are a few of the sheriff's deputies. The area has already been taped off as a possible crime scene and assessable only to law enforcement. A police officer stops her from entering into the restricted area.

What a puffed-up bully . . .I wonder about this guy. She says to him, "I am from Safe Families. Tabitha is a client of mine. I need to enter these premises."

He looks at her with no emotion. "I don't think that will be possible."

"Then, I would like to talk to another police officer."

"I'm sorry. We are understaffed at the moment. You will have to deal with me or no one."

Sarah almost laughs at his pompousness. "Then, I guess I will go with no one."

Just as their mutual stare downs become a standoff, Paul Hines walks up and addresses the officer. "Let her in, Bob. She's working with me."

Bob stands back and reluctantly lifts the crime scene tape for Sarah. No words are exchanged between the two.

Paul pulls Sarah along by her arm. "I take it the two of you didn't exactly hit it off."

"No, we didn't. I think I'm on to him and I think he knows I am on to him."

"We'll discuss that possibility later. Right now, I'm going to take you inside Tabitha's apartment with me. Remember, this place is considered a crime scene. So, don't touch anything. Understand?"

"Of course, I understand."

"Use your eyes and your nose and tell me what you detect. Don't talk around anyone, okay? Wait until we can get alone and have a private conversation."

"Sure, Paul. You've got it."

Slowly and cautiously, Sarah walks around the apartment, in and out of rooms, careful not to touch anything or get in anyone's way. Within a few minutes, she has all the input she needs. She motions to Paul that she is ready to go. Outside, she asks, "Where is Tabitha?"

"She was taken to the sheriff's office for questioning. Let's go so we can listen in on the interrogation." He looks at Sarah. "I know that you don't have any use for me, but will you ride with me? We need to share our thoughts before we get there."

Sarah says, "Yes, I'll go with you. I think it's time we put our differences aside."

Paul walks to Sarah's side of the car to open her door. Suddenly, he decides against it as if remembering how independent she is. Sarah smiles to herself, noticing his impromptu change of mind.

As soon as the two were alone, Sarah begins. "When I first entered the apartment, the first thing I noticed was a strong, unmistakable smell of marijuana. The odor hangs in the air. Tabitha and her boyfriend were smoking up tonight. I also noticed other narcotics on the kitchen table. Purple pills near a bottle with no prescription."

"Probably morphine. You really know how to scope out a place. Just one question: How do you know the boyfriend was there?"

"Two blunts and two empty glasses on the coffee table. Takeout food for two. A man's pair of shoes on the floor. He must have left in a hurry."

Paul nods in agreement, but he looks like he's getting ready to ask something else, thinks Sarah. *He wants to assure nothing was left out.* He asks, "What else did you notice?"

"The house was in the same mess it was in the other day when I was there. The baby's room smelled like poop. The thing that particularly caught my attention was that there was an intense smell of marijuana just over the baby's crib."

"Yeah, I noticed that, too. The whole thing looks suspicious to me."

"Looks suspicious to me, too."

"You are very observant, Sarah. I consider that an asset to your exasperating personality."

Sarah frowns, crinkling her brow.

Paul throws up his arms. "Just kidding! Didn't I tell you I have a bad habit of always saying something stupid?"

Paul backs out into the street. An oncoming car swirls to miss them. Sarah grabs her chest. "Be careful! You could have killed us. Risk your own life. Don't risk mine."

Paul thrusts the car into "drive" and asks, archly, "Why, Mrs. Cole, are you afraid of my driving?"

Sarah smiles. "Let's just say I don't like surprises. At the moment, an early demise would be a big surprise."

Paul looks at Sarah. "My goodness! When you smile, you are quite charming." He cocks an eye toward her. "You are so beautiful, Sarah Cole, even when you're distraught. You know, that's one of the supremely sexy things about you." He throws up his hands. "Dang it, I did it again!"

"What?"

"I crossed that line. I keep pushing you. And I promise," he raises his hand, "I'll never come on to you again."

Rather disgusted with what continues to be his unasked-for flirtation, Sarah replies, "Seems like I've heard that before. Paul, if you would just stop throwing these cryptic messages out there, we might could get along. What exactly is your end game here? You always make your point and you are always diligent when you do. I lower my defense and then you hit me all over again. I was in the process of coming to terms with the possibility of the two of us working together as a team, but you don't leave me with very much wiggle room. I understand completely that you have a problematic background, but we will never be able to move forward and build a working relationship as long as you continuously make passive aggressive comments all the time—"

Paul interrupts, "Only when it concerns you!"

"Well, get over it! I realize I am in no position to judge another man's weaknesses, but you need to ease up on me. I am not a woman out looking for a good time. My priorities are raising my daughter and doing my job to the best of my ability. Not to play "tootsie two shoes" with the likes of you. So, let's put all emotions to the side and work like two professionals. Are you ready to do that?"

Paul hangs his head. "I'm ashamed of myself, Sarah. Of course I am. For the sake of peaceful coexistence, would you accept my apology? I know it is a lot to ask, but I am hoping that one day you can find it in your heart to forgive me for being so outspoken."

"It's your call. Keep your comments to yourself. Because, Paul

Hines, you are not charming. So, give this car some gas and let's get to that interrogation."

Paul says, "I'm hurt. Every time we are together, you remind me how shallow you think I am. I am going to do better and show you that I can be a complete gentleman. Although stunned and whipped, do you think that perhaps we can become kindred spirits?"

Cool and collected, Sarah dismisses his question. "Maybe friends, but never kindred spirits." She casts a stern look towards the man whom she hopes will learn to take her seriously. "Savor the moment. I don't know how long this will last."

"Thanks for standing with me."

"Like I said, savor the moment. I don't know how long this will last."

Paul smiles, shakes his head, and drives on. Soon he pulls into the parking lot of the sheriff's department. "Observe. Don't speak. Understand?"

She nods.

Sarah follows Paul inside. In the interrogation room, Tabitha, sitting at a table, is being questioned by one of the detectives. From the other side of the two-way mirror, Sarah watches and listens. Her thoughts keep drifting back to the baby girl, another child lost; another child fallen victim to such a heinous crime. Her eyes narrow. "How can a mother not protect her very own child? What causes a mother to do the things she has done?"

Paul nods. "It's incomprehensible, isn't it?"

"'Incomprehensible' does not even begin to describe it. What's going to happen now, Paul? What is going to happen to Tabitha?"

"Our goal is to get Tabitha to tell us exactly what happened in that apartment tonight. If she gives up anything or anyone incriminating, we will find a way to hold her for trial. Right now, she is only being detained. But I want her locked away for a very long time."

"Do you think if you find evidence holding her responsible for her baby's death, she will go to prison?

"Hopefully. If I can find an untainted jury."

Sarah's heart sinks as she looks through to the other side of the mirror one more time. "I've heard and seen enough. I'm ready to go."

"Okay. I'll take you back to your car." Outside, Paul stops and puts his hand on Sarah's shoulder. "Are you ready to work with me, Sarah? Are you ready to trust me?" Paul stands back and eyes Sarah. "Look, Sarah. I know I am a louse and a slime ball. For that, I don't blame you if you never want to speak to me again, much less work with me. I hope you can put your feelings aside and don't let them interfere with what is the right thing to do—our taking out the drug guys—to save our children."

Paul bows his head, looking ashamed. He continues, "Enough of this uncomfortable feeling between us. I realize our relationship has been contentious. I recognize I made a big mistake making a pass at you on the first day I met you. My shoulder may be dinged, but my sense of chivalry remains intact. In other words, I am willing to extend myself and move beyond that if you will permit. I need you to work with me on this case. I need for you and your employees to be forthcoming with all information. All of you need to be my eyes and ears in the homes you visit. I need daily reports of anything that might seem suspicious. Do you think you can handle this?"

"I'm not a self-absorbed person, Paul. I can move past our first meeting. Our past is our past. That is where it has to stay. From here on out, we are just two people who have a common objective. My feelings about you are irrelevant to this case. It won't solve the problems we have before us." She smiles at him. "Maybe, we can look out after each other. I want to do what I can to help."

"Thank you for that, Sarah. But, I have to warn you, it's not going to be easy. There is a huge possibility that it might get out of hand and dangerous. Are you and your girls at the office going to be determined enough to help me? Is it your strong desire to go down this road with me to eliminate the threat that is killing our babies, put these sons-of-biscuit eaters in jail, and throw away the keys? Are you with me to bring down the cops who are filling their pockets and casting a blind eye?"

She turns to Paul, the man who at one time she thought to be insulting. Now, she looks at him with admiration and trust. He's kind of awe-inspiring, a, gut-wrenching savior of this little South Georgia town. *For him and all he holds true, I'll stand by his side, follow him to the depths of Hades, to bring justice for Larissa Renew and all those who came before and will come after.*

She wipes her tears. Her answer is quick and crisp. "Yes, Paul. I am more than ready. I want to take the people down who are responsible for this. I'm in this all the way to the end. I am going to finish this. My differences with you are not important. The only thing that is important to me is bringing justice for Tabitha's baby. In this moment, nothing else matters."

11

Happy Endings

"Where are you going, Grace?" Sarah asks her daughter. "Remember the girl I told you about? The one who was being bullied at the grocery store?"

"Yeah. What was her name? Angela?"

"Yes, ma'am. She called and wanted to see me. I'll be back soon." She turns to her mother. "Do you want me to go to the Renew baby's funeral with you?"

"Only if you want to. Funerals are so depressing when they are babies. I've been to one too many in the last few years."

"Are Kathy and Natasha going with you?"

"Yes, but you are welcomed to come."

"I don't think so, Mom. Funerals are not my thing; especially, funerals for babies. If you don't mind, I think I'll pass."

"Okay, you just got a reprieve. See you later, then."

The radio blares as Gracie drove up to Angela's house. The shy young woman is waiting for her sitting on the porch. Gracie bops up to the steps. "Hey. What's up?" Stunned, she stops in her tracks. "What happened to your face? It looks like you ran into a door. Or maybe, someone's fists?"

Without hesitation, Angela says, "Bobby wants to see you, Gracie. He asked me to call you and get you go come over."

Gracie cringed. "Is this a setup or something?"

Angela looks away, careful to avoid Gracie's questioning eyes. "He's waiting for you in the backyard. Gracie, I am sorry. Please be careful."

"I always am."

"No, you are not." She cried, "I told you not to get involved!" Angela jumps up and runs into the house, leaving her new friend in a precarious position.

Gracie takes a deep breath. "Oh, well. The sooner I get this over, the better." As she rounds the back of the house, she spots Bobby, standing beside his truck, waiting. He motions for her to come.

Casually, Gracie strolls closer. "Hi, Bobby. What's up? Angela is in the house. She can't come out to play," she says, trying to act unassuming, with a tint of sarcasm in her tone.

A slow smile lingers across his face. "I don't need Angela to come out and play. I've got you."

"I don't like to play with guys who get their kicks out of knocking girls around."

"And I don't like to play with girls who lie to me."

Gracie shrugs her shoulders. "I don't know what you are talking about."

"Don't try to be so funny with me, Gracie Cole, or whoever you are. I've been keeping an eye on you."

Gracie continues to play her game, acting nonchalant.

Bobby says, "I called you here because I want to talk to you. Alone. I have a few questions to ask. You need to get something straight with me."

"Shoot. I'm all ears and I'll answer anything you have to ask."

"You are a real mystery. First of all, I found out that you don't work at any convenience store on the three-way. In fact, the people who own the store have never even heard of you. What's up with the lies?" He takes out his cell phone and snaps a picture of Gracie. "Just so I can ask around—to see if anybody knows who you are."

Gracie jokes, trying to cover her fear. "Oh, gross!" she exclaims, looking at the photo. "I need a retake. That's not a good picture of me."

Bobby pulls her close and looks into her eyes.

Gracie squirms to free herself. "What are you doing?"

"I am looking at your eyes—one of the supremely sexy things about you." He laughs. "Am I making you feel uneasy? If I am, you need to get used to it. That is, if you are going to be my girl."

Gracie's mind zooms into overdrive. "Aren't you taking things a little too fast, Bobby? I don't want to diminish whatever this is you might feel for me, and I know I said some things that can be misleading, but I am not ready for anything else with you."

Bobby grabs her hand and says, "I've been wanting to hook up with you since the first day I laid eyes on you. Let me take you someplace private and I will show you exactly how I feel."

Gracie chuckles. "There is no rush. Heck, we are not even friends. How can I be your girlfriend? How am I supposed to get it on with someone I barely know?"

"Well, I want more. I can't stop thinking about you, and I think we would be good for each other."

Gracie takes a step back. "Well, I think we need to pull back a little."

"Why? Life is too short. Tomorrow, if I get hit by a bus, I still can't change the fact that I want to be with you. So, let's get something straight. I want you."

"You must be on some serious pain meds. I don't think you are thinking clearly. Heck, Bobby, we hardly know each other. What do you call this?"

"This is the same dance a couple does when they don't want to admit they have the hots for each other. One step forward and two steps back." He attempts to kiss her, but Gracie pulls back. He says, "I am tired of playing games, Gracie. You are gorgeous. I want you."

"I'm not playing games. I'm horrified."

"No, you are flattered and this game is over," he says, as he pulls her closer.

"You really know how to *wow* a woman, but let's not get all warm and fuzzy."

Bobby grabs Gracie by her arm, pulls her to him, and kisses her. Gracie frees herself and jumps back in fear. "Did you just kiss me? Why did you do that? Keep your lips to yourself, please!" She wipes her mouth. "So, what is your excuse for kissing me, Bobby? You're not on drugs, are you?"

Bobby laughs. "Is that a serious question? Didn't this kiss mean anything to you? Or you oblivious to what is happening here?"

"I don't know what you mean."

"What I mean is I am trying to find out if you are for real. You say one thing but act another. I want to know where you and I stand with each other. Don't you think we need to clear the air between us and find out what we mean to each other? I need to know if you can be trusted, and right now, I'm a little leery of you."

"Why, Bobby, you don't trust me?"

"Not one little bit. Convince me that I can." He pulls Gracie into his arms again. The two begin to tussle. Bobby exclaims, "Wow, you got some fight in you!"

"That right and I've got the moves to back it up!"

"Huh! Tough, aren't you?"

"Listen, Bobby, I'm sorry you have been given the wrong impression of me, but you and I have nothing going on together. So, the next time you try to do something stupid with me, for instant, kiss me, then think again, and stay out of my space, okay?"

Bobby ignores Gracie and grabs her once more. He attempts to pull her close but his cell phone rings. *Thank God,* Gracie thinks.

Bobby orders Gracie, "Don't go anywhere. This conversation is going to be continued!"

Gracie tries to think quickly. *What have I gotten myself into? How am I going to get out of this mess?*

Bobby snaps his phone shut and glares. Gracie swallows hard. She asks, "What's wrong? Why are you looking at me like that?"

He snarls. "We've got a lot to straighten out, Gracie. I'm tired of being on the losing end of this. Who are you and why are you sticking your nose into my affairs? Are you a cop or a confidential informant? You had better come clean with me and now!"

"You know, Bobby, this is beginning to sound like an interrogation." She jokes, "I'm not going to say another word until my lawyer is here." She glares at her accuser. "I can't believe you think I am a cop or an undercover. What is this? A theory of some sort?"

Bobby's jaw tightens. "No, it's not a theory. But it is a predictable observation. I've been putting you through a test. And, you are failing."

"Aw, come on, Bobby. Let's don't get so dramatic."

"Dramatic? Do you think I am psycho or something?"

"No! Of course, not! You are not psycho. But we aren't playing checkers, you know. You either trust me or you don't." *I need to make him think I'm in control.* She purrs, "Don't you trust me?"

"I don't know! Let me think. In what universe should I trust an undercover?"

"I'm insulted. I'm even wounded. I don't understand why you are making all these accusations about me. What have I done or said to you to make you think that I could possibly be an undercover?"

"Okay. Tell you what—I'll get over it, Gracie, or whoever you are, if you will lay it all on the line. If not, then there will be some serious consequences."

"Bobby, for some reason, you are giving me the impression that you are threatening me. Maybe, you have intentions to hurt me?"

"I am not going to hurt you, but he will." Bobby motions to his Uncle Ham sitting under the tree, running his fingers on the blade of his knife. "I've caught you in an outright lie—about who you are and what you do. So I guess you can call this a foregone conclusion."

Gracie snatches a glance at the old man staring at her and she gulps. "Answer me this, Bobby. If you are not threatening me, then you need to tell me what you are talking about and what makes you think I am an undercover or an informant? What have I done to make you so suspicious of me?"

"That was my informant that just called me on the phone. He told me that I need to be careful and to watch my back. He says there is an undercover officer on my trail." He smirks. "And you seem to be the only one whom I have caught in a major lie." He begins to rub her back, feeling for wires. "Maybe I ought to do a strip search just to be sure our conversation is not being recorded."

Squirming, Gracie says, "You watch too many *NCIS* shows. Besides, you shouldn't be so quick to judge. You know, I might surprise you and turn out to be the total opposite of what you expect. I am not wired. I am not an undercover officer. What do I have to do to prove it?"

He scratches his chin. He's trying to throw me off my game, Gracie realizes. He swallows hard as he casts a discerning look towards her. "Let's go steal a car. That'll prove you are legit."

Gracie remains calm. "Do you think I am in the business of

stealing cars? I don't think so. Stealing a car is not my style. You are going to have to come up with something else because I am not going to risk spending my life in prison just to prove some blind loyalty to you."

"Well, if you won't go with me to steal a car then how about this?" He pulls her into his arms once again. "If you are legit, then kiss me. Kiss me like you mean it. Prove to me that we are two of a kind." Another kiss. Another pullback. Bobby contends, "Huh! I guess that answers my question."

Gracie brushes herself off and straightens her top. "Exactly what do you want from me, Bobby? I'm not a skank like the others girls you have hooked up with."

"That's a very interesting question. The answer is easy. I want it all. And, if I don't get it all, I get payback. I hoping that payback won't be necessary. I was hoping that when I kissed you, it would light your fire. Then I could tell you are for real and not a fake."

"Yeah, I felt my fire get lit, all right. Contempt, disgust, and so on. I can only imagine. Regardless, what you are wanting from me is absurd. You want me to return your kiss and have serious feelings for you. I'm not wired that way, Bobby. You don't accuse me of being dishonest one minute and pulling me into your arms the next."

Gracie knew she was at a crossroads. Should she run for her life, which she knew would eventually cost her life? Should she play along for her own safety and get away as quickly as possible, or should she hang around to find out enough information to put this hoodlum away, especially for Tabitha Renew's baby? She thought, *I've come this far. I might as well see where this leads.*

Bobby smiles slowly. "You gave me the impression that you needed money and wanted to work for me. I believe we can be good together. I believe you can be an asset for me. My genuine hope for you is that you are smart about your life—about your future. So, if you want to have a happy ending and not have your life cut short, then work for me." He squeezes her arm. "And, never, never cross me."

Gracie stands rigid, not even blinking an eye.

Bobby asks, "What do you say to that? Am I going to be able to count you in?"

Realizing her back is pushed up against a wall, Gracie lies, "I never thought a really cute, sexy guy like you could be into me. I am so taken with you, Bobby, it's really hard to think straight. So, I guess in some convoluted way, you and I are partners. That is, if you are done trying to con me."

Her answer seems to please the thug. Did I pull this off? Looks like it, maybe.

"That's what I wanted to hear. Now, to seal the deal—just to make sure you don't dare turn on me—I want to give you a little gift." He opens the truck door, extracts a bag of money, and hands it to Gracie. "Open it!"

Gracie hesitates, but finally opens the bag. Each step closer gets her deeper and deeper to a point of no return. As her eyes become fixated on the contents, she gasps; eyes widen. "Wow! This is really rich! What are you? A human ATM machine? I've never seen so much money!"

"Then put on your sunglasses so you won't be blinded. I want to impress you because you are low on funds. Didn't you say you needed money to pay off bills? You ought to be pleased."

"Are you for real? I mentioned money and now you are all over me. Yeah, I said I needed some cash, but I'm not accepting this, Bobby. This is preposterous. I don't accept large sums of money like this from anyone. What am I going to do with all of this money? Buy out Google?"

"I don't know. Give it to charity. You can do anything you

want to with it. Buy you a ride like mine. I don't care. Take it and go have some fun."

"Have fun in this town?"

"Yeah. Or, take a trip overseas, the moon, or get on a slow boat to China. I really don't care what you do with it. Just enjoy it. It's a gift."

"Is this a bribe? If it is, you have put me in a risky position. One I don't exactly feel comfortable in. You are making very large generalizations without even knowing me."

"Look, Gracie. You gave me the impression you wanted to work for me because you needed money. Either you are a bad liar or you don't have a lot of know-how. I don't make it a practice of broadcasting my business, but you sure do seem to know a lot about what I do. I'm just asking a few questions to get at the truth. Lucky for me, I have eyes and ears working for me. I have the connections to make sure I get all the answers I need. You keep pushing me away and telling me 'no' to every offer I make. So, right now, I don't like what I am finding out about you. All fingers are pointing to the fact that you are an undercover and wanting to take me down."

Bobby grabs Gracie's arm and twists it hard behind her back. She squirms in pain but tries to make light of her predicament. "It doesn't take much to push your buttons, does it?" She struggles. "What are you going to do with me? You are hurting me and if you don't let me go, I'm going to scream and that will bring in an audience."

Bobby says, "I am going to get rid of you. You can scream as loud as you want because you are not going to have an audience. There is no one around to hear you or to see this." His grip tightens. "If you do scream, the repercussions could be profound."

She fires back. "Then let me go. I may not look dangerous, but, hey, I bite!"

Bobby cackles. "Go ahead. See what happens. Satisfy your woman's curiosity." He tightens his grip. "You know, Gracie, you are kinda hot when you are desperate. It's some shame things aren't going to work out for us. We both know this is not going to work so why prolong the pain? Your pretty little future is about to vanish in a puff of smoke. So much for having a happy ending."

Suddenly, a silver Toyota truck pulls up into the yard. Bobby releases his grip on Gracie's arm. An answer to a prayer begins to unfold. Gracie thinks, an angel sent to my rescue!

The man in the silver truck steps out, extends his hand, and introduces himself—a handsome guy in his early fifties with blue eyes and shaggy brow hair tinged with gray. He speaks in a soft voice. "Howdy. I'm Rick Seager, the new owner of Seager Trash Company, your trash pickup service. You may have seen me driving one of the trash trucks."

Leaning forward, Bobby asks, "Why would you be driving the trash truck if you are the owner?"

Rick laughs. "Well, my man. Just starting this business, I have to be the jack of all trades, even if it means once in a while driving the truck."

"What do you want, Mr. Seager? I'm extremely busy."

"Yeah, I can see you are." He winks at Gracie. "I'm just out and about trying to reorganize my routes. It would save a lot of gas money if I could have my customers place their trash containers on the same side of the road. Then my drivers wouldn't have to spend so much time and waste gas money driving down the road and turning around coming back the same road to empty the cans on the other side. Understand?"

"I guess so. Whatever you say."

"Well, if you are in agreement, I would certainly appreciate it if you would place your trash container on the opposite side of the road on the day of the pickup." He blinks thoughtfully as he turns to go and then pretends to recognize Gracie. "Gracie, how are you? By the way, I looked over your application and would like you to come by the office today. I need a secretary starting pronto. When can you start? Today too soon?"

Gracie has never seen this man before, much less place an application at his place of business. However, she recognizes a way out of this chaos. She decides to go along with this devised plan. "Sure, Mr. Seager. I can start today. If right now is not too soon, can I follow you to your office?"

"That works for me. I can show you the ropes and put you on the clock starting immediately. Come on. Let's go." He turns to look at Bobby. "That is, if you are through here."

"I'm through here," says Gracie as she turns to Bobby, standing with his mouth open, not knowing exactly what to do or say. She hands him the bag of money. "Thank you, Mr. Wright. Since I now have another job, I won't be needing this." She smirks. "By the way, Bobby, you are not the least bit sexy. Enjoy your day—alone."

She pushes past him and calls out over her shoulder. "So much for your happy ending."

12

High Price to Pay

Sarah Cole and her coworkers Kathy and Natasha stand in the back of the small group at the graveside service of little Larissa Renew. Sarah's heart sinks as she listens to the comforting words given to the grieving family of a precious life, taken too early from this earth. Her own consoling hope and reconciliation comes from her faith that Larissa is now being rocked in the arms of angels. A tear trickles.

Kathy squeezes Sarah's hand. "How are you feeling?"

"I don't think I can really describe it. Feels like my guts have been kicked out." She reaches for a Kleenex and dabs her eyes. Suddenly, she notices a suspicious character watching from the hedges. Her heart jumps. She says, motioning to the man, "I have been praying for answers and I think my prayers have just been answered."

Kathy and Natasha strain to see. "Who is that?" Natasha asks.

"It's the man the police have been looking for. The one who bought the drugs for Tabitha." She whispers to the girls. "Call the sheriff. No! Call Paul Hines. Tell him the perp is here."

"What are you going to do?" Kathy asks.

"I am going to go talk to him. I'll keep him busy until Paul gets here."

"Sarah, do you think you should?"

"Don't worry. I am not going to do anything rash. All I am going to do is size up the guy and try to get some answers." Unobtrusively, she ambles her way behind the man lurking behind the bushes. "Hello," she says.

The man jumps. "What are doing sneaking up behind me?"

"I'm not sneaking up on you. I just happen to be the kind of person that walks quietly."

"Aren't you Tabitha's new social worker? I saw you at the house when you came for a visit. What do you want with me? You and I have nothing to talk about."

"Yes. Tabitha is my client. And, yes, we do have something to talk about. Don't worry. All I want from you is answers. You are not the fish that needs to fry. You are just the tadpole in the bigger pond." She continues to watch the man, watching the service. She took a chance, asking a bold question. "Are you Larissa's father?"

He nods, wiping a fallen tear. "Yeah. She was my little girl."

"I'm so sorry for your loss. I can't even imagine the pain you are going through."

He sniffs. "Yeah. I am living out my worst nightmare. If you had a child, you would understand." He points to the flowers carefully placed around the gasket. "It is crazy thinking that flowers will ease the pain."

Sarah feels his grief. She struggles to find words to console him and manages to say, "It's just a gesture to let the family know that they value the person you lost. And I do have a child. She is my whole world and I can imagine what you must be going through." Sarah held out her hand. "By the way, my name is—"

"I know who you are. I remember the day I saw you go into Tabitha's apartment. You are from Safe Families." He chuckles but the sound seems more like a groan to Sarah. "You sure couldn't keep my little girl safe, could you?" A short pause and then he added, "I can't blame you for my Larissa's death. I am the one to blame. I knew the risk of bringing that junk into our house. I knew what it would do to her mind." He sniffs. "And now I am paying the price for the choices I have made. I see the life my baby is never going to live. I see the joy she is never going to have. All because of the choice I made. I took my baby's life. I am responsible. Now, my beautiful little girl is dead."

By now, the tears are beginning to flow almost to the point of hysteria. "Despite my flaws, I loved that baby more than anyone in this universe. I promised her from the first moment I held her in my arms that I would always take care of her. I promised that I would always be there for her, but I failed. I'm just hoping this is a nightmare that I am going to wake up from, but I know better."

Sarah asks, "How is Tabitha?"

"She is lost to me. I tried to warn her about the dangers of doing drugs. She convinced me she needed them to distance herself for all of her troubles." Again, a fake chuckle. "And, now, she's got more troubles than she knows what to do with. I tried to make her see. If she had only listened to me. I am all alone now. I can't go back to her. Right now, I can't even look at her. That's why I'm not down there with her and the family. I am so full of hate right now."

"I understand that your grief is bad, but you shouldn't run out and leave it to her to pick up the pieces." Sarah waits for a response but none comes. She adds, "I know it's not your fault that Larissa is dead.

Sarah places her hand on his shoulder. The comforting touch seems to ease the sorrow clouding his face. "I can understand your pain and I can understand the situations that led up to you and Tabitha making bad choices." She wonders if he knows the "bad choices" she is referring to are the decisions to use drugs around the baby, but she keeps that question to herself. She continues to coax him to a place of trust, even if doing so means using deceit.

"Sometimes, we need to peel back those layers of stress, push the bad memories away, and go to that zombie-like place to leave our troubles behind. I understand that when life is hard, it's easy to turn to a way out." She hesitates before continuing with her act. "Weed, pot, whatever you want to call it, does that for you."

At first, there is no reply from the distraught man. Then his eyes move from the small casket to Sarah. "Yeah, it's a high price to pay, and I don't mean just monetary. How do you know so much about it?"

She lies in hopes of gaining a foothold into this man's psyche. "I've been there. I understand. I know exactly what you are going through."

"Yeah. Then why do you want to talk to me? You think I'm to blame . . ." He points to his baby's final resting place. "Do you think I am to blame for putting her there?"

"Of course not. You are not to blame. You are Larissa's daddy. You love her. Her death is not because of you. You would have done everything within your power to protect her."

She pauses. "You would also do anything to bring down the real threat—the real criminal—the person who only wanted your money and didn't care squat about your little girl's life. The person I blame is the man who never cared about you or Larissa. He only cares about selling you the stuff so he can line his pockets. You are just a means to his end." Her voice softens yet trembles as she continuously plays on his emotions. "What is your name, my friend?"

"Carlos. That's all you need to know."

"Okay, Carlos. Your name is not important to anyone but me. The only name I need is the thug who sold you the junk. He is the only one I desire to take down. Not you. Your baby's death is not in your hands. It's his. He wants you dependent on him, even if it means causing Larissa to die." Her ploy continues. "How can a person like him dismantle so many people's lives? Being thrown in jail is a small price to pay for what he did. He is the one responsible for Larissa's death. Not you or Tabitha."

Sarah watches him as she notices hatred for the drug dealer spawning in his narrowed eyes. Carlos is not only becoming engulfed with sorrow and despair, but with a loathing animosity as well, she thinks. He chokes back tears. Nostrils flare as his dark eyes dart from one tree to another. "I'm going to kill him!"

"No, Carlos. I don't want you seeking some kind of justice for Larissa. Stay out of this and let me handle things, Okay?"

"What can I do?"

"Give me his name—the one who sells the junk to you. I want him to suffer the way you are suffering now. I want him to spend the rest of his life behind bars and get what he deserves because he plays on people's emotions. I want justice for Larissa."

She holds her breath. He holds his. Her steps to lead Carlos into her trust prove to be effective. He leans forward, cuffs his hand, and whispers in her ear. She nods. "Thank you, Carlos."

Quietly, he slips away.

Sarah stands there for what seems like hours—only it isn't. Someone eases up behind Sarah. Sarah jumps a little. "Paul, don't sneak up behind me!"

"I'm sorry. That's another bad habit of mine. I'll work on it."

"Please do and start now! I'm a little jumpy today."

"Enough about my bad habits. Let's talk about why you let that guy get away? Why are you playing nice to him?"

"Let's not argue about my strategy. I needed to handle this the way I saw fit. I had to back off or else it would have blown up in my face. At least, now I have the information I need."

"And, what is the information he gave you?"

"He gave me the man's name—the person who is supplying him with drugs, along with others."

Paul sighs. "We need to go somewhere and talk, Sarah. Somewhere that is private. I need to fill you in on all the sorted details of this case. What do you say?"

"I say, let's go anywhere but the courthouse." She considers, "How about my house? I live out in the country. It's private out there—away from wandering eyes and perky ears."

"Sounds like a winner. I'll follow you if that's okay."

"I have a daughter. She'll probably be there, but we can talk on the porch. She won't bother us."

"Like I said, it sounds like a winner."

Paul pulls up behind Sarah. A Garth Brooks song is blaring on the radio. Sarah meets him at the outside steps. "My daughter understands that we need to talk in private. She'll give us our space."

"That's good. By the way, I made an important call on my way over here. I called the under-cover officer from the Drug Task Force. He's been working with me for some time on cementing this high-profile case. Like me, at the moment, his highest priority is convicting Bobby Wright. He has spent weeks of surveillance time working this case. He'll add a lot of light to this situation."

"So, you knew it was Bobby Wright who was supplying the marijuana and the rest of the poison? That was the name of the supplier Carlos, Larissa's father, shared with me."

"The undercover officer and I have known it all along. In fact, that steel building in his back yard is his growing facility for marijuana and it's not a small garden plot."

"Fill me in on everything. First, tell me how does this operation involve Safe Families?"

"Simple. There is a correlation between some of your clients and narcotic use. Because of that, your clients are easy targets for hitters like Bobby Wright, the man we have under surveillance. Single parents, fragile, less resilient and overwhelmed victims of domestic abuse and financial stress are looking for ways to ease the strains and struggles of ordinary life. They begin with a little recreational drug—marijuana, pot, grass, whatever you want to call it. All of them are becoming junkies, and in turn, the ones who suffer the most are the children. Gradually, they move to the hard stuff which gives more bang for the buck."

"There's been a lot of news media talking about the opioid epidemic going on across our nation. What do you know about that?"

"Opioids are just plain killers and the epidemic is becoming a public health emergency. Deaths from overdoses have already outnumbered deaths by drunk driving."

"We need a fix to this epidemic."

"Correct. It all starts out with needing a prescription for pain meds. Eventually, the patient gets hooked and so it goes. They need more and more and higher doses." He sighs. "And, this drug problem is not only affecting the suffering and unfortunate, it crosses all class lines and cuts through all demographics— suburban, urban, and rural. Drugs have become a major epidemic in our *entire* country. Just recently, the CDC announced that drug overdoses kill more Americans than guns or car crashes."

"Seems to me if you stop the manufacturers, you stop the crisis."

"The problem goes deeper. For instant, there's new synthetic opioid bought in from other countries. Studies indicate that it is fifty times stronger than fentanyl or hydrocodone."

She nervously paces back and forth, hands on hips. "If the major source of problems in this community and Safe Families is drug related, let's take Bobby Wright down right now. Let's do it!"

"Don't be so hasty, Sarah."

"Whatever do you mean, Paul? Time is of the essence.

Especially, if we don't want a repeat of what has happened with Larissa. Why haven't you gone in there and taken him out?"

"I'm not interested in Bobby Wright. He's only a little fish in a big pond. I want the big fish. Bobby not only grows and sells his pot, but he acts as a 'hitter' for the man above him, the dealer. Bobby hands off to the addicts and distributes the bigger stuff—the opioids, cocaine, and heroin—along with his added stash, marijuana. I want that man who pushes the big stuff. I want the man who is responsible for the drug activity in this county. The DEA, the Federal Drug Enforcement Administration, is working on taking down the ones on top of the drug operation—the ones who bring it into this country and sell to the little guys like Bobby's contact. Bobby and this man are at the bottom of the ladder. Get the big bosses and we can put hitters, like Bobby, out of business."

"So you are saying Bobby's operation doesn't warrant taking down?"

"Of course, it does. But in due time. Right at this moment, I don't want to waste my energy on wasted space like Bobby Wright. I don't want to take him now on just a marijuana production and sales case. That would scare off the dealer above him—the one with the hard drugs. Besides, a good lawyer can keep Bobby's case tied up for years. Some may even go lenient since they don't think weed is that big of an issue anymore."

"What do you mean? Not that big of an issue?"

"Although states have legalized marijuana for medical use, it is still classified in most as a Schedule 1 drug—a dangerous substance for a high potential for drug abuse. Yes, it can be helpful with some medical conditions and has a wide range of therapeutic benefits when only containing CBD, the non-psychoactive component of cannabis. However, some states still recognize stout litigations that have found marijuana to be a powerful, and in some circumstances, a harmful drug. Especially, when it contains the THC component. On top of that, there have been some predictions that eventually, more and more states will roll back restrictions and vote to legalize it for recreational use. Personally, I look to see all states eventually legalize it because of the increase in revenue as investors and marketers line up for their cut."

"I have heard news reports that claim there is a rush to accept weed into the mainstream, legitimize, and regulate it as a beneficial new pharmaceutical. Why not just go ahead and legalize it?"

Paul explains his thoughts. "If it was just used for medical benefits, it would be a horse of a different color, but that's not the case. People are using pot to get high, to chill-out, and to calm their nerves." He adds with a chuckle. "In other words, to zonk out and have a ravenous craving for cheese crackers."

Sarah asks, "I'm trying to understand. So you are saying there are serious consequences for cannabis?"

"Most definitely. Relentless research and studies have shown that prolonged use of high-THC can alter the developing brain, provoke serious and debilitating anxiety and depression attacks, and in some cases, with the right compounds, it can trigger suicide. All along, it leads to stronger craving for more efficient drugs—meth, heroin, coke, ecstasy, and the like—sad to say, even prescription drugs like opioids."

He sighs. "It's an uphill battle, Sarah. It's highly addictive, highly toxic, and turns you into a zombie. As long as I have a breath, I will use every tool in my toolbox to get it off the streets. Despite what they say, it's a gateway. There is no other way for the biochemists to get around it. It is what it is. And this—" He digs in his pocket and extracts a wad of money. "This is why states want to legalize it for recreational use. Money! The cause of this never-ending problem. They call it the 'Green Rush.' It's a multimillion-dollar phenomenon. Grow cannabis plant, hemp, as a multipurpose crop and the economic boosts for state governments go through the roof. And while states are lining their pockets, it is sending this country to hell and back."

"Haven't we coped with the addiction of cigarettes and alcohol abuse?"

"*Cope* is mildly putting it. How can you cope with cigarette smoking and alcohol abuse when it is responsible for taking lives? The CDC states that in the United States alone, one in five deaths are caused by smoking, a known addiction. Sixteen million Americans are presently living with a disease, such as cancer, heart disease, and lung disease, to name a few. Worse than that, CDC says that four hundred eighty thousand deaths occur every year just from secondhand smoke." He throws up his hands. "And, why does this country allow it? It's more dangerous than pot, but the cigarettes mean revenue generated in our economy."

He sighs. "It doesn't end there. Alcohol is another product sold primarily to generate revenue. While people are lining their pockets with the sale of alcohol, they don't care about the one in three highway deaths are alcohol-impaired fatalities, or that one in ten working age men will die from alcohol abuse."

"Where and when does it end, Paul?"

"It doesn't, Sarah. Just like the sale of marijuana. As long as money is made and that green stuff lines pockets, so what? It will be around until the Lord comes back." He sighs and then smiles. "If some Americans thought they could make it rich by selling horse poop as chocolate candy, then they probably would do so."

Sarah contends, "So there is no stopping it?"

Paul chuckles. "Like I said, the only thing that is going to stop this explosion is the Lord coming back." He leans closer. "I haven't told you this. Your office does not get the logistics. I received a copy of Larissa's autopsy report along with Tabitha Renew's confession."

Sarah tenses. "And?"

"Do you remember the strong smell of marijuana over Larissa's crib?"

Sarah choked back stinging tears. "Yes. How can I forget?"

"It's a common behavior of partying people. They want to party and get high, but a crying baby demanding their attention needs to go to sleep to give them their space. So they blow marijuana smoke up the child's nose and in his mouth to calm him and put him to sleep. The babies become like a sack of potatoes or a rag doll. Sometimes they never wake up. Those that survive the ordeal, time after time, will have an adverse effect on their developing brain caused by the THC, the chemical found in marijuana."

Tears burn Sarah's eyes. "So that's what happened to that baby? She had marijuana smoke blown up her nose?"

"Yes." Within that instant, Paul's phone rings. "Yeah." His eyes suddenly appear blank as if his heart has hardened. He snaps his cell phone shut. "That call is from my office. There's been another death—another baby." Frustration makes way for righteous anger that floods his face. "A Safe Families client!"

13

The Party Goes On

Paul and Sarah burst through the emergency room doors. Storming down the hall, both make an effort to hide their emotions. Their steps are hurried as they make their way closer. Paul says, "I know God is gracious and merciful, but why, Sarah? Maybe you better keep your distance from me until I come to terms with this. At this moment, being in my presence may put you in danger of eternal damnation."

Sarah allows him to rant for a few minutes. Then she remarks as calmly as she can, "I think we both have a common vendetta—not maliciously self-serving or glory-grabbing but genuinely one of two people who take a stand and pursue the saving of children's lives. The benchmark for each of our life's success is whether we can do that. I'm with you, Paul." She looks around. "Is the undercover officer going to meet us here?"

"No. We don't dare be seen with each other. It will give his cover away and we are too close to nailing this."

"I understand. In the meantime, I am going to call one of the girls who work for me at Safe Families."

"Don't bother! I'm here!" Kathy shouted, busting through to the ER waiting room. "I heard it on the police scanner. I recognized the address the ambulance was called, so I went by the office and picked up the file on Candace Herrington and her newborn baby boy, Kevin—only five days old."

"Great!" Paul exclaims. "My compliments to an efficiently run office."

Kathy motions towards Sarah. "Any compliments go to that woman. If it wasn't for her, we'd all be squirming around."

He agrees, "That's true. Now, since we have both given Sarah's confidence a boost, let's move to another place—more private."

Kathy chimes in, "How about the chapel? When we have finished with our business, we can all say a prayer for little Kevin."

"I'll meet you there," says Paul. "I'm going to find someone that can fill me in about the probable cause of the Herrington baby's death."

As Kathy and Sarah meander their way to the chapel, Sarah comments, "Thank you for that flattering remark you made back there."

Kathy reaches and grabs Sarah's arm. "I mean it, Sarah. Safe Families would be nothing without you. You are an inspiration. You have taught me the importance of listening to my heart and being responsible for my actions. You are like the farmer who has well-prepared soil to produce a bountiful harvest. I am your harvest. Before you came, I always found myself being caught up in a violent, raging storm, but you have taught me how to deal with stressful circumstances without criticizing or misunderstanding me. Your presence with this agency and in my life has been for the good." She smiles. "I will forever be grateful to you."

"I'm not sure I deserve those compliments, but thank you, Kathy, for having confidence in me."

"You got it, boss!"

"Well, you won't believe what I just found out!" Paul says, bursting into the chapel.

Once seated, Paul is the first to speak. "Of course, an autopsy has to be performed, but the doctor on duty says the baby died from suffocation."

"He was strangled?" Kathy asked.

"No. Worse. Blood tests indicate that the mother had high levels of THC in her blood streams, along with heroin. She even topped it off with a little bit of alcohol. She put the baby in a head-to-foot motion swing before she passed out across the bed. Totally unaware that she had set the swing for a faster speed, she caused the newborn to suffocate because he was not strong enough to keep his head up and consequently, he couldn't breathe."

"Same synopsis," begins Sarah. "Parent wants to get high. Places baby in a dangerous position. Baby dies. An endless cycle." She sighs. "I am beginning to excel at suggesting the obvious."

Kathy asks, "So, this is why our agency is under close scrutiny, Mr. Hines? We are not only dealing with ensuring healthy child development and promoting positive parenting, we are up against a population of single parents who are exhibiting negative parenting behaviors because of their involvement with drugs."

Kathy fumbles through the Herrington files. After a brief reread, she slams the files shut. "This client belonged to Jacqueline Karr. It is filled with discrepancies and lies. According to Jacqueline's notes, everything was hunky-dory in the Herrington house." She shakes her head. "When does it end?"

Paul answers, "It won't, Kathy, not as long as we Americans keep our heads buried in the sand. I'll give you an example. A few years ago, one of our outstanding citizens died in a car crash, hit in a head-on collision by an oncoming driver. The family and friends demanded of the governor that the State spend resources repairing the road, which they felt caused the accident. No one mentioned the fact that their friend was hit head-on by a drunk driver. They had rather blame the road rather than alcohol as the cause of death." He sighs. "It's exasperating. Denial like this is what we have to contend with."

Kathy asks, "Why do they even get behind the wheel of a car when they are drunk or do drugs when they know the outcome? To begin with, why does a person even do drugs?"

Sarah's words are blunt. "They view it as a way to escape. Human deprivations and problems have always existed and always will. Users ignore the fact that drugs and alcohol are only a temporary solution, not a cure for their problems. The heart becomes harder as it comes to a place of denial. We always stumble and fall when the heart is hardened. When drugs and alcohol incapacitate the human heart, evil moves in. A person can contrive and dream, obfuscate or deny, but the profound question for personal gratification of drugs and alcohol use does not end in a testament to the unaltered truth that life as we know it may end. Thank God for baby Larissa and baby Kevin that a new life in heaven begins."

The scathing words dig deep. Paul announces, "That's why this job is a calling for me. It is my cross to bear." His eyes dart from one woman to the next. "What do you say, partners? Let's take this to the next level. Let's take them down!"

14

The Heart Speaks

"Good morning," Sarah says, addressing the clerk behind the counter at the gift department of the local drug store.

"Good morning, Mrs. Cole. May I help you?"

Pointing to a special brand of fragrance Gracie enjoys wearing, she asks, "Yes. Will you wrap up that bottle of perfume? My daughter has worked hard lately and I'd like to surprise her with a gift."

"Sure, I'll be happy to do that for you. By the way, is Gracie enjoying her new camera?"

"New camera?"

"Yes. The one she bought here a few weeks ago."

"Oh, that camera. Yes, she likes it," Sarah lies, trying to grasp the realization that Gracie is hiding something from her. She chokes, trying to gather her thoughts. "Do you mind putting this on my charge account and may I take a peek at that account? You know, it is always good thing to stay on top of things."

The clerk turns the computer screen around for Sarah to view. Sarah gasps and says to herself, wow! She's got expensive taste!

The clerk hands the wrapped gift to the flabbergasted mother. "I hope she likes the perfume. She's going to really be surprised."

"Oh, yes! Most definitely! She really is going to be surprised."

Sarah walks into the house with donuts, one latté, one expresso, and a gift for Gracie wrapped up in purple paper and pink bows. She whispers to herself, "Okay, Sarah. Anger is not your friend. Whatever you are feeling now, think about it calmly—that is, if you want to get to the truth."

Gracie bounces to meet her. "Hm. Donuts. A nonfat latté to soothe *me* and a bonus shot expresso to give *you* a boost." She notices the gift her mother is holding under her arms. "Wow! Mom! Did I miss my birthday or something?"

"Something like that," was Sarah's reply.

"What's up, Mom? Should I worry? Bringing home gifts has been a ploy of yours for years, especially when you are trying to outmaneuver me." She opens her gift. "Perfume!" She taps her wrist with the enticing smell that permeated her lungs. "So am I in trouble or is this an expression of how much you love me?"

"That all depends on you, Gracie."

"How much did this bottle of perfume cost? It didn't put you out much, did it?"

"The receipt is in the bag if you want to look."

"Sure," Gracie says, looking through the bag for the receipt. "I'd like to know just how valuable you think I am." At first, she giggles, then freezes. The product was purchased at the same store she procured the camera. Furthermore, it was charged.

Sarah patiently waits, praying Gracie would confess. Instead of acknowledging the charge, Gracie jumps up and begins to run for the bathroom.

"Where are you going, Gracie?"

"To the bathroom!"

"This whole sick routine is not going to fly. Although, I don't appreciate your lack of willingness to come clean with me, you don't have to go puke your guts out."

Gracie stops, takes a deep breath, and slowly walks to the chair, easing down. "I've got myself in a peck of trouble, haven't I?"

Sarah nods. "I suggest you start figuring out how to get out of this mess you are in."

"It's kind of a long story."

Sarah chuckles. "They are *all* long stories!"

"You are not going to let this go, are you?"

Sarah bends down and looks at Gracie—dead in her face. "Do you know me? I don't let anything go. So, would you please just get to the point?"

"Wow. This is not going to be easy. In fact, this is going to be a downer."

"You think?"

"Yes! Even as it is coming out of my mouth."

Sarah sits, folds her hands, and begins sipping on her cup of expresso, hoping for a surge. With quiet confidence, she suggests, "Why don't you begin with explaining why are you freaking out? I want the truth because at this point, I just want honesty. The only way for us to get past this and move on is for you to come clean."

"Mom, will you do something for me?"

"That depends, Grace. Is it legal?"

The comment cuts Gracie to the core. Their mother-daughter relationship has always demonstrated faithfulness, loyalty, and humility, and most importantly, honesty. At this moment, it seems as if this family relationship is in trouble. Gracie silently prays that she can make her mother understand her actions and put the pieces of their connection back together again. She asks her mother, "Does it feel like the forces pulling us apart are stronger than the forces pulling us together?"

"In what sense, child of mine?"

"We've always had a rule of thumb in our household. Never lie. Always trust." She bowed her head, ashamed. "I always considered it a great honor to be ranked at the top of your most-trusting persons you know." She sighs. "I guess I've blown that."

"That depends on how well you rebound." She leans towards Gracie. "I can't help but wonder why you didn't come to me and tell me in the beginning. We have always been honest with each other and you have always included me in the good and bad things in your life." She sighs. "Just out of curiosity, how would you feel if I kept something from you?"

"I realize I should have said something, but I didn't want you to worry. You have every right to be angry with me. I promise to never keep you in the dark anymore if you can find it in your beautiful heart to forgive me."

"How can I trust you again?"

Gracie smiles. "Day by day?"

"Maybe I am a little overprotective. Maybe I should let you live your own life and make your own mistakes. I realize that I can't keep you in a cocoon for the rest of your life. The point is, Gracie, I love you with all my heart, and although I am hurt with you, I'll never, never give up on you. Never." Sarah grabs Gracie's hand. "As your BFF and your mother, it is time you put on your big girl panties and tell me all about your deceptions. I will be with you every step of the way. I want you to do the right thing, Gracie. And, it begins with being truthful. Always telling the truth will save you a lot of hurt down the road. When you are dishonest, you set a lot of ill feelings in motion. So, let's put everything out on the table so we can start picking up the pieces."

Wringing her hands, Gracie begins. "Since I have been working at Safe Families, I have found a genuine appreciation for your job. For the first time in my life, I have taken an interest in helping others. Not just feeling compassion for others, but desiring to be their facilitator when they can't find their way. All of this is part of the goals, plans, and priorities I want to achieve."

Intently, Sarah listens. She must be wondering how the purchase of the camera plays into this, Gracie thinks. She begins to explain. "I overheard you, Kathy, and Natasha talking about taking down the man who drives the black F250. I overheard you telling them you were going to take pictures of this guy making a drug deal."

"Is that why you purchased the camera? For me to take pictures?"

"No, ma'am. For *me* to take pictures. I want to join forces with you and help you take this guy down. Most importantly, I want to be a social worker and do the things you do."

Sarah gasps. "Oh, Gracie! I care about your beliefs, your values, and your ideals. But, Gracie, you of all people should understand the stress behind this job. I speak from painful experience. You can't leave it at the door when you walk out of the office, nor pick it up when you walk back in the office in the morning. The responsibilities of this job tax your very existence. With it comes imminent grief. This is a lifelong commitment. You can't turn it off and on and forget the ones you have lost. It doesn't work that way." She sits down and allows her weary head to rest in her hands. "You don't realize how hard this is—compromising the work you are passionate about, and at the same time, being completely dedicated to your family's needs. For it to be the best of both worlds, you have to make it balance. It is hard to do. My job is not a nine to five. Not only do I bring work home, but I have to be on alert for any emergency. Sometimes I feel like my life belongs to Safe Families, not to me."

Seeing that her mother is not only concerned but deeply worried, Grace assures her, "I understand that. All I am asking is to have the opportunity to try."

"Let's please stop acting shallow and arguing about this. Let it go before you force me to do something crazy—like pull my hair out!"

"Please listen to me. I have confidence in myself, Mom, that

I can not only make a difference in this world, but I can be level-headed enough to control my emotions. Besides, you are not my keeper."

"Gracie, I know I come on hard at times, but I am just trying to keep you from making a horrible mistake."

"So what if I make a few mistakes along the way! I am almost an adult. I am entitled to make my own mistakes. You've always taught me to follow my heart, and that is just what I plan to do." She waves her hands in disgust. "Mom, you are talking out of both sides of your mouth. Just a minute ago, you said you were going to allow me to make my own mistakes and let go of the cocoon. What's up?"

"Yes, but what you don't understand that no matter how perfect your integrity may be or how confident you are, there will always be a situation that tears at your heart. There will always be a face you can't forget—a mother's cry that you can't drown out." She sighs. "I'm not telling you this out of obligation. I am telling you this out of love."

"Then why do you stay? Why do you put yourself through this daily torment? Why is it your job to fix everything?"

"That's what I do, Gracie. I fix families that are falling apart."

"Well, who fixes you? When do you stop taking care of everybody and start taking care of yourself?"

"Gracie, please—"

"No, Mom. Let me try to explain. Regardless of the disappointments, doubts, fears, heartache, and a job characterized by almost daily frustrations, working to make families healthy bulges with blessings. God's grace and goodness surmounts the negative challenges I might encounter, but I will be fulfilling my purpose. I know that at the end of my journey, there will be a reward. What I am trying to say, Mom, is that it is my prerogative to want to help others—just like you. Just like you, I want to be able to reach out to people who are hurting and help them find their way. That is what I feel like I am being led to do with my life. Please allow me to decide what I want in life and have to the freedom to go after it."

"Please listen to what I am saying, Gracie. This job encompasses so many formidable challenges."

"That's what I have been trying to tell you, Mom. Formidable challenges. The severe opposition you find when you're doing what you are called to do is a strength I admire in you. You never give up or cave in. With each step you take, you steadfastly set your eyes on the end of the road. I want to be there on that road with you. I want to do what you do, go where you go, and live the life you live, making a difference, one family at a time." She smiles at her mother. "Besides, I see the way you are with people. You are kind, compassionate, generous, and patient to every one you meet, yet tough as nails." She places her arms around her mother. "I guess you don't really get it—you play a pivotal role in my life." She rolls her eyes at her mother. "What can I say? You inspire me!"

Those words melt Sarah's heart. Subdued, she adds little to the discussion. "You sound very compassionate about making social work a life choice. What happened to your decision about going to college, living a safe life, getting a degree in nursing?"

"I'm still going to college. However, I have made you very aware that I am considering changing my choice of careers. Since I have been working at the office and becoming more and more involved, I have come to the realization that this is what I want to do with my life. And like you, I really have it in for that guy—the one who is passing his poison around."

"So that is why you bought the camera? To take pictures to use as evidence against this person?"

"I want to do what I can to help. You need hard evidence. I can provide that with the pictures I plan to take."

Frowning, Sarah hesitates a moment before speaking. "I can't allow it, Gracie. I'm not going to permit you to put yourself in jeopardy of getting hurt. The person of interest in this case is a pro and he is dangerous. There is no way I am going to consent to your involvement. This problem is resolved. Now get over it. The answer is no! No way am I going to put you in harm's way."

"I don't get a vote in this? You don't trust me enough to manage my own life?"

Sarah shakes her head. "No. The purpose of this conversation was to come to some consensus over this issue. Since we can't seem to find a common ground, then I have to execute my right as a parent. I am the adult in this situation, and at this time, I have to make decisions. Sometimes I get it right and sometimes I get it wrong. But, as your mother, I will always make the decision to keep you safe and keep you happy. I will never make a decision that will be the cause of sorrow in your life."

Gracie grins slightly. "Don't you mean that you will always stand in judgment of me? You are always judging me. Everything you do is perfectly right and everything I do is perfectly wrong. I don't need you trying to manage my life. My decision and my choices, right or wrong, are mine."

"Just to be clear, Gracie, I never judge you. Who am I to judge anyone for being on the wrong side of right?" She sighs. "It is just that you exasperate me at times. You have been sheltered all of your life and that's why I think you are not mature enough to make logical decisions." A frown contorts her face. "I love you. If that's wrong, I'm sorry if I am overly protective." A skeptical chuckle tells the rest. "In fact, I hope you get married, live in a cozy little cottage with a white picket fence, and have a house full of kids!"

"It must be exhausting being right all the time!" Gracie shrugs her shoulders. She pauses. "You get that I am being sarcastic, don't you?"

"Yes, I get it. Just remember that sarcasm is never a good tool."

Gracie frowns, crossing her arms. *Now is the time to make a defiant stand on my rights as an adult.* "I am not an incompetent person." Continuing to authenticate her claim to adulthood, Grace once again tries to make her mother understand the importance of making her own decisions. "You talk about life choices. Mine are mine to make. If I stumble and fall, then I will learn and grow from my mistakes, not let them define me. Give me the opportunity to learn from my mistakes and learn how to move on. Let me learn to rise above whatever it is that knocks me down. This is what one calls 'growing up' and becoming a responsible adult. I'm not asking you to let go of me. I'm only asking you to support me in whatever I choose to do with my life. Most importantly, you must acknowledge that my life choices are mine—good or bad—and I don't need anyone's approval or disapproval. What I want to do with my life is my business. My business! None of your business."

Sarah grumbles, "You are so right. Whatever you think is none of my business, *is* none of my business. That is, under normal circumstances, it is none of my business. This situation is definitely not normal. You say you are in control of your faculties. Then, if you are in control, why did you purchase a camera that we couldn't pay for? Why are you willing to put your life on the line at this point in your life?"

"Okay! Buying the camera was a momentary lapse in judgment and I will never do anything that stupid again. But the fact still remains, I strongly feel that God has a plan for me. For a long time, I have been struggling to define my life, to choose my future. I keep asking myself, am I living in the here and now or am I living to pursue the plans He has for me?"

Sarah pulls her daughter close. "I am trying so hard to see your side of things." She smiles. "You have always been one step ahead of me."

Resting her head on her mother's shoulder, Gracie responds, "And you love that about me, don't you?"

"You have no idea!" She turns to Grace face-to-face so that their eyes meet. "However, the laws of a mother-daughter relationship cannot be circumvented effortlessly. No matter how much I am enjoying indulging with you in our little conversation, I'm done. I am done talking about this. At least, for now. My final decision is that you stay as far away from the situation as possible. Don't think for one second I am condoning your purchasing that camera. What you were planning to do is off the charts and stupid."

She hesitates. "I can't allow you to sneak around and try to capture a photographic moment of a drug deal going down. It is too dangerous, baby. And, like I said, I am not putting your life in jeopardy. This is my final decision." She pauses. "Tell me something. How were you going to pay for that camera?"

Gracie crinkles her eyebrows and shrugs her shoulder. "I was going to sell my Justin Bieber concert tickets."

Gracie's words cause her mother to roar with laugher. "How about just keeping the camera as a gift from me?"

"What about the Justin Bieber tickets?"

Sarah cocks an eye, shakes her head, and waves her off. "Don't push your luck!"

Gracie collapses in her mother's arms. She lays her head against Sarah's shoulder, her tense muscles relaxing. "Does this mean you forgive me? It's a good feeling to let the heart speak."

"I have to admit that I am taking a lot of comfort in knowing that I raised you to fight for what you believe is right. I hardly recognize the young woman standing in front of me. Still, try to understand that when mothers and daughters argue, things seem to get territorial." She smiles. "Did I mention crazy? In the end, we are each other's constant."

"Always remember that a person's character, on the inside, where it counts, stems from the heart—not what she eats or drinks. And when the tongue is used as an instrument to say what's in the heart, it is like the tongue is a barometer. When the heart is filled with erroneous and evil ideas, the heart can harden and we stumble and fall. But when the heart is soft, it speaks the truth, and the heart is filled with grace and mercy."

She cradles her daughter in her arms, much the same way she did when Gracie was a baby. "I am sorry about the third degree, and yea, Gracie, it is good to let the heart speak."

"Mom?"

"Yes, Gracie."

Relaxed in her mother's arms, she giggles. "Are you sure this isn't the donuts talking?"

15

Flames of Discontent

Lilly, the friendly little mix that is never standoffish or suspicious of anything new, wags her shaggy tail as she meets the stranger on the doorstep. The man sporting a crisp, green uniform and tucking his kakis into his boots bends to scratch the ears of the welcoming dog. Carrying a clip board in his hand, he places it under his arm. Just as he reaches to knock, Sarah shoots out of the door.

"May I help you?" she whispers, trying not to wake Gracie on this sleepy Saturday morning.

"Yes," he says, sounding professional. "I am your local trash guy and my company is revamping some of our routes to make them more economically efficient. With the price of gas continuously going up, we have to be extremely conscious about making the most for our buck."

"Of course, what can I do to help?"

"Do you mind if I sit down and go over a few details with you?" With a courteous gesture, he extends his hand. "My name is Rick Seager."

"Pleased to meet you, Mr. Seager. My name is Sarah Cole."

He looks at her questionably. "You don't know who I am?"

"I'm sorry. No. We've never met, have we?"

He cuts his eyes around, making sure no one hears. "Forgive

me for showing up uninvited, but I need to talk to you. I'm the GBI Drug Task Force Agent working undercover with Paul Hines. He and I are collaborating on a certain drug case together."

Sarah gasps. "I'm so terribly sorry. Paul told me about you, but never told me your name. In a backward rather twisted kind of way, I am glad that we finally have an opportunity to meet." Apologetically, Sarah adds, "I would invite you in, but my daughter is still asleep and this conversation needs to be kept private. If you don't mind, Mr. Seager, let's sit out here on the porch."

"Sure, I understand. I have a daughter that likes to sleep in on the weekends, too."

"May I ask you a question? Why the trash business as an undercover?"

"I drive the trucks and I can be around and about in the neighborhoods without anyone being suspicious. I have to be extremely careful because if my cover is blown, the whole operation can fail."

"I understand. Paul explained that this county is infested with drug addicts and because the addiction is so strong, it has become an epidemic. He also explained that at the moment the two of you are not particularly interested in the hitter, Bobby Wright. You are more interested in the dealer who is supplying him with the big stuff to sell?"

Rick comments, "He's right. The real victory comes when we take down the man above Bobby. That will be the real event. I want him sent to prison by a court of law. I want him to pay for all the hurt he has caused by feeding this community his poison." He pauses. "Once we get the dealer, they can offer him a deal to rat on his boss. And, so it goes. In other words, cut off the head of the snake, the rest of the body dies. The problem is that the kingpin is so powerful; his dealers know if they snitch, it could cost them their lives. They are not even safe in prison."

"How soon do you think you will have enough evidence to make a move?"

"I think we are getting ready for a bust. I want to move in on Bobby and his boss simultaneously so one won't have an opportunity to warn the other. Just a few more odds and ends of substantial proof against Bobby Wright and we'll be ready to send these fellows away for a long time."

"What kind of proof?"

"I need to be a hundred percent sure what he's keeping in that steel building in the empty lot behind his house. In this business, you can't be all assuming. You need to have enough evidence to hold up on court. We've got to have enough suspicion to warrant a property search."

"How in this world are you going to get all the evidence you need?"

"Me!" says the voice from the other side of the door. Still, in her pajamas, Gracie moves out onto the porch. "How are you, Mr. Seager?"

"Hello, Gracie. How are you?"

Sarah's eyes, widens, darting from one to the other. Completely taken off guard, she begins to ask, "Mr. Seager? Gracie? How . . . how do the two of you know one another? You have some explaining to do!"

Rick Seager intervenes. "We met some time ago at Bobby Wright's house."

"Bobby Wright's house? What . . . why . . . you better explain, young lady, what you were doing at Bobby Wright's house. And, what about the little talk you and I had about the meaning of truthfulness? Girl, you are just full of surprises! Who are you, by the way? Where is my daughter? Because right now, I don't know you."

"I haven't gone anywhere, Mom. I am right here—Gracie

Cole, alive and well as we speak. So, please calm down and let me explain."

"You'd better! Start now or else I'm going to turn you over my knee. You know, you are not too old for me to spank."

Gracie grins, waving her mother off. Addressing Rick with a slight motion of the head, she says, "She never will let me grow up. If it up to her, she'd install a GPS in my neck!"

Sarah looks from one to the other. "Gracie. Rick. I am waiting. Will you please explain to me how the two of you have become acquainted?"

Gracie volunteers. "Allow me, Mr. Seager." She turns to Sarah, whose face telegraphs, "I'm about to have an anxiety attack."

"Do you remember my telling you about the girl who was being bullied at the grocery store? The one whom that group of thugs destroyed the groceries she was carrying in her arms?"

"Angela? I remember you telling me that you drove her home after that incident. But I don't understand what she's got to do with this."

"Hold on to your britches, Mom. I found out that Angela lives with Bobby. I made the connection between Bobby and the drug business when I spotted the black truck at Angela's house. Besides, there were a few other things that gave the scenario away."

"Like what?" Rick asked.

"I received a bad vibe from his uncle sitting under a tree. It was as if he was watching the place for any strangers coming on the premises."

Sarah interrupts, waving her hands. "Wait a minute. Wait a minute. I never talked to you about the connection between Bobby Wright and a black truck being driven by a suspicious drug dealer. How did you know and have you ever met Bobby?"

"First of all, Mom, the office is small and words carry, especially to my big ears."

"That's an understatement!"

Gracie glares. "That hurt!"

"I'm sorry, honey. Next time I have something you don't need to hear, I'll take it outside. However, please go on. Explain how you met Bobby."

"Actually, I didn't have a conversation with Bobby until I ran into him one day coming out of the drug store. Angela told him I not only liked his truck, but that I was asking a lot of questions. So, he asked me if I needed to make some extra money. I didn't want him to know anything else about me, so I told him I worked at the store at the three-way stop. At the time, I didn't realize that he was actually going to check out my story. He caught me in a lie so he made Angela call me to come over. I thought the call was on the up and up so I drove over to her house. Bobby was waiting on me and began to give me the third degree. That's when Mr. Seager came to my rescue."

Sarah gasps. "Came to your rescue?"

Rick intervenes. "Yeah. I had been scoping Bobby. I already knew about Gracie's relationship with Angela, but I didn't know until that day that Bobby was suspicious of Gracie. When he started getting rough with her, I stepped in."

Sarah jumps up, raging, "Getting rough with her? Don't you understand now, Gracie, why I cannot allow you to get involved with this? Can't you see it is too dangerous?"

Gracie begins to explain. "Mother, I am prepared to handle problems when hit head on. Besides, I am not the one that needs worrying about. Angela does. She must have resisted calling me at first. Undoubtedly, after a few punches to the face, she finally gave in."

"What do you mean?" Sarah asks.

"Angela's face ran into something hard that left a few bumps and bruises, and I don't think it was the door. I'm thinking it was Bobby's fists."

Sarah frowns. "Before this goes any further and *you* are on the other end of Bobby Wright's fists, this thing comes to an end. Furthermore, I am so tired of seeing such a grave injustice to an unforeseeable end for children who fall by the capricious greed of drug traffickers. Their murky logic that recreational drug use is a wave of the future is nothing but bull crap!"

Sarah turns to Rick Seager and says with a tinge of sarcasm in her voice, "I take it you also have your share of grievances against those who are content to become profitable with the lives and safety of others—"

Rick interrupts her. "Of course I have. That's why this investigation has to be carried out carefully and evidence I collect is not fatally flawed. I can't leave anything in question. If I get evidence that is contaminated, controversial, or inadequate, it can be thrown out of court by a good defense lawyer. Paul Hines is a super DA, but even he must have valid and substantial evidence. This county has a judge that pounds his gavel at the least question of invalidity."

"Yes. I've had the pleasure of dealing with him," Sarah admits.

Rick continues, "That's why Paul and I have to be very careful that neither the defense nor the judge can question if we used inadequate procedures to take these people down. Everything has got to be correctly executed and evidence correctly received." He smiles at Gracie. "Although I am a little optimistic about being armed with the new evidence Gracie has just told me, it won't hold up in a court of law unless we can back it up with significant proof."

"My word is not proof sufficient?" Gracie asks.

"Not really. A judge wants pictures, DNA, fingerprints—anything that will show validity."

Gracie eyes quickly dart to meet those concerned ones of her mother's. "I can do it, Mother. I can get everything Mr. Seager and Mr. Hines need to take Bobby Wright down. More importantly, I can even find out what he is hiding inside those four metal walls in his backyard."

Sarah waves her hand frantically and shakes her head. "No, Gracie. Not now. Not ever!"

"So, how many people do you want to suffer? How many children have to be hurt? This is why I don't like to say anything to you. You go all off on me."

"You know the rules in this house, Gracie Cole. We've already had a discussion about this issue and I made my feelings very plain."

"Yes. You are the parent, I am the child, and I follow your rules to the letter." She sighs. "I disagree with you, Mother, though I am inspired by you and I know you will do anything for me. I love you so much, Sarah Cole, but sometimes, you can be a little intimidating. However, you forget that I am now old enough to be considered an adult. Still, you treat me like a juvenile. You are constantly in my face reminding me that I am not capable of making my own decisions. Stop trying to shut me down and give me credit for being perfectly capable of living my own life."

Gracie's tone is solemn as she continues. "I appreciate you always having my back, but you are extremely overprotective. For once, let me grow up. For once in my life, give me the benefit of the doubt." She pauses, waiting for a positive response from her mother. When there is none, she added, "I am not asking for your blessing. I *am* asking you not to interfere."

Sarah glares at her daughter. "Why not just poke me in the eye with a sharp stick? Do you have something else to say that I am willing to listen to?"

"Only if you open your ears, listen, and stop having such a narrow view of things."

Sarah points to her mouth. "As usual, your mouth is moving. You are going to have to translate because I have no idea what you are saying." She points to her lips. "Watch my mouth. These lips say 'no'! Understand this, Gracie. Your life has value. You are living in a moment when all you want to do is to think about the here and now. You are giving absolutely no thought to a future because, Gracie, one bad move on your part and you will have no future."

"Mother, please just calm down. I am going to do what I want to do and that is final."

"Calm down? Listen here, daughter of mine, I will calm down just as soon as you follow the rules of this house. I'll follow my instincts. You follow the rules. Why? Because I am the mother. And, never, never assume you know how it feels to be a mother." She stands up and storms back into the house, but not before yelling over her shoulder, "Here's the thing, Gracie. Since we are having such a hard time communicating verbally, I will just send you a text, slash, warning, slash, exclamation point!"

Gracie looks at Rick. "She is so meticulous. She doesn't let anything by, but she'll get over it. What do you think? I'm eighteen. I'm legal. I can do what I want to do."

"Just give me all the information you have on the homeboy and I will start digging. I just witnessed flames of discontent being fanned between a mother and daughter who love each other very much. That puts you at a disadvantage, emotionally, to be of any help to me. It could make things considerably more complicated if you get involved."

"What do you need from me to make you feel more reassured?"

"You are tenacious about this subject, huh? Besides, you are putting me in a risky position. I can empathize with your situation and I do appreciate your enthusiasm, but I don't want to cause problems between the two of you."

"You are going to have to look over that. I am going to tell you the same as I told my mother. I am old enough to make my own decisions."

He motions towards the closed door Sarah has slammed behind her. "It's going to take a lot of courage, Gracie, going against your mother's will. It's not going to be a piece of cake. Besides, it will be an extremely dangerous mission. It will be like going to war and the only casualty just might be you."

Without hesitation, Gracie asks, "My mind is made up. What do you want me to do?"

"We'll cross that bridge when we get to it."

"What are you willing to do?"

"I want to find out everything I can about the lowlifes and do my part to rid this earth of all the scum."

"There's a lot of scum on this earth, Gracie."

"Then, we'll start in our own backyard!"

Rick Seager nods. "Watch out, Bobby Wright. Victory is imminent."

16

For the Sake of Gracie

"Good morning, Gracie."

"Good morning, Mrs. Cole."

"Come on, Gracie. There's no one in this office but you and me. You can call me 'Mom.'"

A familiar voice rings out from another room. "I'm here," says Kathy. "And, my ears hear all. Call her 'Mom', girl, and get on with it."

Sarah and Gracie chuckle. Gracie says, "Good morning, Mom. Did you sleep well last night?"

"You know the answer to that question. I walked the floor, turned, and tossed most of the night." She pulls up a chair next to her bright-eyed daughter. "I just couldn't figure out why you didn't tell me. You have always included me in the and bad things in your life. You are my baby, Grace, and always will be. One day when you are a mother, you will understand how hard it is to let go. When you have kids, all you want is for them to have a better life than what you had. You want them to make good life choices so their road to success and happiness will be easy." Sarah wipes a tear. "That's all I want for you, sweetheart. I want you to make better decisions than I have." She turns her daughter's face upward and looks deep into her eyes. "I want us to stop arguing about this before it divides us."

"Mom, you and I can never let go of each other. We are joined at the hip—eternally. We can still hang on to each other, be by each other's sides through thick, and thin—as long as we respect each other's space."

Sarah argued, "Don't patronize me. I am frustrated and frankly, more than a little afraid for you. Our little talks about this subject seem to have done absolutely no good."

Kathy walks up carrying Sarah a cup of coffee. "Maybe your perspective will change after you've had your morning coffee."

"Thanks, Kathy. I need to load up on some added caffeine to keep my brain alert when confronting a hardhead."

"Tell me about it," Kathy confirms. "You are not telling anything I don't know. That's why I am a caffeine junkie."

Sarah sips on the steaming liquid. She says soberly. "For once, I'd like for something or someone to walk through that door and make my day."

At that moment Paul Hines walks through the door.

Sarah stutters, "Oh, my gosh, Paul. I didn't mean you! For sure, not you!"

Paul smiles. "With all that entails, this may be the wake-up call I need to finally stop carrying a torch for you!" He looks around. "Did I walk in on something? Is there a problem here?"

Kathy turns back to her desk, muttering, "I don't know. I was just wondering the same. Well, this is my cue to get back to work!"

Gracie adds, "Me, too!" She begins filing.

Paul says, "I didn't mean to run everybody off." He casts a look towards Gracie. "What's wrong with you?"

Gracie grins. "Oh, nothing. I was just decompressing after the usual conversation with my mother."

He looks at Sarah. "Mothers and daughters—I'll never understand them. I'll just let that one go. By the way, Sarah, do you have a minute? I'd like to talk to you in your office?"

"Well, let me see. I guess I can squeeze you in between doing nothing and not doing nothing." She chuckles. "Of course, Paul. Come on back."

Paul follows Sarah into her office and closes the door. "I need to update you on the progress of the case against the drug traffickers. The police commissioner, the county sheriff, Rick Seager, and I had another private meeting. We are almost ready to close in on Bobby Wright's supplier. His name is Theo Harris. Theo lives out in the country, slides out to Atlanta to buy his stuff, comes back, and meets Bobby to push it on for him. Of course, Bobby has his weed on hand to add to the sale. However, Theo is slick. He never takes the same route or meets his supplier in the same place. The Drug Task Force with the GBI is waiting until we arrest Theo, hoping a plea deal for a lesser sentence will encourage him to tell who supplies him. Same with Bobby. A plea deal for a lesser sentence will appear mighty appealing when you are faced with being sent off to prison for a long time."

"So your plan is to try to catch Bobby and Theo making their connection?"

"Yep. There's only one problem. Theo and Bobby always meet at a different location and different time." He pauses. "We have a solution, Sarah."

"You've got my attention. What is it?" Sarah asks.

Paul pulls out a small, black box out of his brief case. He explains. "This is a tracker. If placed strategically on Bobby's truck, we can monitor his every move."

"Great! Go for it. If it helps you catch them in the act, put the tracker on his truck."

"We would, but there are too many obstacles in the way. Bobby keeps that old man, his Uncle Ham, around guarding the place during the day while he sleeps because he stays up practically all night. We presume Bobby spends his time at night "gardening"" inside that metal building. Anyway, he's got spy cameras set up everywhere and watch dogs that will warn him if anyone slips around. Once we catch Bobby with Theo, the judge will easily give us a warrant to search the premises, but until after he is arrested and arraigned, this case has to be airtight."

"So what are you going to do? How can you get someone close enough to put a tracker on Bobby's truck?"

"That's just it. We need someone that has established an inside connection—a reason to visit occasionally without drawing suspicion. Maybe a friend of his sister's."

Sarah does not respond. She sits, staring out of the window, cold and aloof—glacial. Paul waves a hand in front of her face. "Daydreaming? Thinking?"

Sarah glares at Paul. "I know exactly where this conversation is heading."

Jokingly, Paul adds, "Hi. Welcome back. I thought you had zoned me out."

Sarah's voice is calm. "No. I didn't zone you out. However—" She stands up and opens the office door. "I am kicking you out."

"But, why, Sarah? The risk is minimum. I know what I'm proposing is dangerous, but we have no one else in mind that can even get close to that property, much less to Bobby's truck. And we'll have her back." He shakes his head. "I can't believe you are fighting me on this."

"Do I need to point out the potential problems that can occur by asking my daughter, an untrained investigator, to do such a thing? This is not negotiable. I will not allow you to manipulate me and put my daughter in jeopardy."

Paul defends, "I'm probably going to say something inappropriate or do something stupid, but the real one here with the problem is you, Mrs. Cole. You need to stop being so self-absorbed and grow up!"

"How dare you!" She motions towards the door. "This conversation is over. Go find someone else to harass. There's the door. Don't let it hit you in the rear on the way out!"

Paul bows his head as he gathers his briefcase, along with the tracker. "Okay. I give up. Thanks for your time."

Just as he reaches the door, Sarah grabs his arm, pulling him back so that he could feel her breath on his face. She whispers, "If you slip around behind my back, involve my daughter, and put her life at risk, I will use your privates for cut bait on my next fishing trip. This is not a request, an ultimatum, or a demand. It is a fact. Understand me, Paul?"

Red faced, Paul nods and walks out of Sarah's office. He slinks past Gracie's desk avoiding her eyes.

Gracie waits until Sarah's door to her office closes. Then, she races to Paul's car and knocks on his window. He rolls it down. Gracie motions to his briefcase and holds out her hand. "It's obvious to me what I need to do."

As if Paul has read her thoughts, he reaches inside his brief case and pulls out the tracker. "Are you sure?" Paul asks.

"Absolutely!"

Paul hands the tracker to Gracie and quietly drives away.

17

Nowhere to Hide. Nowhere to Run

Gracie glances around her as she drives through town hoping for a glimpse of Angela. I'm in luck, she thinks, as she spots her coming out of the grocery store. She wheels in next to the curb, rolling the window down. "Hi, Angela. Do you need a ride home? It's a hot one today."

Angela bends down and looks through the window at Gracie. She wipes her sweaty brow. "Hi, Gracie. Do you mind? It certainly is hot out here."

"Of course, I don't mind. Hop in." Gracie shoots a quick glance at Angela's face, still showing evidence of an assault, as she thrusts the car in gear. "What happened to you, Angela? Did somebody hurt you? I can't help but notice someone has treated you unkindly. You still have bruises."

Angela attempts to cover her face. "Please don't go there, Gracie. Leave it alone. I don't want you to go seeking some kind of justice for me. It's not worth it."

"Your overmedicated so called brother is an abusive maniac. Nothing but slime beats up on women." She sighs. "You need someone to talk to, Angela. You can't go through life like this—at least, confide in me. You know I am a friend and I want to help, but I can't if you are holding back on me."

"How can you say you are a friend after I lied to you for

Bobby? Please leave things alone, Gracie. If I tell you nothing is wrong, will you go away? It's for your own good."

"No. I am not going away. Like I said, I am your friend. That's the bottom line. So, trust me and let me help you."

"So, I got punched out. My life is nothing but a trash fire, anyway. Maybe I deserved this. Besides, I don't need help or protection from Bobby."

"Tell that to your face."

"But I lied to you, Gracie." She chokes back tears. Slowly, she begins. "Bobby forced me. I begged him not to do it. You never can reason with him. He always does what he wants to do. And he wanted you to come over so he could confront you. I knew that you could possibly be hurt. Still, I did what he said. I put the life of the only friend I have ever had in jeopardy." She looks at Gracie. "I am so sorry I put you in that position."

"I'm not worried about that. The way I see it, you had no choice. I figured out Bobby forced you to call me over. Besides, no worries. The trash man stepped in and saved me." She smiles at Angela. "It's okay. I am not mad at you." She pats the distraught young woman's hand. "What do you say let's talk?

Angela asks, "Where do we start?"

Gracie chuckles. "I am not one for idle chit chat. Maybe start at the beginning and with the truth. Will you do me a favor?"

"What's that?"

"Be straight with me and no more lies. Nothing but truth between us, okay?"

Angela nods. "Okay."

Gracie begins, "First of all, I did a Google search on Bobby Wright. He has no sister. So how did the two of you hook up and what exactly is your relationship with him?"

There was a long silence. Finally, she begins. "I'm embarrassed and it pains me to say this, but my childhood was not standard.

In fact, my life as a child kind of sucked." She chokes back tears. "I came from a dysfunctional family—one that fought and screamed at each other all the time. When I was young, I was a wrecking ball. Growing up poor and with alcoholic parents does not necessarily make for a happy childhood. It seemed that I was always hurt by people I thought cared about me and hurt by people I didn't care about."

She wrings her hands as if struggling to relive her childhood. "I didn't have the clothes and other things that keep other kids from picking on me at school. I hated it when other kids pointed at me and talked about me behind my back. Being bullied was always a never ending battle for me. To make it worse, I have never been able to hide my feelings very well. So, the more they could see they were making me upset, the more they bullied."

"Kids can be really mean."

"Yeah. Tell me about it! Anyway, the first time I saw Bobby, I was immediately drawn to him. It was at a time in my life when I was vulnerable, I think, and I was totally charmed. Besides a physical attraction, I fell for all the nice things he promised to give me. I thought I could be his 'happily-ever-after, stand-by-your-man' girl. It may have been love at first, but now it is mutual self-destruction. I spend most of my time in an empty house with just my thoughts. The thing that bothers me the most is that I allow him to play me. You know, manipulate me."

"How can you allow anyone, much less Bobby, to manipulate you—unless you want to be manipulated?" Gracie asks. "I know there is no answer to that question. I do understand why you are struggling with this and the damage it has done to you, but Angela, people don't define you. You define yourself."

"You don't understand, Gracie. You are not living in my skin!"

"So, explain it so I can understand."

"When I met Bobby, I was not aware he was going down a

very dark path and has been for most of his life. I thought he was a good person, but he is the kind of person that acts on his darkest impulses. At times, he spirals out of control. It didn't take me long to find out how wrong I was. He uses people until they are no longer useful. To my knowledge, he has never done anything out of the goodness of his heart." She wipes a tear. "I made a bad decision and now I can't out run no matter how hard I try."

"What bad decision did you make? I sense something more."

"I fell in love with a sociopath—a useless waste of skin and bones. I left home, quit school, and moved in with him." She chokes back a tear. "I did it because I was different, an outsider, and I wanted love and acceptance." She mumbles, "I thought that one day he might change, but he hasn't and he never will. Deep down in my heart, I always wanted a normal existence. A normal life. I am a realist. I am the one who grew up in this world since day one. But I have dropped the ball."

"My condolences. You were vulnerable, but why don't you end this horrible chapter in your life and put that weasel behind you? If you feel like you can leave, why don't you just let it play out? Relationships generally run their course. I think you are overestimating Bobby and underestimating yourself."

"It's not that simple, Gracie. It's more complicated than that. But the good news is that I don't love him anymore—not since I found out what kind of a man he really is. He is nothing to me. Absolutely nothing."

"Did you marry him?"

"No. Of course you have already figured out that important piece of information, haven't you?"

Gracie nods. "Why tell everyone you are his sister? That I don't understand."

"That's the way Bobby wants it." She sighs. "I honestly think he is either ashamed of me or he wants to be free to play the

field. Girls would be more receptive if they think he is single."
She searches Gracie's eyes for understanding. "I had a moment of
weakness, all right? I thought he was everything I ever wanted.
I thought I finally had someone in my life that loves me and
someone who respects me."

"How does he treat you? I mean, other than the occasional
knocks and bangs."

"Sometimes, it feels like he is constantly trying to push me
away. Other times, it feels like he is trying to keep me close. We
go toe to toe. My relationship with him is like riding a bike. You
never forget how to fall off."

"Although this is totally mind-blowing, I am trying to
empathize with your situation, Angela. But, you are a grown
woman and you don't need justification from a man. So you lost
your way, but you can get back on track."

Angela choked back welling tears. "You don't get it. My life
is not easy, okay? I feel like I have been changed forever. I don't
know who I am anymore or if I'll ever recover. I feel like I am
running around in circles—totally lost. I am afraid of my future
and I don't have hope for anything. My whole life is in chaos.
Maybe, if I was a better person, I could make him a better person.
I am nothing but a major screw-up." She chokes back a tear. "I
wish I could run away." She wipes a fallen tear. "I know in my
head when someone hurts you intensively, they will do it again. I
want to get off this roller coaster. I want it to end. I don't want it
anymore. But I don't know how."

"First of all, you are not a screw-up and there is hope for a
better future. You just had a bad start in life and that can be fixed.
Life goes on and you can still live a productive life. As for Bobby,
he is a grown man. He makes his own choices and that's not your
fault. You have nothing to do with what ultimately happens to
him. What's important at this point is that you no longer have

feelings for him. It's your gain and his loss. I'm proud of you for wanting to face this and find a way to get away from him. You can get it all back, you know. Your life. Your freedom. As for running away without first confronting your problem, that won't help. Regroup, take some time to sort things out, and then when you've got your head on straight, leave him, start a new life, and begin again. I believe in you with all my heart and you just have to believe in yourself. I will help you. I promise."

"You make it sound so easy. You make it sound like getting my life back is simple." She wipes a tear falling from her eye. "However, I don't believe in miracles. I am not a self-sacrificing type of person. I've never believed that suffering makes you a better person. The life that I chose has been all wrong for me. It would be wonderful—I mean, having an opportunity to get it right."

"So, you are not self-sacrificing. Nevertheless, your future depends on you—not Bobby. This is totally on you. You can learn from this and move forward or you just wallow in self-pity, lie down, and die. Over the years, I have learned that if things are meant to be, they work out, and if they don't, there is something better waiting on you. Personally, I think there are better things ahead for you. Stop, wallowing, Angela. Get out of the mud hole and start making moves to get your life back."

"You make it sound so simple, but we both know it is more complicated than that."

"I totally get what you are saying. All I am asking is, just think about it."

For a while, Angela weighs the words Gracie has spoken to her—words of consolation and inspiration, words that offer hope. "Do you know what I think, Gracie? I think that you happening up at this time in my life has been a blessing to me. You make my future sound promising. I want you to know that I would really like to keep you in my life as a friend. I would give anything if I could say that Bobby Wright is dead to me. However, there is one thing you need to understand."

"What do I need to understand?"

"You need to realize that although all of your talk is encouraging, you must save your breath. You can talk to me all you want about this, but I will never be free to live my life the way I see fit. Bobby will never let me go—unless it is in a body bag thrown in the bottom of the swamp. If you aren't careful, Gracie, one of those body bags will belong to you."

Gracie gulps.

"That's just the kind of relationship we have always had. It's complicated. Not simple. I'm his slave, I do what he says, and I obey him. I can never leave, because I know too many of his secrets. If I try to leave, I die. I don't want to die, Gracie. I have no choice but to stay."

"Then don't die. Arise out of this mess and plot revenge. All you are to him is a minor inconvenience. If he truly loves you, you wouldn't be known as a sister and he would give you absolutely no reason to be afraid of him. You are being played. It happens when someone wants to control you. Don't give him an easy shot. Fight for yourself. Make the right choice, Angela, to get as far away from him as you can."

"Believe me, I am listening. You are making some valid points. However, I'm afraid to leave." She bits her bottom lip. "I'm not as brave as you. I don't know what to do or how to do it. I don't have anybody on my side—right or wrong. I am estranged from my family. I don't have anyone to love me and stand behind me."

"Angela, I'll be that person. You can lean on me if you ever need help. We can fix this problem and you will come out of this stronger and better than ever. You may be afraid. Your heart might be broken, but your spirit is intact. You will survive this.

I believe in you with all my heart and you just have to believe in yourself."

"Gracie, I don't want to go to war with Bobby and I am pretty sure you don't want to go to war with him, either."

"No one is going to war. Do you remember the first day we met?"

"How can I forget? We met under a circumstance you probably haven't seen much of. You rescued me from a bunch of bullies. You stepped up, took control, and saved me."

"That's what I am going to do now. Bobby is no different from that bunch of hoodlums that knocked your groceries out of your arms that day. I'm here to tell you that the persecution of Angela ends now. Your life will not be destroyed by that man ever again. He may try to hurt you, but with every ounce of strength I have in me, he will never hurt you again. He has terrorized you and subjected you to abuse and emotional trauma. But never again. I can promise you that."

Angela tensed muscles relax. She takes in a deep breath and exhales. "Thank you, Gracie. I am ready to do something and get out of this situation I am living in. It has taken a long time to get to this point, but I am definitely ready."

"Getting to this point is what matters. Not how long it took."

Within a few minutes, Gracie drives up to Angela's and Bobby's house on the outskirts of town. A little apprehensive, Gracie tries to hide her concern when she spots Bobby's truck. Angela notices. "It's okay, Gracie. He is dead asleep during this time of the day. If I didn't know that, I would never have allowed you to drive me home."

Gracie looks around for Uncle Ham, who seems to always be on duty watching the premises while Bobby sleeps. Angela further explains, "He is not here today, either. He's out of town at a funeral." Frowning, she asks, "What do I do now? You did say you were going to help me."

"The time is now. Do you trust me?" Gracie asks.

"Yes. I am the only one that I doubt. You, on the other hand, are deserving of the benefit of the doubt."

"Then, listen and listen well. Go into the house. Quietly. Make sure Bobby is soundly sleeping." She carefully watches Angela's face, making sure she understands her orders. She motions toward the metal building that she knows Ham keeps under close scrutiny. "I want you to get the keys to that building. Bring them to me, then slip back in the house and make sure Bobby doesn't wake up. If I can pull this off, Angela, you will never have to worry about Bobby Wright again."

"You know what's in that building, don't you?"

"I would bet my bottom dollar. Now go."

Angela eases out of the car, careful not to slam the door. Suddenly, Gracie calls her back. "Please be careful."

Nervous, Angela asks, "What if he wakes up? What do I do?"

Gracie shrugs. "I guess we'll have to leave that up to your intuition."

Angela nods. Before she quietly slips away, Gracie once again calls her back and asks, "No regrets? No second thoughts?"

Angela boldly states, "For once in my life I can say, 'None!'"

Within a few minutes she returns with the key grasped tightly in her hand. She whispers, "He is in a deep sleep. Please hurry— for both of our sakes." Back into the house she goes, to keep watch over the man she has grown to detest.

Your freedom is in sight, girl, thinks Gracie. Angela goes back inside and Gracie quietly opens the door of the vehicle, stopping shortly to grab her camera and a small black box hidden in the pocket of her car. She says to herself, you are on the brink of meeting your demise, Bobby Wright. It is going to be a pleasure knowing you are going to rot in jail. She bites her bottom lip, looking around, careful of her surroundings. *I've got to be on my game if I am going to bring Bobby Wright down.*

As soon as Gracie is near the black truck parked near the building, she quickly scans her surroundings, making sure no one is watching. Kneeling down at the back side of the truck, she hurriedly snaps the tracker inside and underneath the well of the back wheel. Once attached, she eases her way to the locked door of the metal building. The door buzzes upon opening. Once inside, she stands, and her jaw drops in shock. What is before her eyes is more than she ever would have anticipated—an extensive cannabis operation. The building, which hulks against a gritty stretch of outlying woods, from the outside gives nothing to indicate the vastness of this horticultural green revolution going on in the interior.

Quickly Gracie begins snapping pictures, angling her camera and zooming in on the lucrative growing buds. What she appears to be looking at is a business booming beyond comprehension. In this small garden spot, hidden behind metal walls, pulsating with grow lights, fans, filters, trimming machines, and pumps—a profitable crop of cannabis growing. Past a curing room, in all of its glory, are hundreds of plants standing tall, bathing under a halo of plasma lighting and nodding in the breeze of oscillating fans. Gracie leans over and sniffs one of the clustered flower buds with white powdery wisps. "Whew! I could get high just smelling this stuff!"

Towards the end of the building is a propagation room where a young crop beginning with cuttings from other plants is taking root. Continuously, she snaps pictures.

It is at that moment she notices the surveillance cameras hanging from the ceiling. Her heart stops. Oh, boy, she says to herself. While I am taking pictures of this, those are taking pictures of me. She scurries towards the only exit in the building. *I've got to get out of here and now!*

Just as she reaches her hands to turn the knob, the door flings open. Bobby Wright is holding Angela's arms bent behind her back with one strong hand. In the other hand jammed against her forehead is a pistol.

Their eyes lock. Gracie's wide-open eyes and voice of reason tell her she is in deep trouble. Her mind jumps into overdrive as she searches for a way out.

Gracie considers her resources and weighs her options, hoping she'll think of a solution. As fear consumes her, she is reminded of her frailty. There is nowhere to hide—nowhere to run.

18

Prisoners

The weather is placid as the motorized small boat proceeds briskly, gliding through the shallow waters of the narrow creek—its security is its wilderness. A few cigarettes and a couple of bottles of beers later, Ham rams into a clearing, jolting its passengers off balance. Grabbing each girl's arms and tying them tightly behind their backs, he forces them to fall forward.

Gracie, praying for calm, whispers, "Angela, how are holding up?"

"Not very well. How do you think I am holding up? You know, we are not on a picnic here. Do you remember what I told you about what happens in the swamp?"

"Yep. But, look at it like this. There is no body bag. That should be uplifting."

"There is no need for body bags in the swamp, Gracie. They kill you, pin your body under a submerged log, and as soon as your body rots and is soft enough to tear apart in chunks, a carnivore will swim by and have a nice lunch."

Gracie gags at the thought. "Then we need to be thinking of a way to get out of this mess before Uncle Ham decides to feed his pets." She swallows hard. "Do you think you can talk him down?"

"Not hardly. He does everything Bobby orders him to do."

She looks at Gracie with sorrowful eyes. "I'm sorry that I got you into this mess. If it wasn't for me, you wouldn't be here."

"This is not your fault. There is no way you could have known that things would end like this. I take full responsibility for what happens to us. My actions were what put us this situation."

"Shut up!" Uncle Ham yells.

"I thought you said he was the silent type," mumbles Gracie.

Angela whispers, "No. I said he is hard of hearing."

"Hm. That may work to our advantage. I think I'll see just how hard of hearing the old coot is."

As Ham ties the boat to a tree, he orders, "Get out!" He motions towards the bank leading deeper into the woods. "From this point on, we walk!"

Gracie mutters, "Go drown yourself, you ol' lard butt."

A wooden staff finds the back of the mouthy target. Moaning, Gracie bends over. As she straightens up, she whispers to Angela, "Wow! That was a slight miscalculation. Anyway, that settles that. There is nothing wrong with his hearing."

"Go!" Uncle Ham commands, pushing the girls forward.

"Okay, okay," Gracie growls. "I get it. You are punishing us because I do not play nice."

The move is on. Crashing through the terrain and impeded by dense vegetation, stumbling over roots, and slipping through mud and crowded moss-draped trees, the girls are pushed through the trackless wilderness. Occasionally, dark, long limb-like shapes, most likely deadly snakes, flit through the murky waters.

Deeper into the waters of the river's over-spill they trudge in the perfect hush of wilderness, leaving behind the rhythms of solid soil and rock. An occasional push with Ham's wooden staff spurs them forward. Each step takes the young women closer to their darkest time—that time when they could suffer and die. Gracie knows that even though formidable challenges are ahead, she will steadfastly set her goal on not giving up or caving in.

Finally, they reach a miniscule opening through the overwhelming and inaccessible landscape. A small shack on low stilts protrudes out of the scene. The walls, floor, and ceiling have been roughly crafted out of wood that is beginning to rot. In one of the corners stands an antique blackened stove.

Gracie looks up through the tree tops hoping for some familiar object or sight that might tell her where they are. Instead, in the onset of darkness all she sees are the shining eyes of thousands of insects and a harpy owl on the chase of a bat, setting up ownership of the oncoming night sky. Slowly she becomes well aware that they are deep in the swamp, far away from any intrusions of a population, untainted by civilization, prisoners in a primitive and isolated setting.

The lumbering bull called "Uncle Ham" pushes Gracie and Angela inside the shack hidden among the trees. With loud grunts, slaps, and thuds, their young bodies slam onto the floor. Angela asks, "Uncle Ham, can we have some water? I am so thirsty."

Uncle Ham only stares, emotionless. The silence is soon interrupted by the rutting sounds of a couple of wild pigs roving through the area.

"Whew!" Gracie says, as soon as she is made aware the noise is not alligators on the prowl. She turns to Angela. "Maybe the noise will keep the gators away."

"Or draw them closer," Angela whispers, and she begs Uncle Ham again. Exhausted from the ordeal, she continues to play upon his sympathies. "Please let Gracie and me go. Please don't leave us here to die. You can tell Bobby that you got rid of us and we can slip away and never come back."

Ham barks, "No! That's not how this works. Bobby has a rule—anyone that interferes with his business dies."

Gracie's reply seems to surprise him. "It is nice to know there are still some gentlemen in the world."

Uncle Ham snarls, "Am I supposed to do something nice like apologize to you or something?"

"No. Definitely not, Mister Macho Caveman. No public apology from you. However, I would be forever grateful if you would do as Angela asks—let us go. We have no leverage here and you have it all. You've got our number. But, if you play it right, Bobby will never know what happened here, or do you have a better idea in mind?"

"Maybe. I don't want to kill you, but it's a necessary evil in order to leave no witnesses behind."

"How gracious of you," Gracie replies. "However, you do have a choice. You can save our lives or take our lives. You have to pick one."

Uncle Ham grumbles as he ignores the remark. He begins to rummage through his back pack. He takes out a hammer and a few nails.

Unsure of what to expect, Gracie whispers to Angela, "Pretend like you are not afraid."

Angela sniffs. "Yeah, you can write 'honey' on a bottle of rat poison and it will still kill you!"

Uncle Ham points to Gracie and says, "I heard what you said—telling her not to be afraid. You are a brave person. I can respect courage when I see it. I could shoot you like a dog, but a brave person deserves to go out fighting."

"I do appreciate that compliment, Mr. Ham, but listen to me. If I am not back soon, someone will come looking for me."

"No, they won't. Even if they do, nobody is going to be able to find you."

Gracie trembles but manages to control her fear. She continues to reason, motioning towards Angela. "You don't need to kill her.

Take her back to Bobby. Explain to him that none of this was her fault."

"Bobby says she has to die." He glares at Gracie, his aggressor. "He says you have to die, too."

Gracie continues to bargain. "Listen, Ham! You don't want to kill us. You don't want to kill anybody. Face reality and think about the outcome. The GBI, sheriff's office, DA, and everybody else in law enforcement is onto Bobby. They know all about his operation. Sooner or later, they are going to catch up to you and my mother will squeeze your manly parts until you squeal our whereabouts."

"The only reason I am telling you this is because I don't want my mother going to prison for killing someone who is a pansy for Bobby Wright. Do the smart thing. Keep us alive to use as a bargaining chip. That way you can make a bargain for a lesser sentence. Otherwise, if you leave a pile of corpses in here, you will be hunted for the rest of your life. If you kill us, you will go straight to death row. You will never be free."

Ham glares. "Who are you? Who would want you?"

"I am Sarah Cole's daughter. Sarah Cole is the supervisor over Safe Families and she is working with Paul Hines, the DA, and Rick Seager, an undercover agent for the drug task force."

Ham frowns as she forces herself to go on. "Don't be a fool, Ham. Consider the outcome of this situation. Keeping us alive will lessen your chances of spending an eternity locked away in some prison. Think about it. You don't deserve to go down for a crime Bobby is responsible for."

"If I go down, trust and believe, he goes down with me."

"But, *you* don't have to go down. Not unless you are some monster and you have some sinister plan to destroy us."

After glaring at them wordlessly for a moment, Uncle Ham shuts the door behind him, leaving the girls frightened and alone.

Soon, they hear hammering. "The brute is nailing the door shut with strips of boards," Gracie says.

As they realize that this tiny shack may become their grimy morgue, both women's eyes fill with tears. The sky is dark—not a ray of light. The darkness consumes them and magnifies their fear. The young women blink trying to adjust their eyes to the gloom in what may be their death chamber.

Gracie listens while Angela sniffs back tears as she becomes more and more traumatized. "How did I get to this place?" she asks the room. "How did I get to this place where I feel so paralyzed and helpless?"

"Angela, what's going on? Why are you crying? What is that going to help?"

"I'm being overcome by regret, Gracie. I'm afraid for what comes next."

"Well, we can either be very brave or very stupid. I just have to figure out which comes first. All I know right now is that we are not going to panic. We are going to find a way out of this." Gracie lays her head back against the wall, squirming to free herself from the ropes that bind her.

"Why didn't he go ahead and put us out of our misery? We are done."

"Far from it. Sure, we are in an extreme situation here, but we are going to rally. We will get through this."

"You make it sound so simple, but we both know we are not getting out of this. Are we going to die, Gracie?"

"Only in the literal sense."

"Oh, my God!" Angela screams.

Gracie quickly recants, "No! No! We are not going to die. Sorry for the gallows humor. I'm just trying to keep my spirits up."

"I wish I could believe you."

Gracie whispers, "Yeah, I wish I could believe me, too."

"What did you say and what are you doing?" Angela whispers back.

"I am trying to untie this rope around my hands. Why don't you try to do the same?" She grunts and groans. "This thing is tighter than a well-digger's behind." Finally, exasperated, she gives up. "I can't do this. I'll have to wait until the morning when I can see what's in front of my face." Heavily, she breathes, "Maybe then."

Suddenly, an owl hoots. Angela jumps. "What was that?"

"Don't be afraid. It was only an owl. Try to get some rest. When it gets daylight, we've got to come up with a plan."

"I have the feeling that your plan, as clever as it may be, will not work."

"Listen, Angela, this picture doesn't exactly scream closure. Your unquenchable pessimism screams out at me, though. I am getting a little tired of all this browbeating. So, please, with all due respect, shut up!"

"Shut up? I can't help it if I don't believe in miracles. Besides, you know you can't fix this, so stop trying to be my savior." She shudders. "In fact, you are not calming me. You are the reason we are in this mess. If you had only minded your own business—"

"You're right. This is all on me. You cannot blame yourself. If I hadn't forced your hand, none of this would have happened."

"No, I am not right. Like you said, I am a pessimist. A downer. I've always been a pessimist, not an optimist like you. I never believed in dreams coming true or happy endings. Dreams are just dreams, right? Not every dream is supposed to come true. So, why start now believing in all that hogwash?"

"Don't you remember the story about the little train when you were little? 'I think I can, I think I can'? There is a lot of power in the words, 'I can.'"

"There were no childhood stories at my house. In fact, there were no hugs and kisses. I didn't have much to look forward to unless it was when my dad finally passed out from all the booze. Then Momma didn't have anyone to yell at unless it was me, and I always pretended like I was asleep."

"So you had a bad time of it as a child. You have to stop dwelling on the past right now, girl. Think about the future and all the great and wonderful things you are going to accomplish with your life now that you are going to be free from Bobby."

"I'll never be free from Bobby. And, my opinion of him will never change. I will always hope he will just self-destruct." In the dark of the night, Angela whispers, "Oh, I love it when you refuse to allow me to feel sorry for myself. Just for that, when we get out of this, let's go out to dinner, and you can pick up the check."

"Ha! That's not the way this thing is supposed to work. Tell you what—when we get out of here, we'll do some retail therapy. All the stores will have great sales after the Fourth of July."

Angela mutters, "Why do you do that?"

"Do what?" Gracie asks, continuing to strain to untie the ropes that bind her hands.

"Deflect! Pretending that nothing bad is going on. Our lives are falling apart, death is inevitable, and you are talking about shopping!"

"Listen to me. You are not going to die on me. Understand? You and I are survivors. We are resourceful, capable, maybe a little flawed, but survivors just the same. You remember that." She flinches as the rope cuts deeper into her wrist. "Look on the bright side. Ham could have killed us before he left. Instead, he gave us a fighting chance to get out of this mess. So stop being so negative." Pensively, she adds, "Repeat after me: 'My name is Angela. I am a survivor. Nothing. Nothing. Nothing is impossible for me.'"

She listens as Angela repeats the message. She asks, "Do you believe that?"

"Not even as it comes out of my mouth."

Gracie is quiet. *Discouragement is overwhelming me right now. I have courage. I have courage. I am confident. I am confident. We'll get through this . . .*

After a brief silence, not hearing Gracie's attempts to struggle with the rope anymore, Angela asks, "Gracie, are you giving up? Just because I am a senseless idiot doesn't mean you have to be. Please don't give up."

A chuckle. "I'm not. Not even close."

"I figured that much." She hesitates. "Tell me about yourself. Who has been your inspiration? You know, the person you credit for making you the strong person you are."

Gracie smiles as she begins to explain. "I guess that would have to be my mother. She is all I am and all I ever hope to be." She chuckles. "Not too long ago, we really got into a big argument. I was accusing her of being outrageously sanctimonious because she thinks she is right all the time. Funny thing is, she *is* generally right all the time."

Gracie chokes back a tear. "I feel so guilty. I made a mistake—I mean arguing with her. A mistake that I hope I won't regret and hope I get the chance to tell her. I'm a stickler for believing the mistakes you make to people you love always come back to haunt you. I hope I'm wrong. Maybe you will get a chance to tell her you are sorry."

Gracie smiles, bristling with grim vitality. "Of course I will. And you'll be with me. She taught me to embrace adversity whenever its ugly head arises. And she taught me the importance of listening to my heart. Right now, my heart is telling me we are going to rise above this."

Angela yawns. "I am so tired. Will you tell me some stories, Gracie? You must have tons of stories. Talk to me so I can calm down a little and go to sleep. I know you have some great memories that outlast and outnumber the argument between you and your mother. Tell me about those memories. Tell me about your life."

"Well, I guess I can talk you to sleep. My life is that boring."

"Of all the word used to describe you, Gracie Cole, *boring* is not one of them. Besides, I like *boring* and *uncomplicated*."

"Okay, here goes. Let me see where to start." She pauses. "I think I was three, no, four years old when my dad and mom divorced. I always thought it was my fault. I thought if I had been a better child, they would have stayed together. Anyway . . ." Gracie stops and listens to the echo of croaking frogs across the swampy terrain and the whish of a gentle wind blowing through the wooden planks.

Suddenly, Angela crumples up in a corner asleep. Gracie begins to yawn and smiles. "See? I told you my life is boring."

19

Fear Me

Sarah paces back and forth under the morning sun as it begins to set the sky ablaze. Gracie was expected to be home by twelve o'clock last night. Now, after a restless night of walking the floor, there is no word from her daughter. To add to Sarah's distress, Gracie's cell phone goes directly to voice mail. "Please call me, Gracie. I am out of my mind with worry. Get in touch with me. Send up a smoke signal or something." Sarah's mind plunges into despair and goes into overdrive. Tension mounts and she begins to pray, not to focus on her own power, for in her own strength, she could not overcome this obstacle—this heaviness in her heart. Instead, she focuses on His faithfulness and His power. She gives this burden to God, thankful for the reminder that she needs to let go and trust in Him. Finally, after waves of anxiety, countless tears, and ceaseless prayers, the phone rings. Nervously, Sarah grabs the phone. "Gracie?"

"No. This is Paul, Sarah. I've been trying to reach Gracie. Her phone has gone dead. Is she there with you?"

Sarah begins to wail. "Paul, Gracie is missing. I know in my heart, she is hurt or . . ." She cannot say the words she feels in her heart. "Paul, I am so worried."

"Frankly, I am, too." He chokes on his words. "Hang on,

Sarah. I'm sending a car to pick you up. I'm bringing you back here to the sheriff's department."

"Don't bother. I can drive myself over. I have a very important stop to make first."

"Okay, but get yourself together. We are going to find her." He pauses, listening to the woman's sobs. "Sarah."

"What is it, Paul?"

"Persevere."

"Persevere? A truism for a reason, Paul? A reason for what? How dare you tell me to persevere? I feel like I have a hole in my heart and it won't go away. How can I persevere?" Sarah clamps her phone shut.

She meanders her way to her dresser, carefully opens the drawer, and pulls out her Glock 17. Holding the pistol against her chest, she whispers, "Yep, I have a very important stop to make."

A few minutes later, Sarah walks briskly up the short walkway to the Bobby Wright's front door and taps on it. She takes a deep breath when the door is opened.

A physical manifestation of wickedness is standing before her. "Well, hello, Mrs. Cole, mother of Gracie Cole. Everything was going so amazingly well until you appeared at my door."

Ignoring the threat in his comment, she asks, "May I come in?"

He waves his arms around the room. "I'd rather you not. The place is messy. Oh, I have plenty of time to keep things tidy. It's just that I'm lacking in motivation."

Sarah pushes him to the side.

Bobby steps out of her way. "Looks like I don't have a choice," he admits. "I don't like for people to come into my house uninvited. So don't start trying to order me around. I'm not your lackey."

"You should be afraid of me, Bobby." She motions around the cold room. "I am your worst nightmare."

"Will you sit down?" Cautiously, Bobby sits. He motions for

her to do the same. "Wow! Feisty, aren't you? Are you always this pushy, Mrs. Cole? In fact, you remind me a lot of your daughter."

Sarah feels herself go faint. *Stay in control. You have a purpose. Concentrate.*

"Oh, really? In what way?"

"Do sit down." He sits across the room. "Charming. Beautiful. Yet smart. Just like Gracie." You know, I really liked that girl. She thought I was cool. She really liked me. In fact, I bet if you hung around me for a while, you would like me." A smile crosses his lips. "I am sitting here counting my lucky stars. He scratches his chin as he leans back in his chair. "What you say that you and me bust out of this town, go on down to the beach, and savor this moment?" He leans forward, seductively gazing into her eyes. "Are you with me on this?"

Every muscle in Sarah's body trembles. Her temples pound as her blood pressure rises. She forces herself to remain calm and contained. "I can't do that. I don't have my suntan oil. Besides, you couldn't be more wrong about me. I have nothing but contempt for you."

"So a trip to the beach is out?"

"You've got that right. I am not going to the beach or anywhere else with you. Get that idea out of your head."

"Wow! You don't play nice, do you? Why don't you just stick a knife in me and turn the handle? Do you always feel contempt when a man comes on to you?"

"Only when I deal with men like you. I'm not attracted to you. Ugh. No relationship will ever exist. Besides, I don't play nice because I don't play games. But, I am not here to talk about me. I want to talk about you."

"I don't know why." Bobby shrugs.

Sarah notices a black satchel on the table. A drop bag? She

wonders. She takes a chance. "Going out on a drug deal tonight, are you, Bobby?"

"What I do in my spare time is none of your business, Mrs. Cole."

"You need to make it my business."

Bobby scratches his chin. "Why is that?"

"Because it's my job to make sure our families and their children in this community are safe from people like you. I speak in hypothetical terms. So hypothetically speaking, hypothetically, your selling drugs lead to lethargy on the part of your victims. They just don't care anymore, and that most definitely leads to the death and abuse of their children. And, as the narcotics become more accessible, there are more and more overdoses. Don't you even care about the number of people in this country that die each day because of a drug or opioid overdose or the number of innocent children that have to suffer at some dope head's expense? This is not considered a bad thing? It is pure evil."

"I don't twist any arms to buy it and what they do after they have it is none of my business."

"You need to make it your business. This agency, including mine, along with the good citizens of Wesleyville, are fed up with the drug trafficking. They are extremely tired of everyone turning a blind eye to the evil and violence that goes on in their neighborhood. They are all advocates of exterminating the lot of you or letting you rot in prison for decades. Besides the citizens, every law enforcement officer in this town knows you are selling dope and you are nothing but slime. Everybody around you suffers because of you. And, they are going to flush you right down the toilet with the rest of the slime balls."

"So now you are shaming me for selling dope? I'm not the slime ball in this business. This crisis is not caused by me. Why don't you and your mighty DA put the big pharma companies out of business for making the opioids? Why don't ya'll go arrest the politicians who are paid big bucks to pass laws to keep them legal and the doctors who are prescribing them for profit? Are they any different from me? It's all about greed, Sarah. The only difference is that they hide behind a big sign posted in front of their professional building. I hide behind the walls of my little metal greenhouse."

"Like I said, down the toilet with the rest of the slime balls!"

"Like I told you—I didn't twist any arms."

"You may not have cocked the gun or pulled the trigger, but you placed it in their hands."

Throwing his head back, Bobby cackles. "Innocent until proven guilty." He sneers, "I'm not worried. Your accusations are groundless. Besides, other than the judge, I have a couple of police officers in my pocket and they tell me they will make sure I have an ironclad alibi that will cause doubt on where the DA might say I've been."

Sarah's voice is cool. "But we both know that's not the truth, Bobby. I mean about ironclad alibies. At some point you have to accept that things are no longer in your control. In fact, sometimes it is best you *don't* rely on other people simply because you *can't* rely on other people."

"What do you mean by that?"

"Your cop pals are just trying to keep you calm so you won't spill the beans on them. Believe me, when it comes down to the nitty-gritty, you'll sink and they will swim. It's their jobs or your life on the line. Think about it, Bobby, they'll be glad to see you rot in jail. It will keep them from going down. Nope. You will suffer alone and they won't even feel your pain. In fact, they are going to laugh you right into the nearest correctional institution."

Bobby's brow begins to furrow.

Sarah continues to blast. "Don't you think your fake bravado,

Bobby, is putting you way ahead of yourself? You are not innocent. You are far from innocent." She points her finger. "No *dang* moments, Bobby. No twisting the truth. No lying. No trying to convince everyone you are perfectly innocent. We all know what you are. You are a fraud. You may think you have a judge in your pocket, along with a couple of policeman, and your tracks are covered, but the truth of the matter is your high and mighty back end is going to end up exactly where you belong—in prison!"

Sarah squeezes her hands tightly; her knuckles turn white. Still, her voice is controlled and calm. "You sound almost as if you think you are invincible. Why the confidence? In fact, you should be concerned. Very concerned." She leans toward him. "Yep, you *should* be afraid. The sheriff and the Drug Task Force have enough compelling evidence on you to put you away for the rest of your life."

"Not really, Mrs. Cole. I'm perfectly comfortable with this. Let's assume, now, I only said, *assume*, that hypothetically, I am dealing, and I do get caught. As soon as I get my arraignment and the judge sets bail, I will be out of there. A free man again. In fact, the judge will exonerate me and I won't even go to trial. I can have all the charges dropped by the very next day. So, Mrs. Cole, once all the technicalities have already been taken care of, you can color me innocent. You are getting way ahead of yourself by accusing me of selling drugs."

Sarah makes a quick decision. *I'm going to force Bobby to underestimate me. Then I can weasel him and leave him crying.* She begins to talk about going to hell, not just as a leverage, but as collateral to obtain more information.

"You are so transparent, Bobby. I can see right through you— just like a plate of glass. You are by far from innocent. If you have killed my daughter, you will be sent to the prison. They will inject you. And, when they inject you, you will go to sleep—forever. The best part is you won't stay asleep forever. No. No."

She shakes her head, turns back to face him, and waves her finger. "You are going to wake up—in hell. Forever and ever, you will be eternally damned, consumed in hellfire—in agonizing pain for eternity. In fact, hell is so hot, your eyeballs will melt out of your head."

Perspiration begins to bead the man's face. Muscles tighten and Sarah can almost see his throat burning. He stutters, "Why do you not have human kindness? What right do you have to judge me? No human condemns another person to hell. Besides, I do some good in this world."

"Why, Bobby? You are getting all sentimental on me. However, the truth of the matter is that you *are* going to hell. Inadvertently or intentional, sin is sin. No matter what good you think you might do in this world, it will always be outweighed by the bad."

Sarah hopes for the effect on Bobby she is trying to achieve. Methodically, she begins slow-walking it. *Now I need to pick up the pace and eventually obtain all information I need as to the whereabouts of Gracie. I can't wear my heart on my sleeve.*

Sarah analyzes the options. After all, communicating could be the factor in finding her daughter. Besides, Sarah thinks, *this schmuck is the only one who knows where Gracie is.*

Sarah continues dragging the hoodlum through the prospects of being hell bound. She throws her head back and laughs, continuing to rag on him.

Then she stands and turns her back so he can't see the desire for retribution on her face. She inhales deeply to regain her composure and slowly turns to face her challenger. "What about vulnerable young women, Bobby? Are you innocent of them?"

"Aw, come on, Sarah. Are we going through this tiresome pantomime again?"

Sarah slowly stands, picks up her purse, and withdraws her Glock 17 pistol. Arms straight, finger on trigger, she aims at Bobby's head—right between his eyes. "Fill me in, Bobby, on how you took advantage of a vulnerable young woman. Gracie Cole."

"She was not vulnerable. If anything, she was a little spitfire."

"I know my child might be dead and I know you did it. Deliberately. Cruelly. Part of me keeps thinking that I could not have saved my daughter, but I want you to know what it feels like when you think *your* life is about to be over. What does it feel like, Bobby? Do you feel vulnerable? Is this how she could have felt when you held the trigger on her? Is your life flashing before your eyes? Do you have any regrets?"

Silence from Bobby Wright.

Sarah lowers her weapon. Tears trickle as she admits to herself she cannot possibly pull the trigger and take someone's life regardless of what he could have done to Gracie.

Bobby snatches the opportunity and grabs the gun, pulling Sarah around, pressing her body against his. "I never have regrets."

Sarah doesn't struggle. Instead, she relaxes in his arms. "Did you kill my daughter?"

"No. I speak the truth."

Softly, she mutters. "You wouldn't know the truth if it jumped up and bit you. And, one day, everyone will know your lies."

Bobby motions to a video camera set up in the ceiling in the corner of the room. "Never pull a stunt like this again. All I have to do is show it to the sheriff—you pulling a gun on me—I win. You lose." He grits his teeth. Suddenly, he pushes her towards the door. "Get out of here. Get out now, before I change my mind."

As Sarah nears the door, she turns. Her face remains stoic, unyielding, and cold. "This morning, I looked to see if there was any black cloud looming on the horizon and there you were. I am sure you don't believe in karma, but karma works whether you believe it or not. Just enjoy this little victory for now, but Bobby, you will be looking over your shoulder from this point on, and sooner or later, your past will catch up with you."

She begins to walk away but turns around. "Fear me."

Bobby shrugs.

20

I Rise

Thirty minutes later Sarah storms through the doors of the county sheriff's office. Irate and with grief flooding her soul, she walks up to Rick and slaps the startled man hard across his face. Stunned, he shamefully bows his head, understanding her anger. Then, gesturing to Paul, she moves towards him. He stands bracing himself for the same. This time Sarah doesn't slap—she balls her fists and punches the man's face. She rages and bellows. "If something has happened to Gracie, I blame the two of you! It's your fault. Both of you will shoulder the blame." Her eyes glare like pommeling, fiery darts. "If she is hurt, I promise, I will hurt you!" Fingers are shoved in their faces. "And, if she is . . ."

Sarah collapses in Paul's arms. He grabs her just before a fall, carries her to the sheriff's personal office, and lays her on the couch. Rick scurries to get a glass of water. As Sarah regains her senses, she cries out, a mother in grief. "Why? Why did you encourage her? What compelled you to do something selfish and stupid?" She glares at the concerned men. "Yes, Rick. You and Paul encouraged her. By emboldening her to assist you in this investigation, you set off a chain reaction that affects all of our lives. You planted an idea in her head, and now it has escalated. Did you honestly think that Bobby Wright was not going to retaliate? Didn't you realize that man is a danger? Men like him use violence as a solution. If something has happened to her, the two of you will be held responsible and you will be damned to hell!"

Uneasiness and guilt contort both men's faces. Rick attempts to place his outstretched arms around the grieving woman.

Sarah, jumping back, yells, "No! Don't touch me!"

Rick backs off. "I admit responsibility for my part for the way things turned out. However, I am a realist and I'll do just about anything to get these scumbags off the streets. I do what the situation requires, and Gracie was determined to help."

"And, what exactly did the situation require when you got Gracie involved? What justification was there using an inexperienced person to do your dirty work?" Before he can answer, Sarah retaliates with more scathing words that bite to the bone. "I abhor sentiment, Rick. So don't sound like you really care. There is nothing you can say to ease my pain. It won't bring my daughter home to me."

Cautiously, Paul reacts in defense of Rick. "Gracie knew there was substantial risk but she wanted to get the guy behind bars. She wouldn't take 'no' for an answer."

Ponderously, like a great blue whale, Sarah feels her massive anger and frustration rise once again. "Don't patronize me! You are the very definition of despicable. So, what if she did know there was a risk? Don't you think she depended on you to have her back? But you've let her down. You didn't have her back. You never did. She had her whole life ahead of her and now she may be gone because of you. Whatever has happened to Gracie is on the two of you. And I will never forget it!"

Paul whispers the truth. "You and your daughter are not a means to the end. You are our friends."

"Friends? You and I are not friendly, Paul Hines. Not after you lied to me and used Gracie the way you did. Besides, I don't need feckless, miserable friends like you and Mr. Seager. I need my daughter. My tolerance is getting really low so get out there and find her before I pull your hair out by the roots!" Nerves frayed, Sarah begins to gag. "I've got to throw up!" She runs out to find a bathroom.

"Rick, no matter how we respond, we're gonna meet opposition from her," Paul says when they find themselves momentarily alone.

"I know. We're going to stand condemned until her daughter is returned," Rick agrees.

Within a few minutes, Sarah returns. Still filled with righteous anger, fear, and frustration, Sarah's next question is two-pointed. "Why aren't you doing something? Why are you just standing around? Why don't you have Search and Rescue out there looking for Gracie? You say you are my friend? Then, prove it. Get out there and find my daughter."

Before Paul can answer, the sheriff sticks his head in the door, motioning for Paul and Rick to step outside. "What is going on in my office?" he demands.

In the same moment, Kathy and Natasha burst in the door. Kathy agrees. "What *is* going on? You guys sound a little bit intense. Do you think you can converse like, well, let's say, non-screaming adults in a public place? Sarah, you need to lower your voice. We can hear you screaming down the hall."

After hearing the details, Kathy and Natasha throng around Sarah, embracing their heartbroken friend. Natasha tries to console. "We are here for you. Lean on us. You can't handle this alone."

Sarah explodes into deep, urgent cries. "Why, why is this happening? Where is my Gracie? How can this be happening to us? I can't let go of this anger, grief, and sense of loss."

Kathy, rubbing Sarah's shoulders, adds, "Whatever you need.

Whatever you want. We are here for you and we are not going to leave. Use me as a punching bag or whatever. But I am going to sit right here. You are not in this alone. We are with you."

Natasha also tries words of comfort. "I know you are afraid, Sarah. I feel you. In fact, you are beyond afraid and the only way to deal with it is to face it, but not by thinking negatively. You are not the kind of person that acts out and thinks irrationally. You have always been so great dealing with adversity and every curve ball life throws your way. You are spiraling out of control and this is definitely not you. You have to have faith that Gracie is going to be found—alive. For now, think positively and try to hold it all together. For yourself and everyone that loves you."

Kathy steps forward. "Natasha is right. You have to see that you are spiraling. Everybody else can see it. This is not like you. Try to get a grip on yourself, okay?"

"How can I think positively? Thinking positive is going to be a challenge because I know what kind of people we are dealing with. They are the kinds that leave no witnesses alive." Sarah continues to cry. "I am living my worst nightmare. This is a parent's vilest fear, isn't it—the possibility that she will outlive her child." She looks at her staff. "You're my only friends. How do I move through this?"

Sarah's supporters place their arms around her. "Let us help."

"Thank you, but at the moment, all I can think about is Gracie. The horrible thing about becoming a parent is that they don't warn you about all the things that can go wrong. All the heartaches. You never dream that your child can become a victim of a chain of very terrible circumstances. A parent's job is to love and protect. That's it. And as a parent, I have failed miserably." Sarah dabs her red, teary eyes. She mumbles. "I think I feel guilty to some degree. Maybe that's the reason I can't get a grip. Maybe I am blaming myself for all that has happened. I was so wrapped up in getting Safe Families back on track that I didn't pay attention to what was going on in my daughter's life. I took my focus off of my priorities and now I am suffering the consequences."

Kathy hesitates and then says slowly, "I'm thinking of what I learned as a girl and tend to forget. Often we stumble and fall when we are put into the furnace. I understand your feelings of hopelessness, but you've worked through seemingly unresolvable problems before. Where is that woman who has led Natasha and me through our toughest battles? That woman who teaches us to dig deep and use all of our faculties to climb every mountain and soar through every valley? Where is the woman who tells us to believe and trust that our trials are just stepping stones to make us more in God's image? The woman who tells us to look at the other side when we are being forged in the fire. The woman who tells us to look for the calm in the face of the storm. Find her, Sarah, we want her back."

Natasha adds, "I remember one of the first days you came into our lives. 'I rise,' you said, 'Though you slay me, I will rise again.' You are not a quitter, Sarah Cole, so stop acting like one. What some people might call stubbornness, I've heard you call perseverance. You told us that suffering produces perseverance and perseverance produces hope. Maybe, like Job, you are being tested. Just like Job, when darkness overwhelms you, have faith to follow the path that has been carved out for you. Don't stumble and wander off the path, Sarah. Trust and rise."

Sarah nods, finding comfort and a faint sense of well-being in their enlightening words.

Suddenly, Paul storms back into the room. Jubilant, he informs the women, "The sheriff has put all his deputies at our disposal. I hate to break up this little reunion, but I've got some great news. Bobby Wright is on the move!"

Sarah jumps up. "How do you know?"

"Someone managed to place the tracking device on Bobby's truck. Someone who you probably gave up on." He smiles at Sarah. "Don't you know by now never to count out Gracie Cole? Gracie Cole does not surrender! She made it possible for us to rally the troops and stage an intervention."

Sparking with renewed energy, Sarah beams, "Well, go, go, get out of here! Go get my baby!"

Paul whispers to Kathy to step outside for a minute. "How do you think she is doing with everything?"

"She is hurting a lot. However, the news you just gave her will help."

"Just in case, you and Natasha stay close to Sarah, at least, until this is over. I'll keep you informed."

Sarah's heavy heart lifts as Kathy returns to her side. A few seconds ago, she lurched between war and peace, perilousness and goodness, uncertainty and security. Now a sense of hopelessness begins to fade. She sees her pathway illuminated and her world enlightened.

She whispers, "I rise."

21

Takedown

The Drug Task Force officers, along with the sheriff's department, position themselves for a drug bust. Nerves on edge. Law enforcement officers on high alert, well aware that the mission is extremely dangerous—every dealer and hitter are always armed to the hilt.

Rick whispers to an officer standing next to him. "We've got contact between Bobby and Theo inside that house. Make sure everyone is in position. Then watch for my signal." Just as the officer turns, Rick grabs his arm. "No mistakes. Understand?"

Cautiously yet anxiously, the officers surround the small building, ready to intercede. The signal is given. Nervously, Paul makes sure the narcotics search warrant is in his possession. He yells, "GBI. Search warrant!" Quickly, they move forward, busting through the door.

The takedown is swift. It catches Bobby and Theo by surprise. Pointing his gun, Rick commands, "Put your hands up on top of your head. Step away from that table. Slowly."

The hitter and the dealer are caught red-handed. Bags of heroin, cocaine, synthetic opioids, and money are lying on the table. Bobby shouts obscenities at the officers during his arrest, as both men are frisked and hands are cuffed behind. Miranda rights are read.

As each man is whisked away to separate vehicles, Rick Seager orders, "Get the sniffer dog in here. After he checks out the house, take him to their vehicles. Check for any residue, prescription pills, heroin, or whatever is on the menu for tonight. I'll meet you back at the station." As he walks by the deputy's car with Bobby in the back seat, he stops, yanks the door open, and leans in towards Bobby. His eyes are glacial and intimidating. "Where is Gracie Cole?"

Bobby smirks. "Wouldn't you like to know? You know what happens to snitches and informants, don't you, Mr. Big Man?"

Rick loses his composure and grabs Bobby around the collar. Squeezing it tightly, he begins to choke him. "You are looking at twenty, but if anything has happened to Gracie, I will make sure you get what you deserve. You'll never see the light of day." He shoves Bobby backwards against the seat.

Unscathed, Bobby asks a deputy standing near, "Hey, did you see that? This man was not only choking me but he threatened me! What do you call that? 'Unnecessary force'?"

The officer shrugs his shoulder. "I don't know what you are talking about, man. I ain't seen nothin'!" Briskly, he walks away. The officer asks Rick to come over to the side of the patrol car. He whispers, "Mr. Seager, don't you think you need to be a little more cautious with the way you handle that thug?"

Rick bites his bottom lip. His brow furrows. "One thing about me you need to *forget*—I am never cautious when it comes to saving someone's life." Rick motions to the edge of the woods. He says to the officer, "How about you taking a leak over there in the woods. Take your time, hear?"

The officer nods, walks away, and Rick goes back to the patrol car that holds Bobby sitting inside. He slides in on the driver's seat, looks through the review mirror, and stares Bobby coldly in the face. "I want to tell you something before they take you in, Bobby. There is no video inside this vehicle or audio. Anything you say against me will be disputed. After all, it is your word against mine." His eyes remain fixed. "When we take you in to interrogate, you need to come clean. Squeaky clean! We have the evidence and there is no way you are getting out of this. Understand? And as for Gracie Cole, if I find one hair on her head has been hurt, you won't see prison. In fact, you will never see another day. *Comprende?*"

Bobby Wright says nothing.

Inside the interview room, the audio and video are turned on. Nothing said or done will go unnoticed.

Rick and Paul watch in real time as Bobby awaits his lawyer. He taps the table top in a sort of rhythm, much like a drummer's as he beats on his drums. Rick asks, "He's more scared than he's trying to act. Are you ready for this?"

"Ready as I'll ever be."

Just before they enter the room, Bobby's lawyer, an elderly man wearing a tight-chested suit and carrying a briefcase placed snugly under his arm arrives. "I want to see my client alone for a few minutes."

"Sure."

"Turn the sound off," the attorney directs.

Upon entering the interview room, the lawyer, Mr. Cain speaks directly to Bobby in a low voice. "I've read the reports. The most important thing we need to concentrate on is the disappearance of Gracie Cole." His eyes squint as he looks directly into Bobby's eyes. "If she is found dead, you will be charged with murder and they will nail you to the wall. They will make you pay. Understand?"

Bobby nods.

"I am going for a deal. If you have any hope of getting a lesser sentence, you and I need to come to an agreement and accept the deal. Give them any information they ask for and I will arrange to have your sentence lessened."

Sarcastically, Bobby asks, "How can you get my sentence reduced?"

Mr. Cain smiles and winks. "Let's just say I'm friendly with the DA."

As he watches the video, Paul grins. He looks at Rick. "Can you believe it? We are cousins!"

Rick exclaims, "Hey, I thought you cut off the audio?"

"Oh, was I supposed to do that? Oh, golly gee, I'm sorry." Still grinning, he cuts off the sound.

Inside the interview room, Bobby smirks, "I'll take my chances with the judge. I'll be out of here before you know it."

"You are not going anywhere. You are not going to be exonerated. You are not going free." Slowly, Mr. Cain's words burn into Bobby's soul. "They are going to throw the book at you. As we speak, they are getting a warrant to search your property. You are going down, Bobby. You will be considered a flight risk and no judge is going to allow you to leave the premises. And if they find Gracie Cole's body, you will be up for a murder charge."

Bobby smirks. "You must not know the same judge I know."

"You sound almost sure you are going to be released. Why the confidence? In fact, you should be concerned. Very concerned." He throws Bobby's files down on the table. "Mr. Wright, you have been under surveillance for months, and they have enough compelling evidence on you to put you away for the rest of your life. Understand what I am trying to tell you. Being exonerated is not happening, but I will make sure the court knows you are cooperating."

Boldly confident, Bobby sneers, "You think I'm in denial but I'm not. And I'm not worried. The accusations are groundless and like I said, in twenty-four hours, I will be out of here. Other than the judge, I have a couple of police officers who will vouch for me, and they tell me they will make sure I have an ironclad alibi that'll cause doubt on where the DA might say I've been."

"Listen to me, Mr. Wright. As for the accusations being groundless, there has been more than enough evidence accumulated on you to throw away the key, especially after they conduct a search on your building."

"They can't do that! They have to have a search warrant."

"Mr. Wright, they *have* a search warrant! You're mistaken if you assume that a search warrant cannot be authorized." He rubs his crinkled forehead. "As for the judge you claim to have in your hip pocket, his actions have been monitored for months. In fact, the DA has requested another judge be assigned to this case."

Bobby eyes widen and he sighs loudly, which seems to pull the air out of the room.

Mr. Cain continues. "All the DA has to say in the courtroom to the judge is that you are a desperate person and an incredible flight risk. He'll come up with some criteria, and well, you won't be walking the streets a free man." He slams Bobby's folder down on the table. "Believe what I say, Mr. Wright. It is all here— enough evidence on you to secure a conviction." Mr. Cain pushes his chair back and stands with head bowed and hands on hips. "The way I see it, you might as well go ahead and admit the charges, plead guilty, take the lesser deal, and save the taxpayers the expense of a trial. With all that drug stash they found on you, I'd say you are pretty much cooked!"

"Plead guilty? Why would I want to do that?"

"For one thing, for peace of mind. For another, you need to

start refocusing your energy because there is no way you will be getting out of this."

Bobby leans over and whispers to his lawyer. "If I cut a deal, will the court find that's an admission of quilt?"

"Mr. Wright, regardless, with all the evidence they have on you, the court will know you are guilty. Walking away from this is not going to happen. As for what happens next, you will be formally charged at an arraignment before it goes to trial. The judge will ask if you understand the charges that have been filed against you. He will ask you how you plead."

Bobby snarls, "I am not going to plead guilty. Now that I think about it, I am going to stand trial and be acquitted."

Mr. Cain blurts, "Get real, Bobby. May I introduce the DA's next opening statement—the people vs. Bobby Wright. The DA has enough corroborating evidence against you and witnesses to testify."

Bobby stammers, "If—if you are thinking Angela will testify against me, that is not going to happen. She loves me and will do or say whatever I ask her to."

Mr. Cain stands up and attempts to explain the reality to him. "It is my understanding that this girl, Angela, is lost to you. Not to mention she's disappeared. She does not want to speak to you or even hear from you ever again. Not even a postcard. You are dead to her. If she is found, she will testify against you and she is going to blow the jury away just by telling the truth. In fact, she hates you so much, she will bury you."

Bobby yells, Sit down, Mr. Cain! Please. You've got my attention. Let's talk terms. You've got to help me. I want a deal. The sooner I can get out of this mess, the better."

"Now you are using your head." Mr. Cain looks up at the video camera and motions for Rick and Paul to enter.

Bobby looks up. "Is anybody watching us?"

Paul flips on the audio as Mr. Cain winks at the camera. "Only sneaks and weasels eavesdrop on people's conversations."

"Ouch! That hurt!" Paul says from the other side. "Smile, Bobby, you are on *Candid Camera*! Let's go."

Rick and Paul enter the interview room and state their names and titles. Eyes narrowed, Bobby looks at Rick. "Yeah, I've already had the pleasure."

Mr. Cain is the first to speak. "I've talked to my client and he is willing to cut a deal and save the court the cost of a trial. He understands the consequences if he refuses the deal."

Bobby speaks up against his defense attorney's orders to remain quiet. "That's right, and until I get a deal, you don't find out where Gracie Cole is."

Rick says, "You have made a wise decision, Mr. Wright." He looks at the lawyer. "I am going to lay out our specifications on the table. We want a handwritten and signed statement from Mr. Wright for the following: the names of the two policemen who are on Mr. Wright's payroll, his association with them, and how much they are being paid. We also want Mr. Wright's association with Judge Sloan, along with amount he is being paid. Third, we want the location of Gracie Cole."

Mr. Cain takes the paper from Rick's hand and reads. After a minute to contemplate, he inquires, "We want the deal. What will be the terms of his sentence?"

"Reduce his sentence by half. Place him in a minimum-security system away from the hardened criminals."

Bobby chuckles. "Hey, my homies say those minimum securities have all the luxuries of home, plus more. Make sure I get in minimum security with the gym and a T.V. Heck, I might decide I like it and want to stay." He takes the pen and paper from Mr. Cain and begins to write down all the information requested. After a substantial amount of time, he passes the signed confession over to Rick, who passes it to Paul. Paul quickly reviews the papers. Suddenly, he speaks up. "You answered everything we requested except for the location of Gracie Cole."

Bobby, with a slow, certain smile, nods. "That's right. I'll give that information to one person and to this one person only. Sarah Cole.

22

Karma

S arah parks in the back of the sheriff's office and jumps out
of her car. A familiar officer bumps into her at the entrance.
"Mrs. Cole, what are doing here?"

Sarah explains, "I came to get some answers from Bobby
Wright." She motions towards the jail. "I understand that
arrangements have been made and agreed upon by all parties. I
am actually going to get to visit with the thug."

"Mrs. Cole, are you absolutely sure they are going to allow
you to visit with Bobby?"

Sarah smiles. "Is Paul Hines in there?"

"Yes."

"That's all the confirmation I need."

At that moment, a patrol car pulls into the back parking lot.
Sarah moves to the wall and watches. "What's going on?" she asks.

"We're moving some prisoners to different locations. The
sheriff thinks it's best to separate them." In a few seconds, another
person on Bobby's and Theo's payroll leisurely strolls out of the
building surrounded by deputies. For a moment, the man stops
and stares at Sarah with cold, unblinking eyes, before climbing
into the back seat of a patrol car. She shivers as her eyes remain
locked on those of Judge Sloan's.

Sarah asks, "Who are they taking and where?"

"Sad to say, two of my fellow police officers, and of course, Judge Sloan. They are being moved to a facility upstate until their arraignment. It will be safer for them there."

"Huh," Sarah says dismissively. "That's too bad. All snakes belong in the same pit."

"I agree, but someone said it's the humane thing to do."

"Tell that to baby Larissa Renew and little Kevin Herrington."

At that moment, Paul Hines steps around the corner. "Sarah, I am glad you came."

"I understand you have some unfinished business with Bobby Wright. So do I. I've been told I need to see him before he's moved."

Paul hesitates briefly, and then explains, "Okay, Sarah. I hate for you to have to do this, especially at this time, but he's going to be moved upstate in a couple hours. Like I explained on the phone, one of the deals Rick had to make with Bobby Wright in order to get more information is for you to talk to Bobby. You are the only one he will tell where to find Gracie. If this is going to be too hard for—"

Sarah interrupts, "So, Bobby is still here in lockup?"

"Confirmed. The despicable Bobby Wright is inside in jail."

"You mentioned Rick made another deal with Bobby. What kind of deal?"

"As I said, Bobby wants to talk specifically to you. Added to this privilege, he is willing to give us some more ammunition to help take down the top guys. Since you are here, do you feel up to it? I mean, if this is a bad time, then—"

"No. The timing is perfect. In fact, I want to talk to Bobby. I want to ask him questions about why and how things happened the way they did. This is the only way I can find some peace."

"You need to be careful what you are asking for. You may not like the answers."

"I can handle this. Anything to find out where Gracie could be." She hesitates. "Dead or alive."

Paul remains silent, knowing very well of the possibility Gracie might not be found alive.

Sarah clears her throat. "Isn't it illegal for anyone to talk to Bobby without his attorney present and any statements he makes will be inadmissible without counsel?"

Paul contends, "Not in this case. His attorney along with the presiding judge gave us permission. We have all agreed that this is not a matter of legal principles. It is a matter of ethics and trying to save someone's life before the worst can happen."

"For whatever reason, thank you. I'll try not to question your legal prowess again."

"So that's why you admire me so much? For once, you are not questioning my legal prowess or making light of my ethics." He smiles just a little.

For the first time in days, a sweet smile slowly creeps across Sarah's face. "It's just the way my brain is wired."

"You know, Sarah, I have always admired your tenacity and courage. I have never seen you back down from anything. So, if you are ready, I am going to take you back to the visitor's room. You will be the only visitor in there. Don't worry. A couple of deputies will be right outside the door. You will have a guard in the room with you and Rick and I will be in the room next door. Unknown to Bobby, the phone to a suspect is always tapped. We'll be listening in if you need us."

"Another one of your ethics? Taping the conversation?"

"Whatever it takes." He grins. "No one else knows this bit of information, so be careful not to share."

Sarah inhales deeply. "Lead the way."

Dressed in an orange jumpsuit, Bobby sits across the Plexiglas window dividing the cubicle, waiting. Sarah sits down in the cubicle and picks up the phone attached to the wall. Bobby does the same.

"Hello, Sarah."

"Bobby."

"Your timing is impeccable."

Sarah nods. "How is jail?"

"I've had nicer accommodations. So how does it feel to see me here? Is it everything you dreamed of?"

She confesses, "I can tell you this—it is close."

"Part of the deal was for you to see me like this," he says, once again waving his arm around the small, dingy cubicle. "I thought you could use a little lift." He sneers. "You know, Sarah, I don't appreciate the ambush you pulled against me during our last little visit. Remember? You dealt harshly with me. You manipulated more information out of me than I should have given." He throws up his hands. "What a mistake! Letting you walk out that door. Talking about screwups, who knows better than me about making a mistake—one that I will regret sooner than I would have thought."

"Don't be too hard on yourself. You actually did the right thing."

"Maybe. Wouldn't you just love to see me wiped off the face of this earth? Come on, Sarah, you know you can tell me. I can't help but think that you wish you did shoot me." He glares, waiting for a comment. Then he adds, "You think I am pathetic, don't you?"

"Pathetic? Maybe. Mostly, a lowlife, a hypocritical snob, and a man with no soul. Other than that, sure. I think you are deserving—deserving of whatever punishment they will give you."

Sarah's cell beeps. She takes it out of her pocket.

Annoyed, Bobby rolls his eyes and then looks at Sarah's cell phone, "Am I boring you? Why don't you swipe right? I am paying for this time with you. Remember the deals?"

Sarah snaps the phone shut and looks directly at him.

She bites her bottom lip. "I'm all ears. Let's cut the crap, Bobby! I'm not here to play games with you. I'm here because I want to talk about Gracie."

"Yeah, let's talk about Gracie. That girl got guts, you know. She could be a regular Magnum P. I."

"*Magnum, P. I.* was before her time."

"Well, then, she's a little MacGyver."

"Let's focus on the issues at hand. I want the details on where my daughter has been taken and by whom." She pauses. "I want to know if a hit has been ordered."

"I can't be specific."

"Since when does Bobby Wright does not say or do anything he does not want to do? This is strictly between you and me, Bobby. Understand? It goes nowhere."

Bobby motioned to the guard standing on the other side of the room. Sarah glances his way and with one quick flick of the head, the man leaves.

Bobby asks, "Are you wired?"

Without hesitation, Sarah stands, unbuttons her shirt and drops it to her waist, exposing her bra. She turns around for Bobby to see there are no wires.

Rick and Paul look at each other. "What the heck is she doing in there?" Paul asks.

"Sounds like she's taking her clothes off!"

"What?"

"Listen, listen! Here it comes. All the evidence we need!"

Although excited, both know without a shadow of a doubt that any evidence obtained illegally will not be admissible in a court. Still their excitement is piqued.

"As you can see, I am not wired. All I care about is finding my daughter. Her life is involved here. So, if you think this is espionage, you are more naïve than I thought."

Bobby smiles as his eyes absorb her body. "I see. You realize that Theo is still in control, even from his jail cell."

Sarah nods, "Without a doubt."

"Before we were arrested, Theo ordered a hit. When he was informed that one of our men went soft and didn't complete the job, he gave orders for another to finish it."

"Why Gracie?"

"He needs to get rid of her. She knows too much. He has to take out any witness to what went down."

"And Angela?"

"Collateral damage."

"No remorse?"

"Of course, if anything good can come out of this tragedy, it is that I realize and appreciate what a good woman I had. I would give anything—well, almost anything—if she was back in my life."

"Sometimes wishes don't come true." Sarah bites her bottom lip. Taking a deep breath, she desperately tries to regain her composure. The thoughts of something horrible happening to her daughter sicken her. "I'm feeling queasy, Bobby. I have to go throw up. Please excuse me." Sarah grabs her shirt, puts it on quickly, and jumps up, running out the door and slamming it behind her.

She leans against the wall, bracing herself for the inevitable. From behind, a familiar voice asks, "Are you okay, Sarah?"

Shaking her head, Sarah thinks, I can't lose my cool here. She answers, "You still have a knack for slipping up behind me, scaring me to death."

"Sorry."

Rick and Paul wait for her to finish buttoning her shirt and regain her composure. When she does, her tone is cold. "Don't think I'm not still put out with you two." She pauses and then asks, "Am I doing enough to proceed with a case against Theo?"

Paul answers. "All evidence obtained illegally is inadmissible, but we can use it to get under his skin. Maybe draw him into a confession, especially if he thinks we have something on him that is incriminating. If we give Theo the information we have and he knows we have a solid case against him, maybe, we can scare him into making a confession. We can use it as leverage to make a deal with him and get the names of the men above him."

Rick adds, "Nothing can be left to chance when you are trying to bring down the big guys, the ones above Theo. So far, you are having a productive conversation with the piece of trash. Keep it up. As soon as you get the location of Gracie, get out of there."

Sarah's glare at the two men is stern and cold. "Not before I have my say."

Sarah turns to go back into the visitation room, but Paul calls her back. "I'm proud of you, Sarah. What you are doing takes guts. You are what we refer to as 'a crafty negotiator.'"

Sarah responds in a voice edged with sarcasm. "That all depends on how you look at it." She cringes as she eases her way back into the visitor's room.

"This business is sickening, huh, Sarah?" Bobby smirks.

"You've got that right. Listen, I came here today because of the deal you made with the DA." She sits down and takes out a note pad and pen from her purse. "Tell me where I can find Gracie and Angela."

"Hang up the phone," Bobby demands.

"Why?"

"I'm not taking any chances. That DA is not exactly the most honest person I've ever met."

"I agree to that!" Knowing well that Paul and Rick are listening in on the tapped phone, she continues to insult them. "Not an honest bone in his body."

Paul says to Rick, "Ouch! That hurts."

Rick shrugs his shoulders, almost in agreement.

In the cubicle, Bobby hangs up the phone. Sarah does the same. Without hesitation, she leans across the table, watching Bobby lips meticulously move as he mouths the letters "H – A – M." Quickly, Sarah scribbles the letters down. She repeats the letters and suddenly, it dawns on her. "H – A – M is not a code or a location. It is a name. Ham!"

Bobby picks the phone back up. "Read it, then burn it. Don't walk out of here with those letters scribbled on a piece of paper."

"Don't worry. I'll take care of it."

"You know, you need to be a little bit nicer to me. I'm giving you a lot here today." Bobby grips the phone he is holding in his hand. "Let's lay down our armor and not retaliate. I'm simply suggesting that instead of trying to balance the scales, you should let it go. We have both suffered enough. I am going to lose Angela and you lose Gracie. I don't want to look over my shoulders wondering who is coming at me with a shank or pick while I'm in prison. Violence only leads to more violence. I know you have the will and determination to make that happen if you want to, so I'm asking you, Sarah. Let it go."

"You have a lot of nerve, Bobby, asking me to let it go. How do I let go of the fact that my daughter is possibly going to be murdered, if not already? How is the pain eased there? You may not be the number one suspect, but I still detest you."

Sarah squeezes her hands tightly as she grasps the phone she holds. Her knuckles turn white. Still, she remains controlled and calm. "I am the one whom you really need to be afraid of. I am a lethal weapon and I won't hesitate not one minute to blow you away. I will shoot you—ruthlessly. In fact, Bobby Wright, 'overkill' would be an understatement because you are nothing but a disgusting piece of dirt. The fact that I am in the same room with you, breathing the same air as you, sickens me."

Her nostrils flare; her temple pounds. "I am glad I came in here today to see you. Now I can find some clarity. I learned that you and I are a lot alike. Neither one of us knows the difference between not telling the literal truth and being honest. If my beautiful daughter is dead, Bobby, you can rest assured that when you are in that prison, you need to keep one eye opened all the time. I just might balance the scales—not only because I want to, but because I can." She heaves a sigh of relief now that she has brought fear and dread into his psyche. "Do you have anything else to say? If not, I am done talking to you." She turns to walk away, but Bobby calls her back.

"Hey, Sarah. I just want to tell you something about Gracie." Sarah's ears prick.

Bobby's words bring her to a halt. "My only regret is that I never had the chance to do her."

Sarah cringes, trying desperately to dissuade herself from running out in the hall and grabbing the officer's gun standing nearby. Standing with her back to him, harboring an undeniable desire for retribution, she inhales deeply to regain her composure and slowly turns to face her challenger.

At that moment, she notices that in the hallway behind Bobby, another detainee is ushered in, waiting to be locked up, perhaps in the cell with Bobby. He wears eyeliner and his movements are effeminate, but he is large and even robust. Sarah looks over her shoulder, motioning to the man who may be Bobby's new cellmate. "By the way, Bobby. This is Karma biting you back."

Sarah flashes the piece of paper on which Ham's name is written. "Thanks for this."

"Wait a minute!" Bobby yells anxiously. "You said you were going to burn that paper!"

Motioning towards the ceiling, Sarah leans over the table. "Not in here. Have all those fire alarms go off? Don't worry. I'll take care of it outside. I know just where to stick it!" Sarah storms out of the visitation room and brushes past Paul and Rick, anxiously waiting.

Paul exclaims, "Wow, Sarah, you put the fear of God in him."

Sarah glares. "I had to play it smart. He holds all the cards." She shoves the paper in Paul's hand. "My opinion of you still hasn't changed. I'd rather push you in a ditch." Her eyes cut down to the paper with the evidence Paul needs to put the lawless away. She adds, "You know where to put this!"

A frown etches its way across Paul's face. "Where?"

"You know the place. It's the place where the sun doesn't shine!" And, then she was gone.

Paul and Rick solemnly watch as Sarah speeds away. "Where do you think she is going?" Rick asks.

Paul responds, as he reads Gracie's location, written in one word. "Ham! She's going after Ham."

23

Handle with Care

Sarah Cole holds a pistol pointed directly at Ham. She glares at the flustered, burly man, hoping he is wondering if this wake-up call is a sign of doom. "Where did you take her, Ham? Where is my daughter?"

He chokes, "Do you know how to shoot that thing?"

"I've had a few lessons. Enough that I know if I hold my aim steady and squeeze slowly, I'll hit my target."

"Which is?"

"Straight between your eyes. So, consider yourself warned." She points the gun straight for his head between his eyes. "Think about what I have said."

"Believe me. I have."

Leaning forward, elbows on knees, Sarah blurts, "Would it surprise you that I have no qualms with seeing you dead? It is not beyond me. You see, the situation is like this: The cost between saving my daughter and pulling this trigger is not even a consideration. I don't have a problem with killing maniacs. Furthermore, if I find that you have so much as hurt one hair on her head, you will." She motions with her head. "Let's go or start thinking about an early demise."

"Go ahead. Let me have it. If not by your hands, then Bobby's." He grumbles, "I'm just not ready to meet my Maker."

'If I don't find my daughter alive and well, dear sir, you *will* be meeting someone, although I doubt it will be your Maker." She motions with the gun. "Move."

They walk outside of Ham's little bungalow nestled deep in the woods. Sarah sniffs a detestable odor—one coming from Ham. Neither his sweat-drenched clothes nor his overweight body has met with soap and water for some time. *Whew. I'll have to cover my nose if I'll be downwind from him.*

Just as the sun is making its debut, they reach the creek and a boat hidden in the bush. Ham says, "Load up. The place I have them hid is down creek and in the marsh."

For a while, there is silence as Ham rows downstream, with him glancing back at Sarah, who does not set the gun down for even a second. Soberly, he begins a conversation. "I didn't harm those girls, Mrs. Cole. Bobby told me to get rid of 'em, but I just couldn't. Your daughter—she is one of a kind—got more spunk than a bobcat. Got fight in her, she does. Anyway, all I did was tie them up. Thought I would wait until Bobby cools down and then go get 'em."

"Don't worry about Bobby. He's cooling down, all right—in a six-by-six jail cell."

The boat paddle swirls through the calm waters. Occasionally, a plastic bag or Bud Light can floats by. Ham, an enormous man, his bulk exaggerated by his too-tight overalls and his brow pumping sweat, stops for a moment and calmly asks, "Bobby's in jail, huh?"

"Confirmed. In lockup as we speak."

Ham whistles. "So he finally got caught. I knew it would just be a matter of time. That boy ain't got the sense God promised a billy goat. I think workin' around all that weed done got his brains fried."

"Put some muscle behind those boat paddles, Ham. Let's move."

Yes, ma'am," he says and spurs forward. However, he could not resist asking, "You would do anything for your daughter, wouldn't you, Mrs. Cole?"

Sarah nods. "Anything."

"I bet you are the kind of mother who keeps herself all in her daughter's business."

"I guess you are right about that. Staying out of her business has never been my style. Listen, Ham, I don't have time to waste jabbering, so please, put your back into it. Let's get on down this creek."

"Yes, ma'am. Whatever you say. You are the one with the gun."

Finally, they reach the tie-up point. Ham gets out of the boat and pulls it close to a tree. "Follow me," he directs.

Through the marsh they trudge, trampling on vines and plants. Occasionally, just as Sarah is about to fall, she quickly regains balance, never taking her eyes, nor her gun, off Ham. Soon, the small shanty appears in the distance behind the trees. Although her overall impression of the shack confirms that it is a far stretch from a safe haven, her heart skips as her energy soars. Her anticipation exhilarates her. She calls out, "Gracie, I'm here! I'm coming."

At that moment, before another step is taken, the unexpected happens. The shanty explodes, sending up a ball of fire. Pieces of wood fly through the air, followed by a billow of smoke. Flames leap.

In shock, Sarah stands, at first motionless, frozen. Then she cries out as she pushes her way through the thicket. "Gracie!" Stumbling, she loses the gun she once held tightly in her hand. On all fours, she desperately fights to scramble to her feet knowing that Ham now has the advantage. He moves quickly, lifts his walking staff, and brings it down hard across the back of Sarah's head. She groans and collapses onto a fallen log. Quickly, he slips away.

For what seems like an eternity, Sarah is half in and half out of consciousness, holding on tenaciously with only one goal in mind: to get to that burning rubble and rescue Gracie. Suddenly, she hears a voice and feels the hand of another human.

"Wake up, Sarah. Wake up," Rick Seager says as he gently taps Sarah's unresponsive face. He brushes her hair back. "Sarah, it's Rick. Open your eyes."

Groaning, Sarah squints. The smell of smoke and fire burns her nostrils. She manages to point in the direction of the smoldering inferno. Shocked, her voice is weak and shaky as she manages to mouth, "Gracie. Help her." She points to the burning embers. "Gracie."

Rick calls out to the search and rescue team who have followed him into the swampy terrain. "You men get her out of here. We need to get her to the hospital."

One of the men asks, "What about—you know?"

Rick looks up at the man with the persistent questions. He looks back at the place where the shanty once stood. With tears in his eyes, he shakes his head. "She's gone."

24

"Don't say Good-bye"

The ambulance swirls into the drive to the emergency room entrance. Medics are waiting to receive the patient, who they immediately move to the examination room and then on to x-ray.

Nerves frayed, Rick paces back and forth. Within a few minutes, Paul bursts through the door. "What happened?"

Rick begins to explain. "When my team and I couldn't locate Ham, I went back to the jail and got Bobby to draw us a map. Lucky for us, we met Ham coming towards us on the creek. As soon as he spotted us, he tried to paddle in the opposite direction, but our motorized boat was too much for him. Anyway, after we captured Ham, he agreed to take us to Sarah—that is, after a little persuasion."

"What happened to Sarah?'

"Ham hit her in the head and tried to make his escape, but unsuccessfully. The doctors are with her now. Maybe we'll know something soon." He rubs his eyes and shakes his head. "That's not all, Paul."

"What do you mean, Rick?"

"There was an explosion." He sniffs and wipes a falling tear. "Ham says Gracie and Angela were inside." He moans. "No one could have survived that blast. I am almost certain they are both dead."

Endless hours pass. Reclined in a chair in Sarah's hospital room, Paul nods and occasionally snoozes. Quietly, he stands, looks out the window, and watches a lazy sun rise behind the tree tops. After a sleepless night, his body is tired and heart, heavy— almost to the point of breaking for the loss of Gracie Cole and Angela Wright. He whispers, "Such a waste of precious life. I will not rest until everyone involved is brought to justice."

He bows his head and shakes his head. "What a foolish mistake I made. Sarah will never forgive me and how can I blame her? I will regret this for the rest of my life."

Slowly, Sarah opens her eyes, moans, and rubs the back of her head. As her eyes adjust, she looks around the hospital room and at the IV hooked up to her arm. It is then that she notices Paul standing at the window. "Paul? Is that you? How did Rick find me?"

Paul smiles ironically. "Let's just say by the time Rick stopped cutting deals with Bobby Wright, he doesn't have much prison time left to serve."

Rubbing the back of her head, Sarah moans. "I don't understand."

Sarah attempts to stand, staggers, and almost stumbles.

Paul catches her before she falls. "I've got you. I'm not going to let you fall and don't you argue." He laughs. "We've got to stop this! This is the second time in forty-eight hours you fell into my arms." Coughing, Sarah leans her head against Paul's shoulder. Paul asks, "Are you okay? Get yourself together. You can do this."

"You give me too much credit."

"I don't think so and if you can't give yourself credit for being a strong woman, then let me."

Sarah willingly reclines against the pillow. "This doesn't mean there will ever be the possibility of another dinner date."

"Noted. Now lay back. I'm going to call a nurse."

Adrenalin pumping in spite of how tired she is, Sarah shoots up again. Mumbling, she attempts to regain her balance and struggles to say, "It's coming back to me now. Gracie! The explosion! I've got to get out of here! I cannot stay here one more minute. Please help me, Paul. I've got to get to Gracie."

Paul can't find the words to tell Sarah what has happened to her daughter. Instead, he dodges the inevitable. "Sure. Just as soon as the doctor makes his rounds. Then, you can be released," he lies.

Sarah crumbles back on the bed, too weak to stand. She turns her head and stares out the window. After a brief silence, she speaks. Her tone is soft, not full of desperation as before. "Why, Paul? Why did you not listen to me? I begged you not to include Gracie. I tried to reason with you. But you always do what you want to do."

Paul slumps over, shuffling his feet. His heart is breaking and he is well aware of his tendency to think first and ask questions later. He avoids Sarah's eyes.

Sarah continues, "I remember waking up in the middle of the night and thought that maybe it was just a dream. Then the shock and horror wore off and I felt like I was in a daze." A tear trickles down her face. "Have you ever lost someone that you love with all of your heart, Paul?"

No answer.

"Everything inside you becomes numb. You lose yourself."

He grimly mutters, "I've been sitting here all night trying to make sense of this senseless situation, but all I know is that I failed you and Gracie and it is going to hurt me a very long time. You are grieving, Sarah, and you have every right to blame me."

She glances at the man, taking note of his furrowed forehead and trembling lips. "Don't worry. I am not going to give in to anger and bitterness. Grudges are a lot heavier to carry than forgiveness."

He nods his head, thankful that he will escape the wrath from the woman who holds his guilt-ridden heart in her hands. "What can I do, Sarah? How can I make this less painful for you?"

This time, her look is stern. "Things don't randomly explode. Someone put a bomb in that shack. It was purposely done. Do you want to do something for me? Go find out who is responsible."

"I don't want to leave you here alone."

Kathy and Natasha walk through the door. Natasha says, "She is not alone. We are here. Now, go do as she requests."

Paul nods and leaves the room.

As soon as he is gone, the two friends on Sarah's staff from Safe Families collapse into Sarah's arms. One by one, they begin a tribute to Gracie, telling of their love and admiration for their young friend.

Kathy, with tears staining her face, is the first to speak. "I cannot believe Gracie is gone. It seems impossible. Beautiful, beautiful Gracie. So full of tenderness, patience, and love. What an amazing person she was. She was always so full of life. No matter what was going on, she always had time for me. She would brighten even the darkest day."

Natasha squeezes Sarah's hand with one of hers and wipes fallen tears with the other. "I don't how to say good-bye. She became a dear friend—one that would go to the ends of the earth for me. How do you say good-bye to someone like that? I don't want to start because if I start it means there has to be an end."

Boldly, Sarah asserts, "Then don't! Don't say good-bye."

Shocked at the harsh tone of Sarah's order, both women frown.

Sarah glares. "Don't say good-bye," she repeats. "My Gracie is not gone. My daughter is alive! Now please, go get me a cup of coffee, Okay?"

Where has she gone? Natasha and Kathy scurry down the hospital corridor, looking in every nook and cranny for Sarah, though they know hopes are slim. As they round the corner to the main lobby, Natasha bumps into Rick Seager, coming to visit Sarah.

Out of breath, Natasha nervously spurts out, "Rick, Sarah has slipped out of the hospital!"

"Did what? How?"

"The doctor says he came by during his rounds. He told her that she had a mild concussion and needed to stay another day. She had sent us to the cafeteria to get her a cup of coffee. While we were gone, she snatched the IV out of her arm, got dressed, and must have walked out the main entrance. There is no trace of her. What do we do?" Natasha is breathing rapid, shallow breaths.

Rick motions to a chair. "First of all, let's get you seated before you have an anxiety attack."

Kathy holds on to Natasha, leading her to a chair. She asks Rick, "I noticed when we visited with her this morning she was acting really strange—unlike a grieving mother. In fact, she told us that Gracie was not dead—that she is alive!"

"Calm down! Both of you. I don't doubt she may still be in a bit of shock, but on the other hand, sometimes a mother's instinct can be extremely on cue."

"Whatever do you mean?"

"I sent in a team of Search and Recovery, along with bomb and explosive experts. They concluded that there were not any signs of human remains. Not even scraps of clothing that would have normally been blown up to tree limbs. We are almost sure that when that bomb detonated, no one was inside that building."

The women gasp and breathe a sigh of relief, but are still confused. Kathy asks, "Does that mean Gracie and Angela are still alive?"

"I'm not sure. If they were not in that shanty when it exploded and there are no signs of remains, it means they are making all efforts to walk out of that marsh. They won't leave by the same way they were carried into the place. They would be afraid of running into Ham." He shakes his head and frowns. "The only thing that worries me is that the chances of them walking out of that swamp are slim to none."

Kathy comments, "You don't know Gracie. She is tough and tenacious. If anyone can make it through there, she can."

Rick explains, "I'm sure she can, that is, if she were alone. You have to remember that Angela is with her and I am sure Angela is slowing her down. She is not as physical as Grace. Besides, they have no food or water."

"I still disagree. Gracie Cole is a survivor."

"Let's hope so. As for now, I have every law enforcement officer in this county out looking for those girls. The Emergency Response Advance Team has assembled, wearing snake gaiters and insect repellant, following what they hope is their trail and looking for evidence that the girls are still alive. They are using machetes and chain saws to cut their way through the swampy terrain. Some of the search and rescue are on the other side of the swamp, all along the edges. We have men dropped at a site of clear land near the other side, along with air service officers and search helicopters, making over-head maneuvers as we speak."

Kathy asks, "People just don't disappear, right? Do you have an idea in which direction they went?"

"No. Truly, they have vanished, and realistically, we all need to face the possibility that they might not ever be found. That swamp is full of alligators and snakes. We need to face the fact that—"

"That what?"

"That they might be dead. In fact, if we don't find any signs of life in the next few days, we'll have to assume the worst."

Natasha adds, "I feel so helpless. What can we do, Rick?"

"Find Sarah. Stay with her. Don't leave her alone. She needs you girls more now than ever. Stand by her and don't let her lose faith."

"Do we tell her that you have confirmed Gracie was not in that explosion?"

"I'm not sure. I'm not sure what state of mind she is in now. It sounds to me that she is extremely fragile. All I can say is, 'Handle with care.'"

25

Grief

Leaning against the wall of her living room, Sarah sits on the floor holding Gracie's dog, Lilly, in her arms. The black masked, droopy-faced dog with the wrinkled muzzle cuddles up close to Sarah. It has been three days and still no sign of Gracie and Angela, lost in a thicket of mass terrain. The Emergency Response Team has not found any traces of the two girls and is left with no other choice but to call off the search. Officially, they have pronounced them dead.

Sarah's heart is breaking as she cries and gently rocks Lilly back and forth. The confused little dog whines and licks Sarah's hands, trying to comfort the only way she knows how.

Unexpectedly, the doorbell rings. Sarah wipes her drippy nose and yells out, "It's not a good time. Please go away."

"It's me, Sarah. It's Paul."

Slowly, Sarah stands and opens the door. Falling into his arms, she openly weeps. As she slowly regains her composure, she manages to ask, "What are you doing here?"

"You just lost a child and you need someone to help you through this. I know you are feeling unimaginable pain. I wish that I could take away that grief for you, but I can't do it. All I can do is console."

No answer.

Paul continues. "How are you doing?" His forehead crinkles as he looks at Sarah's matted hair and swollen, red eyes. "When was the last time you slept? No offense, but you don't look so good."

"No offense, but you don't look so good, either."

"You are beginning to sound like me."

"Thanks for being insulting." She pauses. "By the way, go to the devil's place."

"Been there."

She stands, begins to pace, and wrings her hands. "I'm sorry, Paul. I promised myself I wouldn't be so vindictive. I am dealing with my loss the only way I know how—anger. Being mad at everyone doesn't change a thing." Her sad eyes search Paul's for understanding. "I shouldn't lash out at you like this. I mean, the grieving will still be here when the anger is gone. I realize that you are not responsible for Gracie's death."

She wipes a tear. Her voice softens. "I am sorry for being so cruel. Can you forgive me? I said those words because I wanted you to hurt the way I am hurting. The things I said were coming from a place of pain and grief. I did not mean anything I said." She looks into his eyes for consolation. "I'm sure those words were harsh, right?"

Paul lowers his head. His response is solemn. "Yeah, they stung." Trying to add a tinge of humor, he says, "I will give you a break but I reserve the right to give you a lecture another day."

Sarah nods.

"May I be honest with you, Sarah?"

She cocks her head, searching his face for the meaning of his words.

Looking up towards heaven in an almost prayer-like state, he admits, "You are not the only one struggling. I would go to the end of the earth to swap places with Gracie. I wish it were me instead of her." Casting a concerned look towards Sarah, he adds. "Maybe knowing that will give you some measure of peace."

"No, Paul. That does not give me peace." She sits down in a chair and calls for Lilly. Paul also sits. Sarah continues. "Nothing gives me peace. I think I am having a complete mental breakdown." She wraps her arms around Lilly. "I can't imagine my life without her. People say time makes things a lot easier. How much time?"

"I can't answer that. I've never lost someone I love with all my heart. I do see how you can lose yourself as you're grieving someone else."

"After the shock and horror wore off, I've started walking around in a daze, not functioning, just existing. Sometimes, I wake up and think maybe it's just a dream. Last night, I dreamed Gracie was alive. I was so convinced that I slipped out of bed and came in here to find her. I just started staring at the door hoping she would come walking through it. But there was no Gracie." She kisses Lilly on top of her head and ruffles her ears. "I still can't wrap my mind around the fact that she is really gone. It is tough seeing her everywhere and knowing she is no longer here."

"I understand."

"All I can think about is my beautiful little girl. She was the sun in my universe, the gravitational pull of my very soul." She wipes a tear. "There is an endless loop of images of her in my mind, from the time she was little chasing butterflies in the park until the day . . ."

"Don't block out her memories. Your daughter will always be with you in spirit."

She begins to weep again. "A few weeks ago, she jokingly implied that I wanted to install a GPS device in her neck." The grieving mother wrings her hands. "Oh, how I wish that would have been possible."

Her questioning eyes search Paul's for answers. "My first instinct, as a mother, should have been to protect my daughter. But I didn't do that. I didn't protect her."

"Don't do this to yourself, Sarah. Try to keep those thoughts out of your mind. This isn't your fault. You have to let go of the guilt and move forward. You'll get past things you can't change. It's hard now to admit it, but life goes on. You know you can move forward. That is what she would want you to do."

Grief floods Sarah's face. "I'm trying to get through this the best way I can."

"You have to find peace in your heart, with the world, and with yourself. That is what Gracie would want. You have wonderful memories that outlast and outnumber what has happened. Allow those to overshadow your grief."

She sniffs as she continues to vent. "It was not enough that she died. It's just that nothing she ever wanted to do with her life is going to happen now. She will never have the opportunity to live out her dreams. You know, Paul, losing someone you love teaches you something about yourself."

"What is that?"

"Not to waste time and not to get caught up in things that don't matter and to say the things that do."

Paul places his hand on hers. "Sarah, you can't handle this alone. Please allow me to take care of you. I have a vested interest that you get back to your old self."

Sarah sighs. "Thank you, Paul. I am glad you are here for me. It means a lot. It's good to have people around you that know how you feel. The truth is I can't do this by myself. I don't know how to get through the grief. You, Natasha, and Kathy are the only ones who understand what I am going through. Maybe Rick."

"Rick, too. All of us know that you shouldn't do this alone. We will stand by you."

She squeezes Paul's hand as if asking for understanding. "I am exhausted, Paul. I need some rest. Will you do me a favor and leave? I want to go to sleep so that when I wake up, for a few minutes I will forget she is not here."

Moved with compassion, Paul stands and walks slowly to the door. He turns around and notices a picture of Gracie on a table. He looks over at Sarah, still holding Lilly, rocking back and forth. Quietly, he closes the door behind. For a brief moment, he stands on the steps of the porch. Welling tears stir his breaking heart. "Good night, Sarah." Lifting his eyes towards the eternal, infinite, and unlimited heavens, he whispers, "Good night, Gracie."

26

Road Less Taken

Sarah jumps into the boat belonging to the county sheriff and rams it into gear. Wind in her face and hair blowing behind her, she guns towards the place where the explosion occurred. Angered by everything that has transpired, her faith in the local law enforcement offices has faltered. A hot temper manifests and now she is after the man whom she believes has underestimated her sensibility and left her in seclusion and ignorance.

Spotting the patrol point on the edge of the creek, she whirls the boat in next to Rick's, who at this point still has Search and Rescue looking for Gracie and Angela. Eyes blazing, she rages, "Why haven't you told me sooner that there is a possibility my daughter might be alive? I was lead to believe the search was over. I thought she was dead! Am I capricious, fickle, untrustworthy? Which is it, Rick? Tell me, why were you not man enough or considerate enough to come directly to me and tell me that Gracie was not in that explosion?" She begins to jerk and tears flow. "I had to find out from Natasha and Kathy. All this time, I have been grieving my heart out and all of that could have been avoided."

His face red with embarrassment at the woman's wrath, Rick excuses himself from his men, jumps in the boat with Sarah, and slowly drives it downstream. "Sarah, not to state the obvious, but if you don't slow down and breathe, you are going to hurt yourself. Calm down, okay?"

He bites his lips. "I'm sorry I didn't tell you sooner, but I thought you were dealing with enough. You were having a really hard time coming to terms with losing Gracie and I knew it would be too much to process if you lost her all over again. So, I decided to wait until I had enough foundational evidence that Gracie might be alive. It was crucial to get all the facts before I presented them to you. I couldn't bear you having to go through the grieving process again. Do you want me to gloss over the truth and tell you that she is alive when I am not sure at this point?" He looks upward for answers to console but not appease her.

"My team has searched and searched. There is no sign of Gracie, Sarah. She may have escaped the explosion, but there are so many obstacles in that swamp. Besides, she has been in there for several days without food and water. I couldn't give you hope just to have it snatched away from you again." He pleads, "Tell me you understand, because in all honesty, I can attest that I was doing what I thought was best for you."

Quietly, Sarah sits, listening to his every word, soaking in the validity of his confession. She stares out into the murky surroundings. "Do you promise that you won't give up? Not until you find her?"

"I promise. Would I lie to you?"

This time Sarah manages a chuckle. "Maybe, not lie, but you would mislead me."

"Okay. I deserve that. I stand corrected. But, believe this—I will be completely up front with you from now on. Whatever happens, I will keep you informed. We will face it together."

In the steaming, smoldering heat and humidity, two young women slush through the water and weeds avoiding stumps and fallen trees—good hiding places for snakes. Gracie's nostrils flare as her dark eyes dart from one tree to the next. Tense muscles tighten as she chokes back tears, careful to hide her anxieties from Angela.

After crossing the murky terrain and passing through areas untouched by humans, Angela gasps for breath. "I don't think I can go any further. I'm all pooped out. Please, let's stop and rest for a while. Maybe if I go to sleep, when I wake up this nightmare will be over."

"We've got to keep moving. We've got to get as far as we can before nightfall. This is no place to be when the lights go out."

"Why don't you just go ahead and leave me here? There is no need for me to slow you down. I just can't go on. I am so tired and thirsty. What I would give for a good ol' glass of cold water—not this germ-infested muck we've been drinking. Besides that, if I have to eat another creepy insect or tadpole, I'm going to puke!"

Gracie wipes the perspiration form her forehead. Feeling an ache in her arms, she contends, "Tell you what—when we get out of this swamp, we'll drink a gallon of good water and then we'll start with some champagne. You know, the really good stuff. And, get this in your head—I'm not leaving you. Besides, we are stronger together. That's why we don't need to be apart."

"It's only going to get tougher on you dragging me along."

"The way I see it, we will do this thing together. Now deal with it. Not that I am complaining, but you've got to stop being so pessimistic. All of your negativism is making me feel trapped, like being stuck on a carousel playing the same old songs. With nowhere to run, the circle shrinks tighter and tighter. So, please, stop beating me down so much that I self-destruct."

Panting, Angela flops down on a fallen log. "Are you saying that I am bringing you down?"

Gracie sits down by the young woman, worn to a frazzle. "No. I am just saying we are going through a challenging time and it doesn't make it easier when you think negatively. Besides, you are not going to fall apart. I won't let you." She catches her breath. "If we keep moving, we'll be out of here before you know it."

"Says the master strategist! You've been saying that for days. Besides, you are asking too much of me. I wish I shared in your confidence, your optimism, and your bravery. How do you do it?"

"I pray. It's called *faith* and it's been my most powerful ally. You should give it a try sometimes. Other than prayer, *experience* has taught me that one shouldn't take anything for granted—especially ourselves. You should look beyond the bad and the scary and look towards the end of the road—towards hope."

"Prayer? Hope? Prayers have never been answered for me and there's certainly never been any hope. I guess I was born under an unlucky star. Besides, I am not as sanctified and perfect as you are."

Kidding, Gracie asks, "Do I hear a hint of sarcasm in your voice?"

"No." Angela begins to cry.

"Hey! What's going on? Why are you crying?'

Despite her despair, Angela manages to joke. "Just having a momentary lapse of control."

"Well, get over it. We are going to survive this. So stop acting like you can't chew gum and take two steps at the same time. You can."

"Oh, that was low! I hope when you grow old, you have stretch marks!" Angela blows the hair out of her face. "How can we survive?"

"By faith and sure force of will. That's how. Now listen to me,

Angela. It's understandable why you have a questionable grasp on reality. But, the reality here is that if you dig deep, you will find you are braver than you think. Sure, we are going through a rough patch but just remember one rule-of-thumb lesson you should learn—that those who keep the faith and those who stay committed, win."

Angela chuckles. "Yeah, some rough patch. Just like the one in my life."

"Yes, but just like the one in your life, you don't let that define you. You define yourself. Don't let your circumstances—past or present—pull you down. Rise above them. And stop procrastinating. Start looking at your own fate. You will be better for it."

"So says my brainiac friend who always has the answers for every problem in the universe."

Gracie sighs. Besides having to deal with the daunting realities of snakes, insects, and mud, she has to deal with Angela's insecurities. "Don't do that. Don't sell yourself short. Gracie hesitates. "Why do you do that?"

"What?"

"Always selling yourself short. It takes all of your time and your energy, and you won't have a life anymore. Besides, you make out of your life what you want."

Angela says dismissively, "I totally get what you are saying, but I keep going over in my mind if there was something I could have done differently. I messed up my life a long time ago by picking the wrong guy." She waves her hand around the murky surroundings with tears collecting. "How pathetic does that make me? All of this is just life getting even."

"Stop it! You are getting too emotional now and you just need to back off. You are allowing Bobby to get the best of you again."

"You don't understand. So, what if I am a cynic? I am eighteen years old. No home to call my own. No job. I'm all alone and worthless. So, what if I go ahead and die? No one will miss me, especially Bobby, who I was over the moon in love with. The same man who tries to kick me out of his life every chance he gets. And, yes, the same person who loves his money, his power, and his business more than he has ever loved me." She throws up her hands. "How stupid does that make me?"

"You are not stupid, Angela. You are only human. But, I have to tell you, you are beginning to sound like a script from the *Jerry Springer Show.* You are the one who is responsible for the decisions you have made in your life. You are the symptom. He is the disease and every time you feel sorry for yourself, it's like putting a pinprick in a balloon. Bobby, on the other hand, can't remove the pinpricks from his life, but you can. So, get over it, okay?"

"I realize it is not Bobby who is threatening me. I am my own worst enemy. All the ways you tried to warn me. All the ways you tried to make me see. I get it now. If I had only listened to you from the beginning."

"You wanted space and your freedom, so you allowed yourself to become a prisoner."

"I guess the good thing is that I am finally going to be free."

Gracie speaks passionately. "See, already things are beginning to fall in place. Your rough spot is coming to an end because you have finally realized you have something to look forward to. What can be better than this?" She motions towards their swampy surrounding. "Are you ready to get out of this hole?"

"You just don't know what the word *quit* means, do you, Gracie?"

"Not even in my vocabulary."

"I wish I was more like you, Gracie. But I'll try." After a brief pause, she asks, redirecting their conversation. "How long do you think we've been here?"

"I don't know. It seems like an eternity."

"So what are we going to do? What would your mother tell you to do? What's the plan?"

"My mother would tell me to follow my instincts and the plan is to stick with the plan, which is this—keep moving. I can tell you this—we are not going to get out of here sitting around talking. I hate to break up this enlightening conversation, but we've got to find a way out of here. Like John Wayne said, 'Daylight's burning!'" She looked through the murky abyss. "The only thing left for us is to keep walking on this road less taken."

The two begin to trudge onward. A couple of hours before dusk and the possibility of another long night under a starless sky, Gracie looks through the tree tops dappling with drifting shadows of clouds. Flocks of egrets gliding overhead thrash against the tree tops. Birds tweet and trill, with their sounds amplified by the surface of the water.

"Look, Angela, do you see?"

Gasping for breath, Angela, clinging to vines and roots, ascends the slippery, leaf-strewn slope and strains her eyes to see through the tops of the trees. "All I see is trees."

Gracie stands entranced, enamored of the sight before her eyes and delighted to see that the possibility of an imminent death by swamp has passed. She laughs out loud. The sight of the egrets and kites makes her fill alive and hopeful.

As the clamor in the upper tops of the immense trees announces the birds' presence, Gracie is full of excitement. "Egrets! We've got to be near dry land." She grabs Angela by the hand and begins to pull her forward—on to drier land and out of the gloomy hole. Trudging through the treacherous landscape, they come upon a cattail-filled marsh with American coots leisurely floating in it. Through the thick brush, Gracie catches a glimpse of what appears to be an opening. "Look! Up ahead! It's a big field. We made it, Angela! We made it."

Washed in wonder, standing on the edge of two worlds, tears stream down their faces as beams of light dance around the two lost young women.

"Hallelujah!" Gracie shouts. "The first thing I am going to do when I get out of here is have 911 put on speed dial, buy a gallon of hand sanitizer, and fill a dumpster bag full of Oreo cookies!"

Suddenly the bright, elated moment turns dreadful as an incessant downpour begins. Several minutes elapse. Soon they are soaked, feeling cold, and all alone among the dense vegetation in the remote environment. Frogs and toads begin to croak, thrumming the forest with their vibrant sounds.

"You hear that?" Gracie asks. "That's a sign for us—that even the living who seem asleep at times come to life with renewed hope. They survive because they are adaptable. Their prospects are changing but they are still alive. That's us, Angela! We have survived!"

At that moment, a loud splashing sound is heard amidst the gloomy surroundings. Something with huge coarse scales and an extremely large mouth is nosing through the murky waters, slithering its way through the jade-colored water to one of the unsuspecting American coots. With one swift lunge at a targeted morsel, it snags its meal and unmercifully chomps with just a few bites.

This is my most frightening moment today, Gracie acknowledges to herself. The knowledge that they are in the presence of carnivorous animals sends shivers through her. "An alligator! I hope that is all he wants to eat for now." Her voice trembles. "I wish someone would assure me that alligators are generally reclusive." Gracie realizes the huge implications of the dire situation she and her friend have found themselves in. Her eyes dart inquisitively from one side of the marsh to the other.

Angela stammers, "What . . . what do you do when you don't know what to do?"

"If it doesn't feel right, you run!"

Wide-eyed, frightened, and speechless, Angela flinches and points—two alligators are slinking their ways toward them.

"Run!"

Closer and closer, across the muddy water, a gator glides. Just as the monstrous reptile comes out of the marsh, shots ring out, sending a bullet zinging past Angela's and Gracie's heads. With a flash of the tail, the carnivore disappears. Gracie and Angela, worn, dirty, and beaten, find themselves near a couple of the men from the Emergency Response Team who had refused to give up on the search.

With a voice clear and poised, Gracie calls out from the murk to her rescuers. Finally emerging from the deep swamp, she takes a breath of the moist pine-sweet air. "We are saved!"

27

The Greatest Comeback

Sitting in the conference room in the sheriff's department are Paul and Rick. Anxiously, they wait on an update about a potential spotting of Gracie and Angela, the two young women who the entire force felt were lost forever. The worried look on Paul's face says it all. His concern for Sarah in her grieving process is eating at his very soul.

Rick, always on cue and incredibly instinctive, speaks. "What is it, Paul? You obviously need someone to talk to."

Paul's answer has a hint of sarcasm. "Unless you can build a time machine, there is nothing you can do."

"Sorry I can't help you there, buddy, but at least, I am your friend and I can listen. I know relationship strife when I see it and you have *relationship strife* written all over your face."

"It's that obvious, huh?"

"Yeah. Is it Sarah?"

"Why do you think that?"

"It's not exactly a secret that you've got it bad for her. Why don't you try to stop hiding your feelings? Now what's up with you?"

Paul stutters, "I am in love with her."

"Then why don't you do something about it?"

"Because I am tired of my heart getting stepped on—over and over again. I think I'll just suffer in silence and bite the bullet."

Rick chuckles. "Huh! Never thought you would be the one for giving up."

Paul nods. "There is no need to try. We can never be together. Too much has gone wrong. In fact, the last time we saw each other, it got confusing." He lowers his eyes, and softly, he speaks. "Guess I'll start going through the countdown and face another year a bachelor."

"Wasn't it you, years ago, who told me to give up on anything but love?"

"I might have said something like that." He chuckles—a fake show of jocularity. "I might be a little jaded, but I have always had the perspective that I had everything in my life that makes me happy. When in actuality, I have nothing. Sometimes the clichés are true. You can't have everything without paying a price."

"Man, I don't understand you. You make it sound like being in *love* is nothing but gloom and doom." He shakes his head. "I don't get what you are saying. Let this woman change the rules. Allow her to show you what love is."

"You don't understand, Rick. This woman dazzles me, she thrills me, she is the most important person in my life, but yet, that scares me. I am so afraid I will mess it up. Commitment is awkward for me and I don't know how to rise above it. Intellectually and emotionally, I want us to grow old together, side by side, but what if that connection becomes lost because a huge proclamation of love and commitment makes my head swim." Elbows on knees, he leans forward, searching for answers in his friend's face. "I really want our relations to go to a better place, but my fears always come back to bite me and I screw up." Another fake chuckle. "So, you think there is some kind of a support group to help idiots like me?"

Rick smiles. "Do you really want me to tell you what I think? It's not going to be good. There are not support groups for idiots like you!" He sighs, looking at his friend for some hint of perception. "Do you really love this woman, Paul?"

"Of course I do. Who wouldn't be in love with her? She is smart, stimulating, and really a great person. You know, I have this fantasy in my head that my life would be so much better if she were in it. And I will be the first to admit, I never thought I'd be one capable of having these types of feelings. I can't even stand the thought of running into Sarah because I can't be with her. It's tough seeing that woman everywhere and knowing our relationship will never be what I want it to be."

"Then, my advice to you is to stop taking your sweet time and do something. If you are grateful she is a part of your life and she makes your life richer, go for it."

Paul pauses to consider Rick's advice, and then shrugs his shoulders. "Can't do it, Rick. This is the operative phase I choose to use at this time. So back off. I am not the man she deserves. Besides, who knows better than me about making a mistake? I've made so many mistakes with her, she won't even give me the time of day."

"Yeah, she *is* a little offish with you."

"That's an understatement. I blew any hope of a real relationship on the first day I met her. She hasn't forgiven me for it yet. And what has happened with Gracie is, of course, all my fault."

"Is this self-pity talking right now?"

Paul rubs his forehead. "Maybe. I guess I just need to accept that this train has left the station. There is no hope. Perhaps if the stars had been aligned differently, I might have had a chance with her, but not now." He looks around. "By the way, you wouldn't have some aged rum lying around somewhere in a plastic jug, would you?"

Rick chuckles. "That's not going to solve your problem. Nope, in fact, the only solution I see is for you to stop pining and tell her how you feel. You might be surprised. Maybe your time has come. Maybe your time is now."

Paul shakes his head. "You don't know Sarah. Let me tell you about Sarah. The mere mention of a relationship scares her. And when something like this scares Sarah, she runs."

"I don't understand. She seems like a pretty intelligent woman. A woman who is stable and has her shoulders set square."

"She is all that. However, Sarah spent years being defined by Gracie's father. I am afraid that if I move forward, she will lose herself in past bad memories and won't be able to loosen up. She is horrified of another bad relationship."

He leans over and looks Rick directly in his eyes. "Listen, I appreciate your concern and all that, but I am a grown man, and right now, I'm not going to pursue this. I'd rather have a friend than an enemy, and to keep her in my life, better a friend." Paul grabs his head, squeezing to prevent the onset of a major stress-related headache. "Look, man. I am going to do everything I can to keep us close. This job, if nothing else, will keep us connected. The point is to avoid a breakup before it happens. I can handle friendship. I cannot handle her out of my life completely." Paul, frowning, asks the man who is staring at him, "Why are you looking at me like that?"

"Trying to measure you up."

"Okay, before this goes any further, tell me exactly what you have surmised about me, Rick, because I know there is no way you are going to let this go, are you?"

Scratching his head, Rick surmises, "I don't want to be forceful or anything. I just want to be honest. I always thought you had too much going on to be so self-absorbed. But, you can't see your nose for your face. You don't do things out of obligation. You do things out of love. Love can turn this whole thing around for you.

Sure, it might get complicated, but isn't life full of complications? What I am trying to say, Paul, is if you don't man up and do what your heart is telling you to do, then your ship is going to sail without you. Savvy?"

"I'm hearing what you are saying."

Before Rick could reply, Sarah bursts through the door. She glances from one man to the other. "Natasha calls and tells me she heard officers talking over the police scanner about a possible sighting of two young women spotted near a swamp. Could they be—"

"Paul and I are waiting on a report as we speak. Sit down, Sarah. Wait with us. We should hear something soon."

At that moment, a deputy sticks his head out of the door. "Mr. Hines, Mr. Seager. You are needed in the communications room. You need to come, too, Mrs. Cole. It's news about your daughter."

Sarah, Paul, and Rick charge through the door entrance. "Have you heard anything?"

"Yes, sir!" says the radio man. One of the helicopter's officers just called in. They are flying in as we speak." Excitedly, he turns to Sarah. "Mrs. Cole, you daughter is on board!"

"Is she okay?"

"I'm not sure. We'll find out soon."

Sarah, overcome with joy and a sense of relief, covers her mouth to stifle a scream.

Paul reaches out and grabs Sarah's hand. "You know, Sarah, Bobby did tell the truth about one thing."

She looks up into his eyes.

As compassionately as possible, Paul continues speaking. "Gracie does have guts. The more I know her, the more I am constantly aware she lives vicariously though you. Walking in the shoes, in the steps you left behind, is the epitome of all things she wants to be." He squeezes her hand tighter. "The most extraordinary thing I know about Gracie is that you can never count her out."

Outside, for what seems like an eternity, they anxiously wait for the helicopter to arrive. Then humming of the helicopter engine and swooshing of the helicopter blades could be heard in the near distance. Soon, flashing lights are seen above. Slowly, the helicopter lands on the landing pad.

The wind is whipping Sarah's hair and clothing. She grasps the collar of her shirt tightly. Eager eyes are searching for any sign of life to exit the flying machine. A door is opened and an officer jumps out, extending his hand for one of the passengers. First is Angela, with a blanket wrapped snuggly around her shoulders. Sarah holds her breath. Then, there is Gracie, also wrapped in a blanket. Gracie looks around and spots her mother. Her face beams.

With one glimpse of her daughter's face, all sorrow is erased. Sarah lets out a sigh of relief and holds her hands out for her daughter, who runs into her arms. For a while, Sarah rocks Gracie back and forth, swearing to herself that she will never again let her out of her sight.

True to Gracie's nature, she jokes, "Mom, I admit I made a rookie move. So, does this mean I won't be getting my Justin Bieber tickets? Am I grounded for life?"

"Yes, to the first question, and yes, to the second question—for life! In fact, Gracie Cole, you are deranged if you think you'll ever get away from me again!"

Gracie grins. "Let's go home, Mom. I need an 'a-ha' moment." She turns around and looks at Angela, standing looking lost, aloof, and forlorn. She holds out her hand for Angela, as does Sarah.

Angela smiles and happily walks into their outstretched arms.

As the threesome walk away, Angela asks, "By the way, what is an 'a-ha' moment?"

Gracie giggles, blowing her hair out of her face. "A hot shower, an expresso, and a handful of donuts! Definitely not acupuncture!"

Paul Hines and Rick Seager gleefully watch as the most extraordinary women they have ever had the joy of knowing exit the scene. Rick says, "Still trying to make me believe a friendship is all that matters?"

Paul laughs as he holds up his hands. "Stop! Stop! I stand corrected and I surrender."

"Great because denial does not look good on you, my friend."

A fist-bump between the two—no less.

At that moment, Sarah stops and turns around to address Paul. "Are you coming?"

Paul looks at Rick. His smile nearly covers his face.

Rick laughs out loud. "Things are fixin' to really get complicated!"

Paul is trotting in the direction of the Sarah, but yells to Rick over his shoulder. "Really complicated!"

Rick salutes and then chuckles. "Amen to that, brother!"